Descended by Blood

A Vampire Born Trilogy

Book One

ANGELINE KACE

AN IMPRINT OF ACCENDO PRESS

Cover design by Robin Ludwig Design

ISBN-13 978-0-9838037-1-3
ISBN-10 0-9838037-1-4

Wholesale orders can be placed through Ingram.

Published by Accendo Press

For Brandon,

It was never a question if soul mates were real,
It was if I would find him.

1

PREDATOR VS. PREDATOR

My sneakers crunched against dead leaves, smashing twigs and gravel into the moist soil. Rain pelted these hills earlier today and whiffs of moss, decaying trees, and other earthly aromas filled my nose.

My best friend, Kaitlynn, would be meeting me here soon for a hike through one of the Blue Ridge Parkway's vibrant trails. The beginnings of fall had started appearing around Buena Vista, Virginia, and my favorite feature about this little settlement lay in the transformation of its trees. The colors splashed the canvas of this town with more brilliance than I had ever witnessed anywhere else. And I'd witnessed many places.

I'd lived in seven different states since the first grade. My mom always thought a better job was around the corner—"I promise this place will be better, Brooke, trust me"—but I often felt she was restless. She finally gave in to my Uncle Garwin's requests that we move closer to him, the only remaining family we had left. I'm glad she did because she's been able to stay here, in tiny Buena Vista, for two years, earning me the luxury of beholding another season of plant life dying gracefully.

My Mazda chirped when I triggered the alarm. I pulled my long, dark hair up into a tight ponytail, and heard the grind and chomping of tires against the rocks leading up to the trail. Kaitlynn swung her yellow Jeep into the parking spot right next to mine.

"Ready to get our Steve Irwin on?" Kaitlynn asked, bouncing over to me

I laughed. "We're not wrestling any crocodiles. We're only

strolling through the forest to look at the pretty leaves."

"Let's call it the jungle. It sounds cooler if we act like we're about to do something incredibly dangerous. Crikey!" she yelled in a bad Australian accent.

It had become our Sunday routine to come up here for a hike before the chilled air grew too biting. Buena Vista had started to get bitter in the mornings and evenings, and the fog began rolling in before the sun rose. Even the rainstorms had been materializing more frequently, hence the moisture left beaded on the tops of leaves today.

I steered Kaitlynn onto my favorite trailhead. I preferred this trail to those closer to town as fewer hikers bothered to venture this far. Plants weren't trampled, and you could still spot squirrels and the occasional deer close by.

"So, guess what?" I asked Kaitlynn, holding in my excitement. It tingled along my arms, and I thought it would seep out through my pores. "We're going out."

"Oh, no way? You finally asked him?" Kaitlynn stared at me in surprise.

"Well, not exactly. Jaren messaged me on Facebook last night and asked me. But the point is, we're going out on Tuesday!"

I'd crushed on Jaren since my mom and I moved here. Even after two years, my breath still caught in my throat whenever our eyes met.

Jaren and his ex-girlfriend had broken up over the summer, and Kaitlynn kept prodding me to ask him out before someone else took him off the market again. I feared the rejection, and asking him out for real seemed like such a huge step beyond my flirting with him in class.

"So, you have to tell me how he asked you out." Kaitlynn relished the details.

"Well, he started chatting with me, and I told him how I was excited to see the meteor shower on Tuesday. He asked me about it, and then hinted at which lucky guy was taking me up to watch it."

"Nuh-uh?" Kaitlynn laughed. "He's such a brown-noser. But it's cute because he said it to you. Continue," she said, waving her hand.

We rounded a hill, following the trail through a field of trees. "I know! I laughed, too, when he asked 'which lucky guy' was taking me. But when I told him I didn't have anyone that I was going with...," I gave her a pointed look. She'd gone with me on the past two, so I gave her a pass on this one. I knew she appreciated the reprieve from *sitting out in the cold watching rocks fly incredibly far away at who knows what speeds across the sky.* "He asked me if he could take me."

"See! I told you he wanted you."

My cheeks heated. "I wouldn't go that far. Maybe he wants to see how big of a fool I can make of myself."

A twig snapped, and I jerked my head to the right. I caught the glint from the eyes of a mountain lion creeping toward us, his ears pulled back, teeth bared.

I froze, hoping we weren't the prey he stalked.

Kaitlynn shrieked. She grabbed my arm and tried pulling me with her as she ran back to the cars.

The lion rose from his crouch and started charging down the mountain straight for us.

We didn't have enough time for both of us to make it out of there alive, and the lion sped up at the site of Kaitlynn running away.

I planted my feet. Something clicked inside of me; heat coursed through my veins. My vision intensified, and I could distinguish the areas of down between the lion's coarse fur as his muscles flexed and stretched.

I'd heard before that you shouldn't look a wild animal directly in its eyes, but my instinct screamed for me to not turn my back

3

on my attacker. I listened to my gut and looked the mountain lion square into his charging eyes.

The lion and I connected on an intellectual level: predator versus predator. Only I knew, and I deemed the lion knew, as well, that I outranked him as the more fearsome predator. How I recognized this, or how I knew the lion realized this, I couldn't fathom. I had never been hunting before, so this instinct didn't come from a belief that man ruled supreme on the food chain. And this moment felt different somehow. It wasn't man versus beast; it was beast versus beast.

"Stop!" I commanded.

The lion skidded to a halt four feet in front of me, his back fixed in its pre-lunge arch. He stared into my eyes, his ears perked back, fangs exposed in a snarl and hackles raised, but he didn't move a centimeter closer.

I towered over him. My pulse pounded at the sides of my neck; my shoulders rose and fell with my deep breaths. My gaze pierced him, welding his toes and the pads of his feet into the ground. Somehow, I had been able to force my command over him, and when I told him to stop, I never considered that he would deny my order.

The nerves along my scalp tingled with the sensation that the lion hungered to attack me, but he *couldn't*. The only thing holding him back from pouncing me was my decree that he shouldn't. My beast had prevailed as the most dominant between us.

Panic filled my lungs at the realization that something stirred within me and it caused me to look at myself as a beast. I yearned for the retreat that Kaitlynn had made. I yelled, "Leave!" before the lion could translate my hesitance and continue his attack.

He hissed, spun around, and ran up the side of the hill, tail flogging behind him. I studied his movements, hoping that he wouldn't change his mind and come back.

4

Kaitlynn rushed up behind me. "Brooke, let's go!" she pleaded, voice shaking.

I stood there, to make absolutely sure. We had some distance to run before we'd get back to our vehicles, and I wasn't going to take any chances on being stuck in that lion's jaws.

The creature was almost out of the small clearing and about to enter into the thick forest when a man stepped out from between two spruce trees. Like a housecat, the lion rubbed his fawn pelt against the man's leg and purred. My hypersensitive hearing digested the happy rumble cascading down the hill. Over the purring, I heard the trill of crickets and further out, the crunch of leaves underneath small feet. How was that possible?

The man loomed, barely outside the shadows, in a dark trench coat, smiling. His malignant stare reached my eyes, and his smirk grew by spades.

Kaitlynn yanked on my sleeve. "Brooke, please," she begged, "can we get out of here? Now?"

I remained, eyes locked on this man who I was sure had sent that mountain lion to attack us. The way he pulled the corner of his lip up in a sneer suggested that he found pleasure in the way things ended with the lion. And it wasn't because we were safe; it had to do with something else about the situation. But I couldn't figure out what it was.

"Come on!" Kaitlynn released me. "It's gone. I'm leaving." Her sneakers thumped along the trail away from me, jerking me out of my trance. I watched her go, and then looked back to the man and the lion just as they turned into the shadow of the treeline. His long jacket snapped with his movement as they disappeared from view.

I trembled, recalling the leer on his face. Nothing about this situation made sense. My blood began to cool, and I spun around to follow after Kaitlynn.

"Kaitlynn! Wait." I reached her quickly.

"Let's just get out of here," she said, refusing to slow down. "That guy sent the mountain lion after us."

"What guy?" Her eyebrows furrowed in confusion.

"You didn't see that guy at the top of the hill? Standing by the trees? The lion stroked up against his leg like a domesticated cat."

"I didn't see any guy. As soon as that mountain lion showed up, I was out of there," Kaitlynn said, picking up speed. "It could explain why there was a mountain lion in Virginia, though."

"What do you mean?"

"We don't have mountain lions in Virginia. It must have been his pet or something. Maybe he called it back, and that's why it ran off."

"No," I said, puzzled, "it was a wild mountain lion. It was definitely feral, and he sent it after us. But why?"

Kaitlynn laughed nervously. "Yeah, that sure explains why a wild cat stopped midattack. My explanation makes more sense."

When the cars were in sight, Kaitlynn slowed and came toward me with her arms out for a hug. "I'm so glad you're okay. I'll call you later tonight." She turned toward her Jeep.

"As she pulled away, rocks and debris flew up from the tires.

I sat down in the driver's seat of my car, but before I closed the door, I heard a guttural growl from the distance. I suspected it was the mountain lion.

A shiver ran up my spine, causing my shoulders to spasm and my head to jerk. I escaped as fast as my old Mazda's four-cylinder engine could carry me.

2
DIMPLES ARE CUTE

"Are you cold?" Jaren asked, sitting on the blanket next to me. We'd come up to this peak to watch the meteor shower.

"Very," I exaggerated. I'd waited two years to get this close to him, and we were finally on a real date. Jaren slid toward me and threw his blanket over my lap.

I smiled and kept my eyes on the stars overhead. I loved meteor showers because the stars came alive. They reminded me of little light creatures chasing each other across the dark sky.

I'd never realized until we'd moved here that the beauty of living in a small town could be found in the stars. Big cities try to produce their own stars with skyscrapers and street lamps, but it doesn't create the same splendor. Plus, the burning exhaust can't compete with the fragrance of pine or the scent of moist soil after an early morning drizzle.

I struggled when we'd first moved here. Starting a new school was harder this time than it had been in the past. Fortunately, there were some remarkable people in Buena Vista. Like Kaitlynn and Jaren.

"So, tell me something else about yourself," Jaren said. "I know about your fixation with the sky."

I glanced at him and laughed. "A fixation is what you call an interest? Man, I bet you're so popular with all the ladies back in town," I mocked.

Jaren flashed me his white teeth in a wide grin. His singular dimple depressed further into his cheek, and my pulse surged. He looked at me with eyes as clear and blue as Caribbean waters, and his messy blond hair shimmered in the star's light. Redrock County High touted him as its star lacrosse player, and the intense sport had given him muscles along his neck that flexed when he laughed, as though he'd been carved by a sculptor.

"No, but seriously," Jaren said, relaxing his smile, "tell me something about Brooke Keller that no one knows."

"Well, what else is there to tell? We live in a small town. You already know everything." I thought for a moment about what to tell him. "I don't know...my favorite band at the moment is Florence + the Machine, and I think guys with dimples are cute." I'd gathered all my bravery for that revelation, and I still flushed as the words fell from my lips.

Jaren laughed. He pulled me into one of those tight-squeeze hugs for a second. Warmth spread up my arms and down my spine, wafting into my stomach and spurring the butterflies to flutter.

"What about you?" I asked.

"Well, I grew up in D.C. and went to a fancy private school. That's where I learned to play lacrosse. They had the best coach east of the Mississippi, and I lived an ideal life until the divorce, seven years ago. Now, it's just my dad and me, but most days it's just me." The twinkle in Jaren's eye took on a distant cloud. I wondered why he told me this if the subject remained raw for him.

"You're lucky to have known both of your parents. I've never met my dad." Maybe Jaren wanted me to see a deeper part of him than he'd shown me the past few weeks. I appreciated that, so I thought I should reveal more than the superficial, as well. "We moved around most of my life and my mom's not even in the military. There's always been a higher-paying job, a better school, or a safer place to live. It's weird, though, because she's never let herself get close to any of the guys she's dated, either." I've often wondered if she was running from a creepy ex-boyfriend or something, but she always assured me that she wasn't.

We sat in silence, Jaren holding my hand. The wind blew a cold breeze across my face and sent a loose strand of hair trembling along my jaw, tickling my cheek. The shooting stars became sporadic, and I wondered when Jaren would suggest we leave. I didn't want to go home yet. Being close to Jaren excited and soothed me at the same time.

"Your mom adores you," Jaren said, "that much is clear. At least you have someone who loves you no matter where you move." He faced me, and I was captivated with his beauty. But it was more than merely his genetic appearance. He had depth in his eyes, and his emotions flickered on his face as he felt them.

The moment would've been perfect for Jaren to kiss me, but it shattered when he spoke. "I'd better get you back to your mom, or she won't let me take you out again."

Neither of us moved to get up.

"Really?" I asked, excitement causing my tone to rise.

"Sure," Jaren said. "Now that we've shared our deepest and darkest secrets, we at least owe each other another date, right?"

"Right," I said, happier about the second date than I was before this one. "So, what are you doing tomorrow after school?" I feared if I didn't make the plans now, he might change his mind later.

"I'm scheduled to work until seven, but I'm free after that. You want to hang out?" Jaren asked with a knowing smile.

I blushed, but he'd already said yes, so I rolled with it. "I have to do some homework with Kaitlynn, but do you want to call me when you get off work? I can pick you up when you're done." Jaren didn't have a car because his dad was a jerk—wealthy, but couldn't care less what Jaren needed.

"Thanks, but I think I can get David to drop me off once we're done."

I frowned. David was Jaren's best friend, or wingman as Kaitlynn liked to call him. I told myself that ten minutes lost with Jaren wasn't really that big of a deal.

"Thanks for inviting me with you tonight," Jaren said. He glanced up at the last of the fading shooting stars then turned toward me. "It was a lot better than I expected. I appreciate the stars now, so thank you."

"Well, I'm glad that you liked it and that you finally asked me out." Embarrassment filled me after the confession.

"Oh, so how long have you been waiting for me to ask you out?" Jaren teased, a wicked grin on his face.

"Quit pretending that you haven't had every girl at school after you, whether you were with Tiffany or not." Tiffany was Jaren's ex-girlfriend. They had dated off and on for a year but had broken up for good this time. The rumor at school was that Tiffany dumped Jaren for a Virginia Military Institute freshman in Lexington and would no longer associate with *the kids* from Buena Vista.

"Like that even matters. I'm here with you now, so don't change the subject. Have you honestly been waiting long for me to ask you out?" Jaren's eyes gleamed with determination.

"Let's just say that I'm not the only one. Kaitlynn kept telling me that I needed to ask you out before someone snagged you up first, but I didn't want to get in the way of you and Tiffany if you guys weren't really over."

"Well, we are. She's already into some college guy at VMI, and I asked you out, so I'm ready to move on."

My pulse raced. The idea of Jaren moving on with me sent a whirlwind through me, and I felt light, almost as if I'd float away.

He turned my hand palm up and straightened out my fingers, analyzing the contours. "Hey, is your pinky crooked?"

"Yeah," I said, pulling my hand away. I put my hands together, aligning the outsides of my palms to show him how the little fingers turned inward at the top joint. I concentrated on steadying my hands, so he wouldn't know how nervous I was about it. "They must come from my dad's side because I've never broken them before and my mom's are straight when she does this." My fingers didn't look deformed. The pinkies merely angled into the third fingers a bit.

Jaren smiled. "I think they're cute."

I relaxed my shoulders. I would've died if he thought it was weird and something was wrong with me.

"I better get you home. I don't want your mom to think I'm a bad influence right from the start." Jaren's cheek dimpled and he stood. I stood after him, pulling the blanket up with me.

He grabbed the blanket out of my arms and started folding it. I snatched the corner, and he pulled me into a hug. He held me close to him, as I stood bright eyed, hoping he'd kiss me. We'd flirted in school for the past couple of months, but I'd never felt more sure that he'd kiss me than right now. My hands shook with anticipation as I clasped them around his waist.

Jaren gazed at me for a few breaths and then slid the blanket out of my weakened grasp. "Gotta build up your anticipation a little," he said, then darted toward the car.

Gah! I didn't think it was possible to build up any more anticipation. I chuckled and chased after him. I'd put up with his teasing as long as there were more dates to come. And he owed me another one.

3
COWARD

The next day at school, Kaitlynn's green eyes were bright with excitement over my date with Jaren. "You guys are going to end up together, go off to college, get married, and have babies."

I laughed. "It was only our first date. I don't think you can jump that far ahead yet."

I loved being best friends with Kaitlynn. I'd never had a friend who meshed so well with me. I'm sure she felt the same way because she's told me before that I was the sister she'd always wished for.

However, Kaitlynn and I looked nothing alike. She had thick blond hair, and fair skin. Her face was slender and delicate with a slight nose, while my face was round, taking after my mom's German side.

I didn't care if we appeared to be related or not. We acted like sisters, and she backed me up like one should. By my calculations we were best friends forever, and that's exactly what sisters should be, anyway.

I spotted Jaren coming up behind Kaitlynn. We were juniors, and he was a senior, so his locker was down a separate hall reserved for seniors only.

"Hey, Jaren, what brings you away from your kingdom on senior row?" I flirted, switching my weight to one leg, and bringing my hands up to my hips. Having Kaitlynn here as my backup gave me that extra confidence to taunt him a little.

He laughed, deepening the dimple in his cheek. He wore a baby blue sweater that brought out his eyes and the light blond tips of his eyebrows.

"I was just coming to find out if you and Kaitlynn wanted to go out to lunch with us," Jaren said, sky blue eyes twinkling.

Kaitlynn peered over at me, her eyebrows raised. I could tell she was struggling to keep in an delighted squeal. I resisted the excitement too; I wasn't going to let Jaren witness us getting all junior high about it.

"Sure," I said. "Who's we, and where are we going?"

"It's just David and me, so I guess you guys can pick."

Kaitlynn wrapped her arm around mine, and we paraded toward the back doors leading to the student parking lot.

I let my gaze linger on her, questioning whether she had a preference. We usually stayed at school and ate in the cafeteria with a bunch of other junior girls, but when we did go out for lunch, we always found ourselves at Momma's Barbecue or Little Italy.

Kaitlynn smirked at me and shrugged. I guess she didn't care where we went, as long as we got to tag along.

"We're good with either barbecue or Italian," I said.

"Italiano it is," Jaren said and led us through the parking lot to David's old Mustang. The car wasn't a classic; I think it was an '89, but he kept it in good condition, and the paint glistened red like your grandmomma's lipstick.

"Hey, David," Kaitlynn and I said in unison, causing us to laugh.

"Looking good, Brooke. Kaitlynn, what's up?" David asked with a head nod, then transferred lacrosse gear from the back seat to the trunk.

Jaren opened the passenger door for us and pulled the lever on the back of the seat, moving it forward.

"Does he open the doors for all the girls, or is he just trying to impress us?" Kaitlynn asked David.

"All the ladies, but that doesn't mean he's not trying to impress you," David replied.

Jaren laughed, but cut it short.

I peered behind me.

Tiffany strolled forward, blond hair shimmering along her shoulders as she came up between David's car and the old Camry parked next to it. She glanced at Jaren. "Sloppy seconds," then she looked at me with disgust on her face. "With a sloppier rebound." Her friends laughed.

My face filled with heat from anger and embarrassment, and I stood, silent, like an idiot.

"Just keep walking, Tiffany," David said, slamming the trunk.

She chuckled along with her friends as they cleared the cars and made their way to her white Audi convertible.

I crawled into the back seat as quickly as I could to hide from the discomfort of the situation. I'm sure Kaitlynn would have said something for me if David didn't tell Tiffany to move on, but I knew I wouldn't have had the courage to stick up for myself. And that's what ticked me off the most.

Jaren got in the back with me. "Don't worry about her. She's a snob." He grabbed my hand, and I nodded.

Kaitlynn slid the seat back and sat in front. "She's evil."

"Yep. That's Tiffany." David squealed his tires when he pulled out of the parking lot.

I felt awkward almost the whole way to the restaurant. David finally broke the tension with his jokes, and I decided not to let Tiffany's remarks ruin my first lunch out with the guys.

"Hey, window please," Jaren said.

"Does it smell like stinky socks back there?" David asked.

It kind of did. "No," I feigned. I didn't want to embarrass him.

"Oh, yes it does," Jaren said, nudging me with his elbow and busting me.

David laughed and rolled down his window. "Sorry about that. I usually keep everything in the trunk, but I was in a hurry this morning because this kid," he pointed back at Jaren, "kept going on about his date with a certain Brooke Keller."

Kaitlynn looked back at me and my cheeks flushed.

Jaren punched the side of David's seat. "Hold up. It's not my fault you've got lead feet."

"Bro, I'm so much faster than you. You're just too chatty. Kinda like a girl that way."

We all laughed. Jaren shook his head.

David parked, and Kaitlynn hopped out of the Mustang. Jaren climbed out first, gracing me with the view of his athletic butt.

Kaitlynn noticed what I was gawking at and snickered.

"What?" Jaren asked, adjusting his sweater as he turned back. Virginia had eased into the beginning stages of fall, so it wasn't quite cold enough during the day for a jacket.

"Nothin'. Brooke was just making faces at me," Kaitlynn lied. I tried to hide the red in my cheeks as I scrambled out of the car.

When we got inside, we were escorted to Shannon's section. She's a good friend of Kaitlynn's mom, so we always sat there.

"Hi, kids!" Shannon greeted us with frosty glasses of water. "Good to see you guys hanging out," she said, looking over at me. Kaitlynn must have told her mom about my date, and then her mom must have told Shannon. Word traveled fast around here.

Kaitlynn and David flirted nonstop. He was funny and had us all laughing.

"Hey, you gals want to come running with us in the morning?" David asked.

"Isn't it cold? Why would you go running so early?" Kaitlynn asked.

"Off-season training," David said. "And it's not bad once you get going. You in or are you gonna be a baby about it?" He raised a single eyebrow and smirked.

Kaitlynn laughed, then looked at me.

"Sure. I'm in."

"Me, too, then." Kaitlynn smiled.

* * *

"I will not be held responsible for you guys missing second bell," David said as he ran his Mustang through the red light and into the student parking lot.

"No, but my mom *will* hold you responsible if you kill me," I pointed out.

Jaren laughed.

"That would never happen," David said. "I'm an excellent driver." He swung the car around and slid it into a tight spot near the school's entrance.

We all climbed out, and David looked back at his car with a proud grin. "See 'Exhibit A,'" he said, pointing to his parking job.

"Second bell. Remember?" Jaren grabbed David by the shirt, and we hustled through the doors.

Kaitlynn and I shuffled to our lockers, while Jaren and David separated from us to go to class. I let my gaze linger on them. I noticed Tiffany stood at the end of the hall, and upon her first glance at Jaren, she turned around, flouncing away from him.

"Ice witch much?" Kaitlynn whispered.

"I can't believe I just stood there when she spoke to me like that."

"Aw, don't beat yourself up over it. She's seriously not worth it."

"True," I said. "And you know, I don't like how rude she is to Jaren, but I think I might prefer this behavior over her pining to get him back." It was easier for me to put up with a rude ex-girlfriend than it was to put up with a rude ex-girlfriend who fought with me to win the boy.

I grabbed my copy of *To Kill a Mockingbird* and then we hurried down the hall toward our classes. I had English for fifth block, and Miss Andersen didn't tolerate tardiness.

"Well, does he want her back?" Kaitlynn asked.

"He said they were done this time, and he was ready to move

on." I stopped in front of my class.

"That's good," Kaitlynn said, hugged me, and then left for her class.

I plopped down into my seat on the far side of the room as the second bell rang. Carley Daniels and Bri Walters dashed through the door to their seats. Both of them had become popular with the seniors, but stayed cliquey when it came to us juniors.

They were the first girls I tried to befriend freshman year when I moved to Buena Vista; however, they weren't much of the befriending type. They tormented me about the flannel shirt I wore that day because it was a regular button down and not a fitted, designer one. They cackled and teased that I would get along great here, in the hills with all the other hillbillies brewing up their moonshine. That was when Kaitlynn stepped in and rescued me. She's had my back ever since.

"All right, students, hand up your assignments from chapter thirteen, and let's begin chapter fourteen," Miss Andersen said to quiet the after-lunch chatter.

I liked Miss Andersen. When we struggled to understand a concept, she would explain it until she felt certain that everyone grasped the lesson. I appreciated her efforts because I never had enough bravery to speak up if I didn't understand.

She walked to the front of the room, stopping at her desk to grab a new stick of chalk. She preferred the new sticks and kept her chalkboards wiped clean to minimize the dust, but I feared she would always wear chalk fingerprints on her slacks. The other kids mocked her for these chalk streaks.

Not me. I knew the discomfort of being bullied and teased. Big city or small town, my generation could be brutal. I never spoke up, though. I'd always responded the same way I did when Tiffany humiliated me in the parking lot—frozen in embarrassment and stirring in anger at my lack of courage.

Miss Andersen reached the chalk board and slid the eraser

along its cradle. She wiped her hand down her slacks and began to write on the board.

As expected, Carley yelled out to Miss Anderson, "Why even bother doing your laundry? White streaks are your signature."

The class laughed.

Miss Andersen glared at Carley, but then brushed the chalk off in wafts of dust. Miss Andersen would say something if you strolled in late to her class, but she kept her mouth closed in a tight line when students disrespected her in other ways.

I wanted to defend her, but I didn't have the guts. I could stand against a wild mountain lion, but I folded when it came to teenagers. What did that say about me? Or better yet, about my peers?

I sat there, thinking of all the things I would say if I wasn't such a coward, ashamed with myself for not speaking any of them.

4
Not Fair

Kaitlynn and I had been researching for our history project for three hours before we started to get giggly.

"You so have the hots for David," I said.

She grinned, not denying it.

"Well, you and Jaren are gonna get married and have babies."

I laughed. "No, we're not."

"Don't doubt me on this. I can see it in your eyes every time you look at him. You wanna have his babies."

"No. That is not an I-want-to-have-his-babies look."

"Oh, yeah?" Kaitlynn sat up, challenging me. "What is it, then?"

"Infatuation. Attraction. I dunno, but it has nothing to do with wanting his babies."

My phone rang. I jumped, excited as a five-year-old at a Chuck E. Cheese because Jaren's number flashed on my caller ID.

I answered the phone. "Hello?"

"Babies," Kaitlynn said.

I gave her a punishing glare and waved at her to shut up. Jaren could probably hear her.

"Hey, I just got off work, and David is going to give me a ride to your place, if that's cool with you?" Jaren asked.

"Sure. Kaitlynn and I aren't getting much work done, anyway, so head on over. Is David planning on staying, too?" I looked over at Kaitlynn. She clasped her hands and looked toward the sky in dramatic prayer that David would stay.

"I don't know," Jaren said, and then I heard a muffled, "You want to hang out with us over at Brooke's?"

"Sure," I picked up as David's answer.

"He's coming, too," Jaren said. I nodded to Kaitlynn.

She got up and started to do a happy dance, throwing her arms in the air and twisting her hips. It was actually quite ugly. I stifled the laugh that tried to sneak out.

"We'll be over in about ten minutes."

"Cool. Come in when you're here. The door's open." We hung up, and I dropped my phone next to my laptop. Kaitlynn ran down the hall to the bathroom, and I followed behind her.

"You're beautiful," I told her, leaning on the door frame of the bathroom. I tilted forward trying to get a look at myself in the mirror.

"I only wanted to make sure," Kaitlynn said, opening her jaw wide and wiping the mascara off from under her eyes. "We were laughing pretty hard there, and I was right. My mascara had run."

We primped in the bathroom until the Mustang's engine roared into my driveway. We ran into the living room and flew onto the couch, giggling and slapping at each other.

"Shut up," I told Kaitlynn.

"I'm trying. You shut up." She laughed harder.

Footsteps sounded on the porch, and we sobered.

Jaren stepped through the door first. He still wore his Computer Technician shirt. Kaitlynn or I would have changed shirts first, but he pulled it off gorgeously, and I didn't think he thought like us girls about that stuff.

"Hey," Jaren said as David closed the door behind them.

"Hey." I scooted over in the hope that Jaren would take the hint to sit beside me. "So, do you guys want to watch the newest *Resident Evil* movie?" I smiled when Jaren sat next to me. David took a seat on the other couch.

"I saw that in 3-D," David said.

My shoulders sagged. "So, do you not want to watch it, then?" I loved Milla Jovovich in that series, and it was supposed to be a guy's movie. All our other movies were chick flicks.

"No, it's fine. It won't be as good as 3-D, but I'm down to watch it," David replied.

I got up to put the disc in the player, and Kaitlynn wandered over to sit next to David on his couch. I smirked at her as I grabbed the remote and took my seat next to Jaren. His shirt felt a bit cold from being outside, but it quickly warmed up against my skin.

My mom came home after the first part of the movie. I pressed pause.

"Hi, Naomi," Jaren said, sitting up straighter as my mom locked the door behind her.

"Hey, kids. Sorry to disturb your movie. Brooke, can I talk to you for a second?" My mom walked toward her room. I got up to follow her since it really wasn't a request.

"Am I not okay to have them over tonight?" I asked, pushing her bedroom door closed behind me.

My mom moved through her room, gathering her night clothes. "It's fine. I just needed to tell you that I want them gone and you starting to get ready for bed by ten thirty."

I checked my watch. "The movie should be over by almost eleven, so can we at least finish it?" That would suck if I had to tell them they had to go home early.

"Fine, but no hanging around afterward. They need to go as soon as it's over," my mom commanded.

"They will," I promised and closed the door after I was out. It was the small victories that made life so sweet. Especially when Jaren was involved.

I strolled down the hall and sat next to Jaren. My mom's door creaked open shortly after, a sign she must be ready for bed and wanting to hear us from her room.

"Is everything okay?" Jaren whispered.

"Yeah, she wanted to make sure I get to bed at a decent hour, so she said no hanging out after the movie." I grabbed the remote.

"That's cool," David said. He put his arm around Kaitlynn, and she snuggled closer to him.

I hit PLAY on the remote, and ten minutes later Jaren put his arm around me as well. I learned fast, so I snuggled closer to him and held his hand.

My mom came out to get a drink of water, during one of the most intense parts of the movie. I think my mom's reason for coming out was more to check on us than out of her need to quench her thirst.

A while after she went back to her room, I looked over and caught Kaitlynn and David kissing. Jaren glanced over when their lip smacking grew louder and then looked back at me with a dimpled grin.

I snuggled my cheek up against Jaren's jaw, hoping he would take that cue from David as well, but he never made the move to kiss me.

When the movie ended, Jaren rose from the couch, and David detangled himself from Kaitlynn. He put her cell number in his phone, and then he and Jaren headed for the door.

I hopped up to walk them out. Jaren grabbed me into a hug and kissed me on my forehead as we stood on the porch. My bare feet were cold standing on the wood planks, but it was worth it.

"See ya bright and early," Jaren said.

I went inside and waited in the doorway while they got into the car, then I pulled the door shut. I turned around, and found Kaitlynn doing another happy dance, this time more discreet so my mom wouldn't come out.

I couldn't hold back the laughter. "You have to go, but call me when you get home and we'll talk," I told her so I would be obeying my mom's wishes, at least as far as everyone leaving after the movie.

She spun around toward the kitchen and snatched her purse from the table. I gave her a hug and peeked between the blinds as she pulled out of my driveway to head home.

After her taillights turned onto Magnolia Drive, I dropped the blinds and sighed. She got a make-out session, when all I got was a hug and a peck on the forehead.

Not fair.

5

HE'S FOLLOWING ME

I shot up in bed from the first buzz of my alarm. No snoozing for me today. Anticipation hummed through my veins at the idea of seeing Jaren. I jumped into the shower and took an extra five minutes of primping to make sure I looked as good as I felt, even though I was about to go for a run.

I sang out loud to Taylor Swift's *Back to December* on my way to school. I listen to all sorts of music. Living in a small town limits your music choices unless you buy a lot of it yourself.

I pulled into a spot near the track and saw that most of the lacrosse players were there. I took a deep breath and released it slowly in an effort to calm my nerves. I hadn't done any sort of exercise or real activity, save for hiking, in a long time. What if I couldn't keep up with Jaren? Would I look like a lazy sissy to all the lacrosse players?

Jaren waved at me from the track, so I got out of my car. Kaitlynn pulled her Jeep into the spot next to me and stepped out.

"It's cold," she said. "Are you sure we wanna go through with this? Maybe we could grab a blanket and sit on the bleachers to watch."

"No," I laughed, "we said we'd do it, and we're already here. I'm more nervous about being able to keep up than I am about the cold."

"Well, you and I can always go slow together," she said, wrapping her arm around mine as we passed through the gate onto the track.

David pulled Kaitlynn into a hug. "You made it."

"Good morning," Jaren said, stretching his quads. He wore a white Redrock County High sweater and track pants, but he still looked way good.

"Good morning to you, too," I said, mimicking his stretch. I looked around, and it seemed that there were a lot more people for me to make a fool of myself in front of than I saw from the car. "Do you come running often?" I asked, nerves getting the better of me.

"Yeah, four times a week, most weeks during the off season."

"Hmmm," I said, wishing I would have taken Kaitlynn up on her offer to sit with a blanket on the bleachers.

I followed Jaren through a few more stretches.

"You ready?" he asked.

"Sure," I said, putting on my game face. Kaitlynn and David strolled up beside us. Some of the lacrosse players were already circling the track.

"Let's go," David said, and we all took off.

We started out at a pace that I didn't feel would be too hard to keep up for a while, but then Jaren and David sped up after the second lap.

I kept up with them and was surprised when my legs obeyed me to move faster.

After a mile, Kaitlynn trailed behind, and I looked back at her. "No. Go ahead," she said, waving me on.

I picked up my speed and easily caught up with Jaren and David. We circled the lap a few more times and their breathing became labored. That was when I noticed that mine wasn't. I felt fine. In fact, I could keep going for a long time still.

"Wanna race?" I asked David because I knew he couldn't resist.

He smiled in the affirmative, and all three of us took off.

I straightened my fingers and pushed off with the balls of my feet. We reached the straightaway, and I pushed myself harder, passing David in seconds. Then I passed Jaren. I pushed myself as hard as I could, going faster than I ever thought my untrained body would go. I slowed down to take the turn and let the guys catch up with me.

I turned around and laughed at them. "You just got your butts handed to you by a girl." I had been worried about looking bad in front of them, and here I was showing them up.

"Wow," David said. "You're fast."

Jaren grinned at me. I'd say he looked proud. "Yeah, you should try out for track. We'd never lose with you on the team."

I beamed. "My mom had never let me try out for any sports or clubs before, but maybe we've been here long enough that she might."

"It doesn't hurt to ask," Jaren said, encouraging me.

"You're right. I should at least ask her." I was thrilled that not only was I good enough at something to be on a team but that I might actually be able to convince my mom to let me try out.

We caught up with Kaitlynn to do a few cool-down laps. When we finished our stretches, we walked to the building to get changed and ready for class.

David opened the door for us, and we walked in.

Tiffany stood with a group of her friends in the foyer. She wore her brown leather jacket and slacks that slimmed her thighs. She looked great, and I was glad to find that Jaren didn't pay any attention to her.

She normally didn't pay much attention to him, either, but when she caught Jaren in her sight, she turned around and glared at him. She'd noticed Jaren and me holding hands. Suddenly, her lip rose and her eyes twinkled with interest in what she saw. It reminded me of the way a hyena would look upon an injured gazelle.

I picked up my pace, pulling Jaren with me as I scurried past her.

* * *

I walked toward sixth block, excited to see Jaren. We both had study hall this block, but we sat on the couch in the corner of the room and flirted instead of doing any studying.

I met him outside of the study hall doors. "Hey," I said.

"Hey. Are we hanging out today?" he asked, looking over at our sofa. We'd claimed the couch early on in the semester. "Or did you want me to leave you alone?"

I smiled, figuring he only asked because he was prompting me to say that I wanted to hang out with him. I gave in. "No. We're definitely hanging."

He laughed, offering me his cute dimple in the process.

We walked over to our couch and plopped down.

Jaren grabbed my hand and traced the lines on the inside of my palm. "So, my birthday's next Thursday. And I'm planning to take you somewhere special."

"What? It's your birthday. I should be taking you out for the big one-eight."

"True, but it's going to be better this way. Trust me."

"Jaren, come up here, please?" Coach Riley called Jaren to his desk. "I need you to run something to the office for me. Seeing as you're not working, anyway." Coach Riley looked at me on the couch.

"Hey, I'm not the culprit." I feigned innocence.

Jaren looked over at me as well. "Can she come, too?"

"I don't see why not," Coach Riley said, shaking his head and then writing us a hall pass.

Jaren took the pass and the papers intended for the office, and we left.

"Thanks for getting me out of class," I said.

"Well, you are my study hall sidekick."

I grinned, and he held my hand as we walked.

We didn't say much else as we made our way to the office. I was just glad to be with him.

Jaren opened the door to the office when we approached it. "Hello," Jaren said to the office secretary when we reached the desk. "These papers are for Principal Williams."

"I'll make sure he gets them. May I see your hall pass, please?"

Jaren handed it to her, and she nodded, giving it back.

He held the door open for me as we walked out.

"What is she, the hall pass police? You did give her the papers from Coach Riley."

"Yeah, she can be sort of strict about that."

"What would she do if you didn't have one?" I asked.

"I dunno. Probably call in a Code Red or something."

I laughed. "What's that?"

"I dunno. It just sounded like a serious last step." He chuckled.

"Hey, can we stop by the photography studio for a sec?" Jaren asked, turning down the hall. "I need to get something real fast. I was gonna get it after class, but since we're here..."

I didn't mind, so we walked farther away from the office and also farther away from study hall.

Shortly before we reached the studio doors, Mr. Kingston appeared in the reflection of the windows, coming toward us.

"Crap. Mr. Kingston's going to kill us," I said. I had him for Spanish and he was super strict and mean.

Jaren pulled me by my hand as he rushed to the studio doors. Once there, he creaked the door open and we hurried inside. He held the door as it shut, making it close as quietly as possible.

"Quick. This way." Jaren led me to another room.

He opened the door, and red light from the darkroom leaked out. I ran in, and he shut the door behind us.

I laughed.

"Shh," Jaren said. "Mr. Kingston really might kill us if he finds us."

I laughed harder, but this time I hid my face in my arm. It took me a few seconds, but once my eyes adjusted to the dark and the red light, I noticed pictures hanging from a string.

I released Jaren's hand and walked over to them to get a closer look. The few that hung before me looked familiar. Probably because I was in all of them.

"Um, yeah," Jaren said, "those are mine."

I remembered that day. It was before Jaren and I had our first date. Kaitlynn and I were laughing in front of the school. The way Jaren captured me in the picture gave me a beauty that I had never before seen within myself.

"Wow. You're really good," I said. "How long have you been doing this?"

"I just started with this class."

I knew photography was one of his electives, but I never knew he could do this with it. "Well, you're really talented." I turned back to him and smiled. He had his eye on me for a while, too, then.

He stepped forward and stood beside me, looking at the photos. "I think it's more the person in the image than it is anything I did with it." He turned to me. I looked at him, but he grabbed me by my waist and turned my body to face him.

My pulse raced and breathing became hard to do. I looked into his eyes and knew that this would be our moment.

I wrapped my arms around Jaren's neck, and he pulled me closer to him and touched his lips to mine. My heart skipped at the contact and then increased twofold.

His lips meshed delicately smooth but firm and sure against mine. He lifted his hand up to cup my face and slowly started to open his mouth. I opened mine, following his pace. His tongue slid into my mouth and brushed my tongue with the tip of his.

Jaren tasted sweet, like faded strawberry Red Vines and bliss. His warm breath tickled my cheek. His hand caressed my jaw, then glided through my hair before cradling the back of my head.

I shivered. I had been kissed before, but never like this.

Jaren's movements were sensual, yet playful, commanding, yet yielding. His arms were strong and reassuring around me. His fresh linen scent felt like home, which drove my intensity up another notch.

His bottom lip was full, and it did wonderful things to me when he gently bit mine, then released it, letting it glide against his bottom lip.

We fell into a practiced and comfortable pace for what felt like ten minutes, but seemed to float away timeless. Jaren pulled back and propped his forehead against mine. He breathed heavily, releasing intoxicating whiffs of sweetness around me.

I lifted my face to look into his eyes. Endearing, violet eyes stared back at me with the blue of his irises and the red from the overhead light.

"I have been waiting for a while to do that," Jaren said, smiling.

I bet I've waited even longer.

He released me and reached for one of the pictures. "Here, you can have this one." He handed it to me.

I grinned as I looked down at the picture, taking in all of its details. That was when I noticed a lone figure not too far from where I had been standing. And he was wearing a trench coat.

I leaned over the long sink and looked closer at all the other photos.

"What is it?" Jaren asked.

The man was in all of them. "See this guy here?" I pointed to the man in the picture I held.

"Yeah," Jaren said, leaning down to look at the picture.

"He's following me."

"How do you know? These were all taken the same day."

"I know. I've seen him before. When he sent a mountain lion to attack me."

"What?" Jaren asked.

I told him the details of my last encounter with the man.

"You need to tell somebody about this," Jaren said.

I thought the same thing. But who would I tell? Once my mom heard about this she would make us move. Whenever things got too hot, she always made us move. Even if it was something as small as the same car circling our street more than what would be considered *normal*. She was a freak like that. Paranoid. I'd lose everything. Kaitlynn. Jaren. My school. My life.

I had to diminish the fear Jaren felt for me. I couldn't have him telling anyone about this. Maybe I was being careless, but I finally had a life, and I would take my chances with this stranger to keep it.

"He hasn't really done anything, though. I mean, no one but you will believe me that he sicced a wild cat on me. And he's only in the background here," I said, pointing to the picture. "He could have been just walking by."

Jaren stared at me, concern etched in his creased forehead.

"I mean it. I overreacted. I get that from my mom," I said and leaned in to kiss him again. I wanted to remember this moment as our first kiss and not when I realized this man was following me. I'd have to deal with the man later.

* * *

My alarm clock glowed 2:32 a.m. in green, blocky letters. Jaren and I had been talking on the phone for the past four hours. I talked in a hushed tone to keep my voice hidden from my mom, who was in the room across the hall.

"What about past boyfriends?" Jaren asked. "Is there anyone that I have to worry about swooping in and stealing you away from me?"

I laughed quietly. "No. I never really had a chance to get to know anybody. There was a guy in Dallas who I liked, but as soon as he showed any interest in me, my mom made me move here."

"That's gotta be rough on you. Moving all the time."

"It's never been easy. But for some reason, this last time was the hardest," I said. "Maybe because I'm old enough that I need to start making lasting friendships, or maybe I'm sick of never having a place to call home. I don't have a specific place to say, 'this is where I grew up.'"

"I can't even imagine. David and I have been best friends since second grade. He was there for me when my mom cheated on my dad and they got divorced. My dad changed after that. He used to be so involved. He really cared about me. But after they split, he shunned me, like I was the one who had the affair and not my mom. I'm still not sure if it's because I look so much like her or because I'm her son, but he's never treated me the same since. And then my mom ended up going off somewhere with her new boy toy and couldn't care less what was left of her family, or the son she helped create."

"Oh, man. I'm sorry."

"Yeah, it sucks, but I can't change him," he said. The other end of the line got quiet for a second. "So, what's your sad story?"

"My dad found out about my mom's pregnancy and took off. She says it was for the best because I shouldn't be a part of what his life was like, anyway, but I would still like to know who he was and why he didn't want me. You know what it's like not to have a father around. Well, yours is there, but not really. But there are times when I think I probably would have avoided a lot of the moves or had a different perspective on things if I would've had a father around. My mom has tried, but she can only do so much."

"Your mom has done an excellent job with you, though. You turned out great, but I know what you mean about wishing for something else. You know that quote, 'It is better to have loved and lost than to never have loved at all'?" Jaren asked.

I turned onto my side and pulled my hair up to fan out over the pillow, so it wouldn't crease. "Yeah, I've heard of it, but I don't know who said it."

"Me, neither," Jaren chuckled, then sighed. "But sometimes, I think it would've been better for me to never have known that my dad could be a great dad. Now, I know that he has the ability to be an awesome dad, but he's not because he hates me. That's the absolutely worst part for me."

"For me, it's the not knowing. I hold onto that feeling of rejection that my dad left because of me, and I'm the reason he's no longer with my mom. With your dad, his animosity is directed at you, but comes from someone else."

"Wow," Jaren said, voice thick with emotion. "I have tried to tell myself that before, but I have always been able to talk myself out of it. When did you become so wise?"

I smiled. I was giddy inside, and didn't feel a tiny bit tired yet. It was like my mind was clear and my eyes were weightless.

"Sometimes, it's easier to see from the outside."

"Well, I'm glad that I have someone like you on the outside," Jaren said.

"Are you saying you want to keep me at a distance?"

"No. You know what I mean." We were quiet for a moment considering all that had been said. "What are you doing tomorrow night?" Jaren asked.

"Kaitlynn and I are going dress shopping with her mom. One of her cousins is getting married and her mom needs to find something pink."

Jaren laughed. "Pink. That ought to be fun. Guess I won't be seeing you after school then."

"Guess not. That'll be kind of weird," I said, missing him already. I had Jaren's jacket snuggled up against my chest, and I pressed my face into the leather and wool. It smelled like him, fresh and crisp, like a breeze blown over a river. He reminded me of summer. Warmth and lazy days. Juicy fruits and fresh cut grass.

"Are you still awake?" Jaren asked quietly. I must have lost myself in his scent for longer than I thought.

"Yes, I'm still here," I said, pushing the distraction of his jacket a little farther away from my face.

"Are you getting tired yet?"

"Not really. Why? Are you?" I didn't want to hang up unless Jaren was getting tired.

"A little bit. I should probably let you go. Just because you aren't feeling tired right now doesn't mean you won't be exhausted tomorrow. I expect you fresh and witty in study hall tomorrow," Jaren said with a stern tone.

"You, too, then," I laughed.

"I'll try. Sweet dreams, and see ya tomorrow."

I snuggled his jacket closer to my face in an effort to comfort myself after we hung up. I fell asleep shortly after with Jaren's fresh scent lingering in my nose and his phantom lips brushing over my mouth.

6
HE WAS THERE

When Kaitlynn and I pulled up to her house the next day after school, her mom was in frantic mode. She was a busy lady, an interior designer, which wasn't a nine-to-five, so I could understand.

"Hi, Rhonda," I said to Kaitlynn's mom.

"Oh, hello, Brooke. You sure are looking lovely today," Rhonda said. She put down some small boxes and gave me a hug and squeeze to the shoulders.

"Thanks. Are we still going shopping?" She looked really busy, and I didn't know if she still had time carved out for shopping.

"Yes. I have to get this stupid dress, so I can stop fretting about it. One less thing to fret about is good, right?" She picked up her boxes and set them on top of the credenza in the office across the hall.

Both of Kaitlynn's parents worked, so they had a nice house. It wasn't very large, but the interior was high end, the floors either dark mahogany wood or Italian travertine, depending on the area in the house.

"Ladies," Rhonda said, "we'll take my car, if you don't mind?" We followed Rhonda down the porch steps and into her Durango.

Buena Vista touted a quaint dress shop called Mary's Boutique. The store was small, but Mary was able to fit a good selection of dresses between her store's tight walls.

Rhonda began by walking around with Kaitlynn and me to search the racks of dresses, but eventually we got to the point of bringing her what we liked. We thought would be limited because we were looking for a pink dress, but Mary assured us that she could dye any white dress to match any color of pink we wanted. She also mentioned that if the style didn't come in pink or white, then she would order it in for Rhonda. Great for Rhonda, but that meant we'd be here all night; Rhonda could be particular about clothing.

"Girls," Rhonda hollered from her dressing room, "no more banana Popsicle colors. I don't care how much you like the style. They all look terrible on me."

Kaitlynn and I chuckled. She put aside her newly started pile of dresses and set out to collect everything "banana Popsicle" colored. I had to walk to the other side of the boutique for fear of snickering too loud.

When Kaitlynn felt satisfied with her putrid pile, she scurried off to deliver it to Rhonda.

"Kaitlynn!" Rhonda squealed. "I said *not* to bring me anymore of these." Rhonda handed back the pile of dresses and turned Kaitlynn around by her shoulders to send them back.

We must have gone through one thousand dresses or more because we were there until Mary had to close. Kaitlynn and I were ecstatic when we finally found the perfect dress for Rhonda. The length would have to be adjusted because Rhonda was short, and she didn't fuss with heels, either.

I wanted to pass out from exhaustion by the time Rhonda finished paying for the dress and ordering the alterations. Jaren had been right about me suffering today for last night's late chat. I stumbled out of the dress shop, triggering the bell on the door when I pushed it open. Mary waited behind us to turn the lock and close the shop for the night.

The air was crisp and had some bite. It jerked me out of my tired fog. I became alert enough that when I looked up and peered across the street, I recognized a figure silhouetted in the shadows. I blinked a couple of times to clear my eyes of any lingering daze, and found the figure to be a man standing in a crevice between two buildings. He wore the same trench coat as the man who sent the mountain lion after us, and his face was shadowed in the dark, but I was sure it was the same man.

"Kaitlynn!" I shrieked, tugging on her arm and pointing. "It's the man who sicced the mountain lion on us!"

By the time Kaitlynn looked up and over at the buildings, the man had disappeared into the shadows. His creepy setup was almost perfect. The only thing missing was the fog and the eerie music. "He was just right there. I swear it—on us."

"You're tired. Let's get you home so you can go to bed."

"He was there."

"Huh, ladies?" Rhonda asked, huddling close to our shoulders to get in on the secret. "What's going on?" she asked as if we were whispering about boys.

"Oh, nothing. Brooke is tired. We should get her home," Kaitlynn said, covering for me.

"I'm so sorry we took as long as we did," Rhonda's face creased with concern as she apologized.

"It's perfectly fine," I said, trying to hurry things up so she wouldn't be apologizing all night, and we could get out of here. "We got you a great dress, right?"

She smiled. "We did." She walked around the hood of the Durango and slid into the driver's side.

As soon as I was in my room, I changed into my pajamas and plopped down on my bed. Warmth escaped me, even though I was underneath my blankets. The chill brought on by the thought of the crazy man following me drilled into my bones, smothering any heat that tried to kindle there.

Piecing together from Jaren's pictures that the man was following me was quite a bit different from actually catching him in the act. I could tell my mom, but I wasn't ready to move. No, Kaitlynn and Jaren were too irreplaceable to allow for any of my mom's rash relocation decisions.

I wouldn't say anything about my stalker unless he got closer to me. He'd mostly been spying from a distance, anyway. I'd have to be careful not to go out by myself anymore.

My exhaustion won over any concern I had for my own well-being, and I was asleep in minutes.

* * *

I startled awake when my cell phone vibrated on my nightstand. I picked it up and found Kaitlynn's number on the caller ID. It was only eleven thirty. What could she possibly want? I had been with her two hours ago.

"Hey," I said, wiping the sleep from my eyes.

"Sorry. I know you were sleeping, but my mom just got off the phone with Shannon. She told my mom that she saw Jaren walking with Tiffany in the park today."

My stomach dropped, and I gasped. My mouth went dry.

"Well, did she say if they were holding hands, or kissing, or anything else?" I asked, trying to hold myself together. I was on the verge of a major freak out.

"She said that they were walking, but them being together can't be good news for us, right?" Kaitlynn sounded really sick about this, too.

"Did Shannon say how long they were there?" I needed more information. No. I needed facts because my mind was playing *worst case scenario* with what I'd heard.

"She doesn't know how long they were together. She was at the playground with her kids when Tiffany and Jaren walked around on the trail toward the parking lot. She didn't go follow them or anything."

"I hate her," I growled. Kaitlynn knew I meant Tiffany. "She was so evil to Jaren before she knew he wanted me. Now, she wants him back all of a sudden because he can't be with anyone else. I seriously HATE her," I spit out and started to cry.

"Oh, Brooke. Do you want me to come over there? I am so

sorry, hun," Kaitlynn said, trying to console me.

"No. It won't help, anyway. I'm gonna cry whether you're here or not, and you don't really need to see me being a blubbering mess tonight. I love you, though. Thanks for letting me know, but I'm going to go now, okay?" I sniffled.

"Okay. I love you, too. Try to get some sleep so you're not stressing about it all night." It sounded nice, but I wasn't feeling like the universe was going to give me any "get out of jail free" cards on this one.

I lay on my bed going from furious at Tiffany, to heartbroken and betrayed by Jaren, to enraged at Jaren, then back at wishing terrible things would happen to Tiffany.

I knew she just couldn't let me have him. I knew it. From the moment she saw him and I walking through the back doors at school, hand in hand, she wanted him back. How stupid could I be? You don't get to be that big of a witch and still get to keep Jaren around for a whole freaking year unless you had some conniving tricks to keep him.

Ugh, I *hate* her. I clenched my jaw, grinding my teeth to keep from yelling.

Great.

Now, everyone is going to know what a fool I've been and that he and Tiffany are back together. I knew he was going to end up leaving me. Same as my dad.

My stomach twisted. My hands shook as I furiously wiped the tears from my face. I was further frustrated because my mom slept in the next room, and I had to keep quiet or she'd end up being another witness to my demise, wrapped in a pretty little pink bow, signed:

Truly yours,
Tiffany XOXO

Arrrrhhhh. Tiffany probably didn't even want him back because she missed him. I bet her only motive was because she didn't want me to have him.

I tried to focus more on my breathing and less on the internal monologue. I kept telling myself that I didn't really know anything yet and needed to stop jumping to conclusions. Eventually, I tuckered myself out so much from all the tears and thrashing around on my bed that I passed out for the remainder of the night.

7
He Tarnished It

The next morning, I had to force my legs to walk to the bathroom. I tried to convince myself that maybe Jaren and Tiffany simply talked and not to jump to any conclusions. It wasn't like they were going to get back together. Right?

Oh, man. My stomach hurt. I jumped into the cold shower trying to shock myself out of this terrifying train of thought.

Jaren and I had made plans before I left school yesterday that we'd meet up today at lunch. I wasn't really sure what was going on anymore. I certainly didn't want to call him and make a greater fool of myself by groaning to him about it. So, you can imagine my surprise when I saw him pull into my driveway with David's Mustang. It must really be serious then. David didn't let Jaren take his Mustang "just because."

I was grateful that my mom had left to go show a client some houses. I didn't want her getting involved in this.

I opened the door before Jaren could knock on it. My face contorted with anger.

"Hey," Jaren hesitated. "Can I talk to you? Can we go for a ride or something, please?" Jaren's face told me what he tried to hide in his voice—regret and urgency.

"Where do you want to go? The *park*?" I crossed my arms.

"That's not fair. At least let me tell you what has been going on with me, okay? If you never want to talk to me again afterward, then I'll accept that. But I can't accept it if you won't even hear me out."

I grabbed my keys from the counter and slammed the front door behind me. "You're driving."

Jaren took Highway 60 and drove until we were out of town. We passed the point where we watched the meteor shower, and I squeezed my eyes shut as hard as I could, demanding they not water.

Jaren stayed on the highway until we were deep into the Blue Ridge Mountains. It would have been nice to have been coming up here with him under different circumstances. The leaves were now brilliant oranges and fiery reds. I loved nothing more about the East than its vibrant fall seasons.

Jaren turned the car into a pull-out. He shut it off and faced me. I met his eyes with daggers in mine.

"It really isn't as bad as you think," Jaren said, but I cut him off.

"Right, like you know anything about what I am thinking right now."

"Okay, let me get this out, and then you can cut in all you want, please?" His eyes took on a pleading shine. I nodded my head in agreement.

"Tiffany came up to me after school yesterday and asked if she could talk to me."

"Before or after I left?" I had spoken to him after school, right before I'd left with Kaitlynn.

"After I talked to you."

I sucked in a ragged, angry breath. She had probably been hanging out, waiting for me to leave so she could swoop in like a vulture.

"Let me finish," he said.

I huffed air from my nostrils and rolled my eyes.

"I know. I was surprised by this, too, because...well, you've seen how she's ignored me or been a complete snob."

I nodded again, and he continued.

"Well, I was curious to see what she had to say, so I got in her car. She took me to the park and asked if we could go for a walk. She kept going over 'remember this' and 'remember that' until I

42

finally told her to tell me what she wanted to talk about."

My heart pounded against my ribs, waiting for the devastating punch line.

"We stopped walking, and she told me that she realized she'd made a huge mistake and that all she'd ever wanted from me were simple gestures, like me holding her hand while we walked down the hallway. She said she really missed me, and all this stuff—"

"Get to the point. Are you guys back together or not?" I said, demanding the answer.

"I'm getting to that. So, after she tells me all that, she kissed me, and I'm not going to lie, I kissed her back." Jaren had to see the hurt on my face. My nightmares from last night were confirmed.

"Here's the important part; I don't want to get back with Tiffany. I didn't do those kinds of gestures for her because she never made me feel like I wanted to. When I'm with you, I feel alive and happy. I never felt that way with her. I told you I was ready to move on, and I had a lapse of uncertainty, but I know, as confidently as I can, that I want to be with you officially now," Jaren said with finality.

"What do you mean *officially*?" I spit back with venom. He flinched. Certainly not the reaction he had anticipated from me.

"Well, we'd been dating, but we weren't official or anything yet," Jaren said, trying to talk reason into me.

"Yeah, well...I wasn't dating anyone else, and neither were you until Tiffany decided no one else could have you," I said, raising my voice and getting out of the car. Jaren got out as well.

I marched toward him. "And what was all that talk the other night about asking if there were any guys you had to worry about taking me away from you?" Fury boiled within me.

"I meant it. I don't want to lose you," Jaren said.

I started to cry because I was hurt, and he sounded sincere.

"I never told you that you couldn't date anyone else, and I never told you that I wouldn't, either. But that is what I'm trying to do now, if you'll have me," Jaren pleaded. He grabbed my hands and brought them to his chest like he hurt, too.

I slid my hands away and looked him in the eyes for emphasis. "I don't know. I'm pretty ticked off right now. The only thing that changes with *official* is that I get to change my relationship status on Facebook to 'in a relationship.' So...just take me home," I said, turning toward the car and getting in. I didn't want him to see how much pain I was in. I also didn't want to have to see his pleading eyes, either.

Jaren stood outside for a moment, stunned that this conversation didn't go as he had thought it would. He got in the car and turned it around, heading toward my house.

"I know this is terrible timing, but I think I'm falling in love with you," he confessed when we were stopped at a light.

I put my hands up to my face because there was no way I could hold back the tears. The hardest part was that I felt like I loved him, too, and he had just tarnished it.

* * *

As soon as I shut the front door behind me and heard the Mustang drive away, I lost all control and the sobbing took over. I slid down the door, hurt and confused. I had never felt this strong for a guy before, so I had never been hurt in quite this way.

I went back and forth from believing Jaren was genuinely falling for me, to believing that he couldn't be sure about anything at all if he kissed Tiffany yesterday and confessed his love for me today. I feared I should have told him how strongly I felt about him when I had the chance, and because I didn't, he was going to run back to Tiffany to take her up on her evil offer.

I wasn't doing any good for myself by going back and forth, so I called Kaitlynn.

"Is everything okay?" Kaitlynn asked. I could hear her concern and love for me in that one question.

"I'm not really sure. Do you think you could come over? I think I need my best friend right now," I sniffled.

"I'm on my way. Do you want me to stop and get some double chunk chocolate ice cream?" She knew the keys to comfort oh so well.

"Please." My lip quivered.

As soon as Kaitlynn arrived, I started to feel better about everything. She had a way of soothing me when I went in freak-out mode.

"The reason why you're so hurt is because you care about him and want to be with him, right?" Kaitlynn asked. She brushed aside some of the mess my hair had become.

"Yeah," I said.

"And he said he didn't want Tiffany, but that he wanted to be with you, right?"

"Yeah."

"So, be with him," she said simply. She had a point. I couldn't change the past. I didn't like what happened, but I couldn't do anything about it. My choices were to either be with Jaren, or not be with Jaren. Even after everything that had happened, I honestly still wanted to be with him.

Kaitlynn and I made plans for her to spend the night at my house. As we got ready for bed, I texted Jaren to tell him I would pick him up tomorrow so we could talk. He texted me back right away saying he was sorry for hurting me, and he was glad he'd get to see me tomorrow.

"I would say it's a good sign he texted back so soon. I think he's been waiting around to hear from you," Kaitlynn said, fluffing her pillow and throwing back her end of the covers. She climbed in, then turned off the table lamp.

I was exhausted from all of the crying, but I felt like things were set right again. Before I passed out for the night, I had the most satisfying thought: Tiffany didn't get the guy.

I guess I had gotten my sweet revenge after all. She wouldn't be made a fool in front of the whole school like I would've been, but *I knew* and *she knew* that she had made her move to get Jaren back, or her sloppy seconds, as she'd called him, and she'd failed. I snuggled deeper into the blankets with a victorious smile on my face.

8

His Mouth Was Warm

Kaitlynn and I got up at ten o'clock to get showered and dressed for the day. She and David had plans and she told me to call her if Jaren and I wanted to hang out with them.

She followed me into the living room where we found my mom. My mom didn't show houses on Sundays so here she was, wiping down the blinds.

My eyes had been red and swollen when my mom came home last night, so I ended up telling her about Tiffany trying to get Jaren back. I didn't tell her about the part where they kissed, though. Even at that, she was concerned with how hard I'd fallen for Jaren.

"I'm going to meet up with Jaren to discuss some things," I told my mom. She knew how much this meant to me, so I hoped she wouldn't try to stop me.

"What time will you be home?" she asked.

"I'll only be gone an hour. Two at the most."

"All right," she said. "Call me to check in after an hour."

"'Kay." I was willing to call her every fifteen minutes if she'd let me go.

I followed Kaitlynn out to her car. "Thanks for everything, bestie," I said, giving her a tight squeeze that lifted her off the ground a little.

"I'm glad you're back to your giddy self again," Kaitlynn laughed, dropping back to the ground. She grabbed her keys out of her purse and got in her Jeep.

My boots crunched the leaves into the gravel drive as I hustled over to my car.

"Call me later," Kaitlynn hollered out of her window as she drove away.

Jaren was waiting for me in his driveway when I pulled up. He made a motion of driving an invisible steering wheel, asking me if he could drive. I laughed and put the car in park.

I stepped out into the crisp, cold morning, and we walked to meet each other. I smiled up at him. I could see the relief on his face that we were on good terms again. My eyes dropped to his chest.

I placed my hand over his heart. His body's heat seeped into my palm. "The reason I was hurt so badly by the Tiffany thing is because I care a lot about you." I looked into his blue eyes. "That is also why I texted you and want to continue to see you. I want to be with you and you to be with just me," I said, a little scared he might have changed his mind after all.

"I want the same." Jaren grinned wider. His hand grazed my cheek. The delicate touch drew tendrils of warmth through my arms and into my gut. He studied me with his eyes and then focused on my lips as if he wanted to kiss me, but his eyes lingered.

He finally gave in by brushing his lips against mine. I smelled his fresh breath before I tasted it. His lips started out cold, but his mouth was warm. Our tongues welcomed each other, and I knew I had done the right thing by forgiving him. I would probably still hurt for a while over this, but I was willing to move forward with him now.

"It's a good thing, too," Jaren said, pulling away from me. "I'd already made plans for us on Thursday."

"Right," I said. Crap. I almost forgot his birthday with all of this Tiffany drama. "You already made all the plans?" That was fast.

"Yes. Now, if my *girlfriend* would kindly get in the car, we could get on with our date."

"Hey, if my *boyfriend* would stop putting moves on me, I

would."

Jaren laughed, and I allowed myself to smile. Both of us were elated to be together.

"Now," Jaren said, starting the car and turning around in the driveway, "what would you like to do today?"

"Well, I was thinking yesterday, as we drove up Highway 60, that I wished we were driving up there under better circumstances."

"It is really amazing up there," Jaren agreed. He turned onto Beech Street and followed it until he turned onto the highway. He put his hand in the center console, palm up, and looked at my hand, then his. "Huh? Huh?" he winked. I laughed and placed my hand in his. We drove in silence for a few minutes, breathing in the energized air between us.

Jaren pulled the car off to the side of the road and parked. He came around to my door. "I thought we were going for a drive?" I asked, getting out.

"I have a better idea," he smiled. His voice vibrated with excitement. We entered through the trees, and Jaren found a trail that he must have known was there in order to find it so quick.

"Wow! This is beautiful," I said, stepping over a large rock and onto the trail. The trees flattered the trail with leaves of crimson, burnt orange, and citrine. Japanese ivy climbed in and out of limbs, covering the branches with violet. The sun filtered through, its rays highlighting rocks and fallen mossy logs.

"This isn't even the best part," Jaren said, building my anticipation. He held my hand as we walked along the trail. I squeezed his, then he squeezed mine, and we laughed.

We turned around a sharp bend and what my eyes beheld sucked the breath out of me. Water glistened as it tumbled from a small waterfall into a pond surrounded by smaller trees and blankets of ivy. The pond flowed into a shallow river that twisted in and out of the trees, to be forgotten beyond this spot of paradise.

"This is amazing! How did you find it?" I let go of his hand to wander closer to the pond and twirled around in an overload of titillated senses.

"My dad and I used to come fishing here before the divorce. I've never brought anybody here. Before you, that is."

I dropped my eyes from the brilliance of this place and focused on the sincerity in Jaren's. The fact that he brought me to such a special spot, one that held only the best memories for him, swelled something warm and delicate within my heart.

I stepped away from the pond and took the few paces needed to touch my toes to Jaren's. My eyes held his for fear that breaking contact would evaporate this feeling that caressed my soul.

Jaren touched my face, and I nuzzled my cheek against the delicate cradle of his palm. "I meant what I said yesterday. I love you, Brooke." I didn't think the warmth within me could burrow its roots any deeper, but that's what happened.

"I love you," I whispered.

Jaren crushed his lips to mine. I felt connected to him in a way that I had only read about. I finally felt what true love meant. I let it embrace me, and I could understand why it was powerful enough to start wars and destroy lives. It was something worth fighting for and something that you didn't realize you would miss as deeply or as painfully as you could until it was there and you couldn't bear to be without it.

*　*　*

I woke to Jaren's ring tone. I squinted up at the clock, surprised he was calling me at six thirty in the morning.

"Happy birthday," I said, hoping I was the first one to wish him a happy eighteenth.

"Thanks," Jaren whispered. Uh-oh. He didn't sound excited about it.

"Hey, what's going on?" I asked, sitting up in bed, rubbing the sleep from my eyes.

"My dad left for a business trip. When he woke me up this morning, I allowed myself to believe it was to wish me a happy birthday before he left." I could hear the bitterness in his voice.

"Oh, no. What did he say?" I knew it had to be really bad for him to not wait until we were at school to tell me.

"He told me I had until the end of the weekend to find my own place, and then threw a couple thousand dollars down on my bed. He kicked me out. On my birthday!"

"Man. I'm so sorry." I ached for him. "That was a really evil thing for him to do, but we'll go after school and look at some apartments. At least he gave you some money to help you get started, right?"

"No. He gave me the money so he wouldn't look like a complete jerk," Jaren said, voice shaking. I'd never heard him like this. I knew his dad was cold, but I never thought he could be this mean and heartless.

I tried to stay optimistic for Jaren's sake. "Regardless of why, you do have the money, and you'll need it to get a place. If you want, we can skip school to start looking this morning."

"Yeah, I want to get out of here as soon as I can. He obviously doesn't want me living here. I tried so hard to stay out of his way, too. I never asked him for money or anything." He sounded vexed.

"'Kay, let me shower. I'll come pick you up, and then we'll make some calls." This was going to be a rough day for Jaren. He was already sensitive about his dad, and this was only going to make it worse. I couldn't understand how a father could do that to his own son.

"Thanks. It means a lot to me that you're here for me like this." Jaren's sincerity broke my heart.

"Of course I'm here for you. I love you."

"I love you, too."

* * *

When I pulled into Jaren's driveway, he was sprawled out on the lawn with a vase of pink lilies propped up against him. He saw me and dragged himself up with a grim twist to his mouth. He walked over to get in the passenger side. He really was in a bad mood if he didn't want to drive. He always wanted to drive. That was another thing about his dad. He had the means to buy Jaren a car as owner one of the manufacturing plants in town. But he wouldn't. He wouldn't give Jaren any spending money, either. That was why Jaren worked after school instead of joining another sports team.

"Are you okay? And what are the flowers for?" I asked, grabbing his hand. I had to wiggle my fingers against the tight fist he must have been holding since his dad dropped the bomb. Jaren's hand relaxed, as did some of the anger on his face.

He handed me the vase with his other hand. "I got these for you as part of the plan for today, I didn't want to leave them here. They're yours and you should have them."

Lilies were my favorite flowers. "Aww, thanks. I'm so sorry your dad did this to you."

Jaren looked at me with a smile that didn't reach his eyes. "I wanted to break everything in the house as a little reminder that he could've had it so much worse."

"You didn't though, did you?" His dad was the type of man who would call the sheriff and demand charges be brought against him. His own son.

"No, but it felt good to imagine it." Now the smile reached his eyes, but it was a bitter one devoid of happiness.

I gave the vase back and turned the car around to get us out of there before Jaren decided property damage was indeed appropriate. "I figured we could go back to my house to find some places that are renting, and then we could go check some of 'em out."

"That works," Jaren said. "It sucks I'll probably have to use some of my college money for things that are not for college."

"I thought you were getting a scholarship?" Jaren was supposed to play lacrosse for William and Lee University next season.

"I did, but it doesn't cover housing or books."

"Well, I'm sure it'll all work out." I had to believe it would. Jaren deserved so much more than his dad had given him.

I pulled into my driveway and shut the car off. I was glad my mom was already gone. I didn't want her hovering the whole time. Plus, she wouldn't be too happy that I was missing school, either.

I set the vase of lilies on the counter and turned on my laptop. "Do you want anything to eat or drink?" I asked Jaren.

"Nah, I'm not really hungry, but I'll take a Coke if you have one?" I handed him his drink and opened my Web browser. I searched for places to rent in Buena Vista.

"What about this one?" It was close to his work and it was the same price as an apartment, but it was a quaint little duplex.

"I could probably swing that," Jaren said with some interest.

He pulled out his phone and called Trish, the lady listed as the contact. "Hello, Trish? This is Jaren Matthews. Would it be possible for me to look at your duplex on Iring?" There was a pause as Trish responded. "That works. We'll be there at ten."

We found a couple of other places that Jaren could "swing" and then set out on a mission to find him a new place to live.

The first apartment we looked at was in his price range, but it reeked of stale cat urine. We didn't have to go very far into that place to know it was a dud.

We drove to Trish's duplex next. The house rested on a well-manicured yard with red and violet Japanese ivy climbing up the planks of gray siding.

Trish, a sweet, middle-aged woman with back problems said she hired out the yard care to the Taylor boys. "I'll give you a discount on the rent if you do the yard yourself," Trish said, unlocking the front door. "Mr. Brackens next door is too old for any kind of yard work, and his eyes and hearing are shot."

We were welcomed inside to a brightly lit yellow room. Light streamed in from the curtains to flutter against the back wall. The place looked dated with the wallpaper and the yellow Formica counter tops in the kitchen, but at least the house had been updated as recently as the '80s. The floors creaked underfoot, but they looked clean and well maintained.

The bedroom had been updated most recently. The wallpaper was gone, replaced by a fresh coat of eggshell paint. New, plush carpet had been laid and the soft brown tones complemented the paint. It felt cozy in here.

"I like it," I said to Jaren. I could tell he liked it, too, by the way he kept opening up the drawers and closets.

"You know, I think this is the one." Jaren showed the first sign of a true smile all day.

9
CATALYST

Kaitlynn, David, Jaren, and I had been moving Jaren into his new place all weekend. David couldn't get over how cool it was that Jaren had his own bachelor pad, and I think some of his excitement rubbed off on Jaren.

Jaren's dad let him take all the furniture out of his room, so it was nice Jaren didn't have to buy everything from scratch, although Jaren thought it was so his dad didn't have any reminders of Jaren lying around.

Kaitlynn and David had been gone for a couple of hours when I began to make dinner. Jaren put on one of the *Fast and Furious* movies to watch while we ate. I was glad he was finally settling in.

The doorbell rang, and I jumped, spaghetti sauce splashing over the sides of the pot. Kaitlynn and David had already become accustomed to walking in, and neither Jaren nor I expected anybody else.

"Can I help you?" Jaren asked the person at the door.

I came around the kitchen wall to see who Jaren spoke to.

It was him. The man who had been following me. My heart raced at seeing the same trench coat, and the same sharp features that were now casting shadows in Jaren's porch light. I dropped the glass I'd been holding. It shattered on the tile. Fear punched me in the gut.

"Brooke," said the man. "My Lady requires that you come with me." He swept his arm to the side and out toward the walk as if it was already decided I was going with him.

He stood under the porch stoop, looking as menacing as I

remembered. I shook my head, which was the only course of action I could take in my terrified state to nullify going with him. A tickle crawled along my scalp, and my mind took on a weightless, floating sensation. My body urged me to go with this man.

"No." My mouth was dry, so it came out as a rasp. I shook my head, trying to clear the fog and strange urge. When it was clear I wasn't leaving, the man pushed Jaren aside, marching in after me.

"Hey!" Jaren demanded, grabbing the man by his arm.

The man turned back at Jaren, *hissing* at him, like a cat but more threatening. Jaren's eyes widened with fear.

"What the...?" Jaren breathed.

The man grabbed Jaren with one arm and launched him, as if Jaren were a small dog. Jaren landed hard on the end table, smashing it to pieces.

"Uggghh," Jaren whimpered.

I ran across the room to get to Jaren, but the man stepped in front of me. Face to face, I saw his fangs.

"Whoa!" I froze. I wanted to believe he was some psycho who thought it cool to brandish fake fangs, but he wore them with a confidence a creature could only get from knowing how to use the real ones.

Jaren crept up behind the man, with his pocket knife out. "You need to leave now, or this isn't going to turn out well for any of us."

The man turned back at Jaren and cackled at him. "You trying to get yourself killed, boy? I *am* leaving here with the catalyst," the man said, pointing at me. "I'm sick of trying to procure her without any casualties. You can either survive it or not. I don't care anymore." He spoke with a thick accent that sounded European.

Jaren lunged at him in warning, but the man was fast. He

snatched the knife out of Jaren's hand and threw it, stabbing the wall behind me. My heart pounded in my ears.

Who was this guy?

The man attacked Jaren, grabbing him by the throat and squeezing. With one arm, he lifted Jaren clear from the floor.

A squeak leaked out between Jaren's lips with what I feared might be his last exhale. Heat scorched my veins.

I grabbed a hold of the knife stuck in the wall and struggled to yank it out. I leaped at the man, swinging the knife in as large of an arc as I could to gain momentum, and sliced it into the side of his throat.

I expected him to release Jaren, drop to his knees, and gurgle to his death.

He dropped Jaren, but instead of falling to his knees, the man turned to me with malice on his face. His intentions for me now were much worse than taking me to his *Lady.*

He sprung at me with incredible speed.

I followed his movements and dodged him.

He turned around, fangs glinting in the overhead light, and his hands came up with his fingers curling into the likeness of claws. He lunged at me again, catching me on my shoulder with one of his sharp, clawed fingers. Pain burned down the back of my shoulder where the flesh tore.

Adrenaline spiked through me, intensifying the heat and heightening all of my senses. The pain in my shoulder numbed.

I sped toward the fanged man with all of my strength. I ran three steps up the side of the wall to give me a better angle and propelled myself off, lunging through the air toward him. My hands reached out, locking onto the sides of his head. I held on as tight as I could and used my momentum to swing around him.

Crack!

His neck snapped.

He finally drooped to the floor, arms slumped at his sides,

fingers relaxed to a less deadly posture.

* * *

I ran to Jaren, needing to know if he was all right. He sat up, shook his head, and stared up at me in awe and confusion.

"How did you do that?" he asked, stunning me out of action mode and into *Oh my God! What did I do?* mode.

The strength and speed I used should have been impossible. Fear unfurled with the rapid beat of my heart, and my hands shook. I turned to look at the man who I'd killed.

He lay on his side with his head twisted back at me. The menace was gone from his eyes, but the life in them was, too.

"Oh, my God. What do we do?" I verged on hyperventilation. A dead man lay in Jaren's living room. A dead man who I had *killed*. "I killed him. What do we do?" I looked at Jaren with fear and hopelessness. My fear must have spurred him into action.

"We have to get out of here. More of those monsters might be coming for you when he doesn't return with you, or return at all, for that matter." He started hustling through the house grabbing things and shoving them into the duffel bag he had just unpacked hours ago.

I stood, frozen, staring at the lifeless form that seconds ago had been about to rip my head off. "It was self-defense, wasn't it? He was trying to take me. Then he almost killed you. I had no choice, right?" I thought out loud, hoping Jaren would tell me I wasn't a monster.

He didn't say anything, though. He only ran in and out of the room, grabbing clothes and supplies.

"Why are you packing? We need to call the police. The police will protect us if the man's friends come for us."

Jaren set his bag down and looked at me. "And tell them what? That you had superhuman strength? That you were able to give this guy a complete one-eighty degree makeover of his head. They'll never believe what we just saw, which means they will never be able to properly protect us, either. We have to get out of here. These people can't find us. Do you understand this?"

"Mm-hmm." An invisible vise tightened around my throat.

"Call your mom," Jaren said. He picked up his bag to continue his packing.

I walked to the kitchen on legs that wobbled as I stepped over the shards of glass. I didn't trust that I could stand much longer so I turned off the stove, grabbed my purse, and sat on the floor next to the sink. I dug my shaking hands into my bag and grabbed my phone. I hung up twice because my quaking fingers called my friend Monica and then my friend Molly before I stabilized them enough to hit "Mom" in my contact list.

"Mom," I sobbed when she answered. Fear smothered me, and I wondered how she would see me once she knew I had killed a man.

"Brooke? Honey, what's wrong?"

"Mom," I cried, "a man came to Jaren's—" I tried to collect myself, because I was sure she didn't understand me.

I tried again. "There was a guy who came to Jaren's saying I needed to go with him. When I didn't want to, he stormed into Jaren's house and tried to force me. Jaren tried to protect me and almost got himself killed." I took a few deep breaths trying to delay what I was about to tell her.

"Are you okay? Did you call the police?"

"Well...he had Jaren by the throat, so I stabbed the guy, but it only ticked him off. Then he came after me, and we fought, and I killed him. Please don't hate me. I'm so sorry," I said, pleading with my mom to not disown me. I needed her right now.

"Slow down. I could never hate you. Now think. Why did he want to take you?"

"I don't know. He said I had to go with him to some lady. He had fangs. And he was super strong and fast. And when I fought him, I was too."

"Oh, no. We've stayed here too long. You and Jaren need to head straight over to Garwin's house. Right now." Terror in my mom's voice set me on edge even further.

"What about the man in Jaren's living room? I killed him."

"Leave him. We'll take care of it. Don't call the police or anything. You get over there right now, and I'll meet you guys as soon as I can." Images fluttered through my mind of my mom and my uncle Garwin packing up the body in the back of Garwin's truck to go bury it somewhere no one would ever find it. I shuddered at the thought.

"'Kay. I'm sorry, Mom," I whispered, still worried she would never look at me the same.

I pulled myself up off the floor, wiped at my eyes, and went to find Jaren. He was in his bedroom. He looked up from zipping his bag. "What did your mom say?"

"She said we have to leave here now and go up to my uncle Garwin's. She's meeting us there."

"Who's this *Uncle Garwin*?" Jaren's forehead creased.

"He's not really my uncle, but he's a close family friend, and he's been there for my mom and me whenever we've needed it. My mom said they would take care of the man, so I'm pretty sure you can trust him because we can't leave a dead body in there for Trish to find, and you and my mom are telling me that we can't call the cops. So, really, the only option I can think of is to go to Garwin's." Anxiety caused me to ramble.

"All right." Jaren sighed when he realized that was our only real option at the moment.

I gave him the keys and followed him as he booked it through the living room. I took one last look at the man lying dead on the floor. I couldn't stop myself. I didn't want to look, but the muscles in my neck and eyes had a mind of their own. As soon as I registered the knife in his neck with blood thickening around it, and his head turned in such a way that you knew his neck had been broken, I wished I could have just ran out of there without looking back. The image of the prone, lifeless body seared into the darkest depths of my mind.

* * *

"Turn here," I said, directing Jaren past Lexington and into the hills where the really rich people lived.

"Wow," Jaren whispered in awe of the lavish neighborhood.

We reached the end of the street and rolled up to the gates leading to Garwin's house. "Who is this guy?" Jaren's dad was rich, but nowhere near as wealthy as Garwin.

"The code's 4-9-7-7-6-5-8," I said. Jaren typed it into the keypad.

The screen beeped and flashed "Code not accepted."

"What? I've always had the same code. Buzz him," I said, fearing the worst. A few seconds later, Garwin answered.

"Yes?" Garwin asked.

"My code isn't working. Is everything all right in there?"

"Yes, dear. I changed it due to the circumstances. I'm glad to see you're okay. Who's that with you?" Garwin had cameras around the gate so he could see I had a stranger with me.

"My boyfriend. Mom said for us to meet her here."

"She's already here," he said and hung up. The gates disengaged to grant us entry.

If Jaren was awed from what he saw through the gates, then he was overcome with what sprawled out before him as we drove up the drive to the house.

A white mansion spread across an endless parcel of well-manicured property. The house's second story was supported by four large columns that stood in front of the entrance. Intricate details in the moldings surrounded the windows and framed the house, giving the property a regal feel.

Jaren drove the car up to the front door and gawked at the house. I stepped out of the car to go inside because I was scared and didn't have the patience to wait for him. I could not shake the vision of the dead man lying on the floor, and I wanted this night to be over.

I strode up the stairs, Jaren finally trailing behind me as I walked into the foyer. I turned down the hall, making my way toward the den. My mom and Garwin would be in there.

Jaren lingered behind me to stare at what I'm sure were the chandelier, the marble statue in the foyer, the paintings in the hallway, and everything else his eyes probably feasted upon. He finally composed himself and grabbed my hand, walking beside me with purpose.

When we reached the den, I found my mom and Garwin sitting in the lounge by the fireplace.

My mom looked up before we passed through the double doors. She stood and ran to me. "Honey, are you all right?" she asked, hugging me then checking me over for injuries. I slipped Jaren's jacket down to reveal my shredded shoulder.

She gasped. "We need to get that cleaned up. We'll be right back," she said to Garwin and Jaren.

"Not yet." I planted my feet. "What did you mean when you said 'we'd stayed here too long'?" My mom knew something about why the man was after me, and I was going to get it out of her, even if it meant my shoulder might fall off.

"Are you sure you want to talk about this now?" she asked, looking over at Jaren.

"Mom! He just had a monster *with fangs* try to strangle him to death because he was protecting me. Then he saw me fly in the air only to catch myself on said monster's head with enough force to torque the guy's skull around, snapping his neck, and killing him! I think he can hear what the hell is going on."

"Brooke, don't talk to your mother like that," Garwin said, still sitting in his chair and swirling a glass of brandy and ice. He didn't raise his voice, either. He didn't have to. His voice held an authority that didn't need volume to communicate business.

I looked at Garwin, then to my mom with apologetic eyes. "I'm sorry, but we've had a really rough night, and I'm a little freaked out." I shook, on the verge of tears by the end of my apology.

"Oh, Brooke. It's fine. Sit down, and we'll talk. Okay?" My mom led me over to the couch she'd been sitting on. Jaren sat on the other side of me, across from Garwin.

"Hi. I'm Jaren," he said, getting up and offering to shake hands with Garwin.

"I'm sure you already know I'm Garwin," he said, grasping Jaren's hand, ice clinking against his glass.

"Let's start by you telling me everything about your attacker tonight," my mom suggested.

I had to tell her now. I couldn't hide my stalker from her any longer, not with him lying dead on Jaren's floor. I swallowed, afraid of confessing the truth of my prior run-ins with this weird stranger, but I needed to know what was going on.

"Well, I first saw him while hiking with Kaitlynn, and I'm convinced he had a mountain lion try to attack us."

Garwin's head tilted to the side. "*Try?*"

"Yeah," I nodded. "I told it to stop, and it...did. It froze. It wanted to attack me, but it couldn't."

"Why didn't you tell me? You could have died, and we could have avoided it if you would've told me," my mom said, agitation thick in her words.

"That is exactly why I didn't tell you. The man freaked me out, but I didn't want to believe my life was at stake, and I knew you would flip out about it and not let me go out with Jaren, or worse. You'd make me move again." I adjusted on the couch to ease the throb in my shoulder. "And I think he only sent the mountain lion after us to test me."

"What makes you think that?" my mom scolded.

"Well, when I stopped the lion from attacking us, the man had a smirk on his face, full of approval."

My mom looked at Garwin.

"Yes, this makes things interesting," he said, then sipped his drink.

"Why?" I asked.

"We'll get to that. What happened the next time you saw him?"

"Ugh," I grunted, frustrated they weren't telling me *anything*. I sighed. "I'm pretty sure that I saw him lurking outside of Mary's dress shop the other night." I didn't tell them about Jaren's pictures. I already felt stupid and guilty that I'd risked Jaren's life. I never thought the man might try to hurt someone else. I figured if I never went anywhere alone, always used the buddy system, the man wouldn't be able to touch me.

"And then the next time I saw him was tonight, and I already told you what happened with him," I said, lowering my head so I wouldn't see my mom's disgust with me.

She grabbed my chin and forced me to look her in the eye. To my relief, there was only love and concern.

I felt a little better, but I still wanted answers. "'Kay. Your turn. What's going on?"

My mom dropped her hands into her lap. She hesitated, but she spoke anyway. "I know this is going to sound insane, but the man who came for you tonight was a vampire. We call them Pijawikas."

"What?" I laughed.

"I know it sounds unbelievable, but it's true. He's a vampire."

"Well, what on Earth would he want me for? Do I have some extra special blood that makes me tastier to them or something?" This really was crazy.

"Not exactly," she said. "But your blood is special."

"Okay...," I stared at her, waiting for her to tell me this was all a joke, and I would wake up from this nightmare. When she didn't, I recalled she had the same blood. "Well, what about your blood?

Is someone after you, too?"

"My blood's not special in the same way, so I'm not sure if they're after me, too, but I don't think so," she said, looking over at Garwin for confirmation.

"I'll have to find out what's going on, but if they were after your mother, they would have moved in on her, as well," Garwin said.

"So, what do you mean my blood isn't special in the same way yours is?" I still felt like nothing was getting answered. I was more confused now than I was when we arrived.

"You're half Pijawikan, Brooke," my mom confessed, relaxing the tension in her shoulders that must have weighed heavily on her for ages.

I laughed. "No way. It's not even possible. I've never been bitten by one of those...*things*, and I sure as hell have never had fangs. I'm fine in the sun, too. In fact, I love it."

"Vampire myth has it all wrong," she said. "The sun thing comes about because they used to hunt at night to remain a secret. And you don't turn into a vampire because you get a virus from being bitten by one. It's descended by blood; Pijawikas are born. They're an evolved race of humans, but they can still procreate with us. That's how I got pregnant with you."

"You're telling me my dad is a vampire? Yeah, right."

"It's true," Garwin said. "How do you think you were able to fight that guy tonight? Anyone else wouldn't have stood a chance against his strength and speed, but you did. In fact, you were able to defeat him."

I recalled how fast I was in dodging the man, and how much strength materialized in my muscles when I broke his neck. I looked at Jaren to my right. His complexion had gone pale. His mouth hung slack in shock.

I turned, glaring at my mom. "I have never had any sort of real stability in my life, and the only thing that remained the same for me was who I thought I was. You shattered that. Why would you keep this from me?"

"I didn't know how much Pijawika you'd have, so I didn't want to say anything unless you started to show traits of your Pijawikan side. It is forbidden for Pijawikas to mix, or even have romantic relationships with humans. I did it for our safety." My mom sighed, as if it was all for nothing now.

I sat stunned. Was this why she never let me try out for any sports teams? Had she been too afraid that it might reveal this awful part of me? "So, what? You watched and waited? Hoping, praying to God, that I would never reveal the monster inside of me, is that it?" Bile rose in my throat with the knowledge of what I was, and that disgust transferred to her for not telling me about it.

"You are not a monster," she said, grasping my hand.

"Oh, yes I am. I fought that thing that tried to take me tonight. Did you forget that? Because I'll never be able to forget. And to make my night even worse, you're telling me that half the stuff that runs in that guy's veins also runs in mine."

"You can't judge what you are by meeting only one Pijawika. It's like saying all Mexicans are this, or all Canadians are that. You can't make these judgments on people after only meeting one of them. Your dad was a great man, and I've met many other Pijawikas that were great, too."

"Right, my dad's a great *man*. That's why he's here now, right? That's why he was there when I was born, and there to watch me at my dance recitals. Such a great dad, in fact, that he was there to teach me how ride a bike and to drive a car, and there for me for all those other big things a great *man* should do to be there for his daughter, right? He left us. He left because of me." I slumped my shoulders, my anger transferring to disappointment. I was the reason he'd left.

"Oh, honey. Is this what you've thought all this time?" my

mom asked, eyes blinking with heartbreak. She shook her head. "Of course you would. I haven't told you anything to help you think otherwise." Regret etched in the small creases around her eyes.

"Let me set you straight." She wiped her eyes. "We, Garwin and I," my mom said, nodding over at Garwin, "come from a long line of families that are kind of like the Freemasons. In that, our families are part of a secret society that knows all about the Pijawikas. Part of this society's job is to feed the Pijawikas. I was the one who fed your father." Her eyes grew distant and sparkled as if they visited happy memories.

"I loved him and he cared for me, probably more than I did for him because Pijawikas feel emotions on a stronger and deeper level than we do. But as soon as I found out I was pregnant with you, I ran away. I couldn't risk his life, nor mine with yours developing inside of me, so I ran. I'm sure your father was crushed when I left, and I'm sure he would be even more upset to learn I had you, and that he didn't get to know you. So you see, he didn't know about you. He didn't even get the chance to walk out on you."

"So...you're saying you used to be what? You were basically a call girl who would come over to let some vampire bite on her neck whenever he wanted?" I hoped I offended her. I was irate at how this conversation had gone, that neither my mom nor Garwin had told me about this, years ago.

Garwin stood. "How dare you? You have no idea of the sacrifices this family has made. Go upstairs." This time he did raise his voice.

I figured this conversation was over, anyway, so I turned to Garwin to let him see the rage on my face and headed toward the room we called mine. It was actually a guest room, but I was the only one whoever stayed in it. Plus, I kept clothes in there for when we stayed over.

Jaren got up and followed me out of the den. The walk to the foyer and up the grand staircase to my room was silent except for Jaren's sneakers that squeaked across the travertine. Once inside, I slammed the door.

"I cannot *believe* what I just heard! I find out my dad might have really wanted me, but the kicker is I also find out I'm a monster." I turned around to look at Jaren and found his eyes cast to the floor with guilt.

"Oh, no," I said, letting him know I caught it written on his face.

"I don't know what to think about this," Jaren said. "We've been through a lot in a short amount of time. Maybe we should cool it between us for a while to let this all settle in."

"God! Can this night get anymore fantastic?" I screamed, throwing my arms in the air. I looked him directly in the eyes. "You know what? If you didn't want to be with me because you wanted to be with Tiffany or someone else, that would hurt. Really bad. But to not want to be with me because of something I was born with, something in my DNA that I can't even change, is a little too much."

"I know it seems wrong, but you can't even accept it. How can you stand there and expect me to?"

I plopped down on the bed defeated. He was right.

"I'm not saying it's permanent or anything. I just need some time to think about this."

I wanted him out of here before he could see me break down. "Well, there's a room down the hall on the left you could use." I was sending him to the furthest room away from mine. "You probably don't want to go anywhere else right now—now that you've been associated with the half-vampire everybody's after."

"Brooke...," Jaren started, but I don't think he knew what to say.

"Just go," I told him, closing the door behind him. He gave me one last conflicted look before the door met with its frame.

The latch clicked with decisiveness, and I let my life crash down around me as I fell to the bed.

I squeezed my eyelids shut, trying to ebb the flow of tears. When that didn't work, I pushed against them with the palms of my bloodstained hands, thinking if I could just stop the tears, then the pain would stop, too. I failed at both.

My mom was right. I'd fallen too fast and much too hard for Jaren. Maybe that was the curse that came with being a vampire—feeling too deeply. He was everything I had dreamed about in a boyfriend, or at least that's what I thought before. Maybe he still was, but I couldn't recognize that right now. The only thing I was sure of at this moment was that my feelings for Jaren hadn't changed, but everything else around me had.

What was the point of all this, anyway? What did the vampires want with me, and why did they have to come for me now, when everything was going so great with Jaren?

My shoulder burned and throbbed with the tempo of my broken heart.

10

I'M MIRKO

I stood in front of my mirror, adjusting the lame attempt at a bandage I'd made last night for my shoulder. Tears blurred my vision and made it impossible to get the gauze on right. The harder I tried, the more it reminded me where the injury had come from, and why Jaren had broken up with me.

Around nine o'clock, I decided to head down for something to eat. The prior evening's carnage had left me desolate, and I needed the fuel. I hoped to at least appear strong when I saw Jaren today.

I stopped in the entryway of the kitchen.

Great.

Everyone was in there. Awkward much? I didn't want to talk to Jaren, at least not yet, and I didn't want to talk to my mom, or Garwin, either, because they had lied to me about who I was my entire life.

I grabbed the Cheerios out of the cabinet and set out to make some cereal in angry silence.

"You better hurry," Garwin said. "I've arranged for you guys to meet an associate of mine at the Lynchburg airport."

That stunned me out of the planned silent treatment they were supposed to get. "Why are we meeting with one of your associates?"

"This is an extremely delicate situation. Pijawikan society is very prejudiced against humans. They are even more so against mixed-bloods. It's rare for one to survive long after they have been ousted to the Pijawikas. We can't let anything happen to you, and despite my resources, I can't offer you the proper protection for what you're up against. My associate can."

"How do you know what we're up against when we don't even know who's after me?"

"Someone attempted to kidnap you in my own back yard. Whoever it is must be high up for them to even attempt it." True. You had to be hard core to risk pissing off Garwin. He had the resources to make life miserable for those who crossed him.

"I've called your father's stražar—or his head of security— Emerik, to inform him of the potential threat. If the Pijawikas know about you, then they might know who fathered you, too. If they do, your father could be in danger."

My stomach tightened at the mention of my father. Garwin had a number to contact him? I wondered how he would react when he found out about me. Would he try to contact me? Protect me? Harm me to save himself?

"What about the guy at my house?" Jaren asked.

Right. The man I'd killed. I didn't forget. It was still there, hovering in the dark shadows it'd created in my mind, but it had been pushed aside by the knowledge that I was a vampire. A monster incarnate. And the first guy I'd risked giving my heart to had handed it back to me because he was afraid. Afraid of me, the monster who killed other monsters.

"Taken care of," Garwin said, referring to the body. "That reminds me, did you see a necklace on your attacker last night?"

I thought for a moment and tried to picture the guy's neck without being mind-slapped by the image of the knife sticking out of it. "I don't remember seeing anything around his neck," I said, recalling the night's events one more time to be sure. I looked over at Jaren to see what his response would be.

He shook his head. "That guy knocked me so hard last night that I'm not sure I could remember a necklace. Why is that important? And does this associate have a name? If we're to go anywhere with this guy, we should know his name." Jaren said.

I leaned against the counter wondering why he thought he was coming with me.

"Mirko's his name. And it's not the necklace that is significant, but what is on the necklace. Most of the Pijawikas that hold any kind of power have what is called a znak, or a symbol of their power. Whoever came for you did it as an order or as a close favor for the *Lady*. There are only a few Pijawikan women who hold any actual power, so this further limits the possibilities. If the kidnapper was wearing a necklace, he would have been wearing his 'master's,' for lack of a better word, emblem. A necklace wasn't with the body when my crew went to clean up, nor did they find one lying around had it been torn off in the fight. But had you been able to describe the znak, we could have pinpointed who's after you."

"What's with all these funky names—Pijawika, stražar, znak? Is it some kind of secret code or something?"

My mom answered. "It's Croatian. Pijawikas originated from there and a lot of the terms have remained."

"Now eat up." Garwin said. "You're meeting Mirko at eleven. It'll take you about an hour to drive there, so you'd better hustle." He walked out of the kitchen.

That was a lot of information to process and again, brought up more questions. I asked Jaren the one I couldn't hold back any longer. "Why are you coming?"

"Garwin thought it'd be best if I go with you and lay low for a while. Plus, I didn't think you should go by yourself. Once we meet up with Mirko, we're flying to Utah."

"Utah?" I asked. That seemed like a weird place to hide out. I'd gone snowboarding there once when we were moving from California to Colorado. Utah didn't really seem like a vampire hideout. Jersey, New York, or maybe even Cali, but Utah didn't scream vampire sanctuary to me at all. Maybe that was the point, though.

"Yeah," Jaren said, "there's some kind of reinforced compound there that Garwin thinks will be able to better protect you."

I looked over at my mom. "Are you coming, too?"

"No, honey. Rumor will take longer to spread about us if I don't go there with you. I'll be going up to Toronto." Her lips curved down in regret. "I trust Mirko to take care of you, though, and I'll come for you as soon as it's safe."

"This sucks," I said, finishing my last bite of cereal. I didn't even feel like drinking the leftover milk. I tossed my almost empty bowl into the sink and skulked back up to my room to get some stuff. I left my door open, but Jaren knocked, anyway.

"Come in," I said, not as nicely as I used to talk to him.

"Just because I'm not sure what to think about us doesn't mean I don't care for you anymore."

I really didn't want to hear him say he cared about me if he saw me as a freak. "We have to go soon, so I need to focus on getting ready," I said, turning back to the closet.

Jaren left, and my heart cracked all over again. I decided to let it out a little since I was going to be stuck in a car with him for the next hour.

My mom came in, surprised to see a tear running down my cheek. "Oh, Brooke. I know this is a lot to take in, but everything will work out fine."

I threw down the blue sweater I held in my hands. "I'm not scared. Jaren broke up with me."

"He did?" Jaren must not have told them anything about the breakup. My mom got up, anger creased in her lips.

I grabbed her arm, stopping her. "No! Just leave it, please?"

"Fine, but when he comes crawling back to you after he realizes that you're still the same girl, I hope you remember what he's doing to you right now."

"Give him a break. I can't even accept this part of me; how can I expect him to? We just need a little time to figure things out." I was mad at Jaren, but that didn't give liberty for everyone else to be, too. She gave me a hug.

"You better get going. You don't want to keep Mirko waiting." She grabbed my bag and walked with me down the stairs and through the front door.

When I stepped out onto the porch, I startled, seeing my car gone and Jaren in the driver's seat of Garwin's Land Rover. Garwin leaned in the passenger side talking to Jaren.

"You're taking this since whoever was after you has to know your car," Garwin said once I approached.

I nodded.

My phone rang. It was Kaitlynn. I wasn't sure what I was going to say to her, but she was my best friend, and I probably wouldn't see her for a while. Fear sliced through me as I thought about what Kaitlynn would think if she knew I was a half-monster. I answered anyway.

"Hey, I know you're hanging with Jaren today, but I needed to know if I left my history book in your car—"

"Um...," I paused to take a deep breath. "I'll have somebody bring it over to you. I have to go out of town for a little while, and I'm leaving here shortly, so I really have to go now. I love you." I felt like this was a forever goodbye to my best friend. It was a lot harder than all of the other goodbyes I'd given when I moved.

"Wait!" Kaitlynn demanded. "What do you mean you're leaving town? Where do you think you're going on such short notice, and why am I not going with you?" She paused for a minute and then asked, "Who's going with you?"

"Jaren, but I really can't explain it all right now, and—"

This time Kaitlynn cut me off, "Oh, no. Jaren does *not* get to go with you if I don't get to go. What's going on? What's wrong? And don't lie to me because I always know when you're lying." She was right.

I sighed, defeated. She wasn't going to let it go. "Someone's after me. I'm in danger, and so is Jaren because of me. If I stick around, you will be, too."

"That's stupid. Just call the cops. They'll handle it," Kaitlynn said. Best friends really do think alike.

"It's a bit more complicated than that. You stay put. Okay? I need to know you're safe."

"Un-uh, you're obviously going somewhere you think will be safer than here, so if you and Jaren are in danger, what makes you think I'll be safer here? By myself? I should be going with you."

She had a point. If whoever was after me had been having that man follow me, Kaitlynn would be the next target. If she was with me, she would be one less target they had, and I would know for certain where she was, and more importantly, that she was safe.

"'Kay, pack your bags. We'll pick you up on our way out of town, which is in ten minutes." I hung up.

"Slow down," Garwin said, holding up his hand. "You can't bring her or tell anybody about this. Pijawikas operate very similar to the way the Mafia does. More like the Mafia has taken after the Pijawikas in their methods of secrecy, but parallel nonetheless. I have to call Mirko and get this cleared with him first."

"It's only Kaitlynn. We can trust her. And what are they going to do? Kill me? They're already after me, so what more can they do?" I asked, stunned he even considered I wouldn't tell Kaitlynn about this.

"A lot. Trust me. And we don't want to burn any bridges with the ones willing to help you, now do we?"

I sat in the Land Rover while Garwin spoke with Mirko on the phone. Wow. The Mafia. Really? I didn't want any part of this. At all.

* * *

I was on edge the whole drive to Kaitlynn's house. I knew I had to tell her what I was before we left. I owed it to her to tell her now rather than when we were on the other side of the country. I couldn't begin to comprehend what I'd do if Kaitlynn wouldn't accept me. I'd probably want to crawl into a deep dark hole somewhere and let myself wither away.

Jaren wasn't any help in comforting me. I mean, what could he tell me? That everything was going to be fine? That she would see me the same as always? Yeah, right.

He pulled up in front of Kaitlynn's house. She came running through the front door with a few bags busting at the seams. Her mom followed behind her to the Land Rover. I rolled down my window so she could talk to me.

"I'm so sorry for your loss. Please give my regards to your mom, okay?" Rhonda said as she grasped my shoulder right where the guy left his claw marks. I hissed through my teeth.

"Oh, I'm so sorry," Rhonda said, backing up. "What happened?"

"Um, I tweaked it a little moving Jaren's bed into his new place," I lied.

"I hope it's nothing serious." Rhonda's forehead wrinkled.

"It's not. Just a little sore is all. I'll be sure to tell my mom you send your condolences." I was ready for her to go back inside. I looked to Kaitlynn in the back seat, wondering what she'd told her mom.

"You kids be careful, and Kaitlynn, I want you to call me daily," Rhonda said as Jaren backed out of the driveway.

"What did you tell your mom about where you're going?" I asked Kaitlynn.

"I told her your grandma died."

I looked at her, astonished she would make up something like that.

"Well, what was I supposed to tell her?" She gave me a pointed look. "She asked me a million questions before she would let me go. I had to tell her something."

"Good point," Jaren mumbled as he turned off her street, then parked.

I faced Kaitlynn. "There's something I have to tell you before we go too far."

"Yeah, what's going on? Are my mom and dad going to be okay? And what about David? Are we picking him up, too?" I looked over at Jaren, unsure about what to do with David.

He chewed on the inside of his cheek for a moment. "He hasn't been around you very much, so I think he should be okay if we leave him here."

"Why are we at risk? Brooke?" Kaitlynn asked, tugging on my sweater. "What is going on?"

I took a deep breath. "Here it goes. Remember that guy who sent the mountain lion to attack us?"

"I still don't think he sent it after us, but whatever. Yeah, I remember him."

"Well, he came to Jaren's last night demanding that I had to go with him. When I said no, he tried to force me and we fought. He tried to kill Jaren, and then he tried to kill me, so I killed him." I gave her the short version. I already knew she was going to be freaked out about what I was, and giving her a detailed image of me in action wouldn't help my cause.

"We're on the run?" she asked.

"So, you're okay with what I just told you?" I asked her.

"Well, yeah. It was self-defense, right?"

I nodded.

"Then, yeah. I'll always back you up. But I still don't understand why you just didn't call the cops."

"Here's where it gets complicated. The man I killed," I said looking at her, hoping she wouldn't hate me. "He was an honest-to-God, real vampire."

Kaitlynn laughed.

"I laughed, too, when my mom first told me, and I witnessed his fangs, strength, and speed, so I know it's hard to believe."

"I'm sorry," Kaitlynn said, trying to compose herself, "it just sounds so crazy." She continued laughing.

I should get it out while she was still in denial. I hoped she wouldn't believe what I was telling her, and we could act like it never happened. "I also found out that I'm half-vampire."

Kaitlynn quit laughing.

My hands shook and felt clammy when I rubbed them together.

"You can't be serious. No way." She stared at me.

"It's true," Jaren said.

Kaitlynn turned and looked at him.

He arched his brows. "I was there."

Kaitlynn looked at me.

My stomach turned. "Uh-huh." I bit my bottom lip.

"But you don't have fangs," she reasoned.

"No, but I do have the strength and serious speed. I never needed it that bad until last night, so I never knew about it, I guess." My stomach clenched tighter now than it had last night. I didn't think that was possible, but I really couldn't lose my best friend. And I couldn't wait any longer. I had to know. "Do you hate me?"

"Hate you? No, we're still besties. You being a half...," she said, waving her hand in the air, "whatever would never change that."

"Oh, man, I love you." I was so relieved. I reached between the seats and Kaitlynn met me with a hug.

"I love you, too," Kaitlynn said.

"All right, then, ladies. Shall we go?" Jaren asked. I gave Kaitlynn one last squeeze and let her go.

I looked at her to see if she was still on board.

She nodded that she was.

I smiled. "Then let's go meet Mirko!"

* * *

After only a half an hour on the road, we had to stop at a gas station so Kaitlynn could have a bathroom break. Jaren parked the Land Rover and went into the convenience store to get some beef jerky.

I followed Kaitlynn to the restroom. There was no one in any of the other stalls, so I figured now was a good time to tell her about Jaren breaking up with me.

"It seems like you're taking all of this better than Jaren is," I said to Kaitlynn while I leaned against the sink.

"What do you mean? He doesn't seem that freaked out about it to me," she replied from behind the stall.

"Well, last night, after we found out about everything, he tells me he needs some time to think about us and broke up with me."

"No!" Kaitlynn said.

"Yeah, which sucks because there isn't anything I can do to fix the other half of what's in my blood, you know?" I asked, wiping tears from my eyes. I needed to focus on something else and ended up scratching at my shoulder for the bazillionth time. My shoulder had been itching nonstop since we were barely outside of Lexington.

Kaitlynn came out of her stall. She pulled me into a hug. "I'm sorry Jaren's being an idiot." She pushed me back a little to assess the damage. "You seem to be handling this better than you did the Tiffany episode."

"Oh, it hurts. I wanted to die last night. I just have so much other crap going on right now, too. And I don't really have the option to bawl my eyes out over Jaren when we're going across the country with him." I gave her a half-smile, wiping more tears from my eyes.

Kaitlynn pulled me into a tight hug. When we drew apart, her hand slid across my shoulder.

I turned around and pulled my sweater up to check on the

scratch. "Can you lift the bandage a little so I can see how it looks?"

Kaitlynn stepped around me to peel the tape back. "What happened?"

"Fight with a vampire," I said, like it explained everything that was wrong with my life. Strange that it actually did.

I looked in the mirror at the raised, pink line. "What the...?" I asked, shocked. "These scratches looked like raw meat last night." I looked Kaitlynn in her eyes through the mirror. "I have always healed fast, but never this fast." I was more of a freak than I thought.

Kaitlynn shrugged. "So what? Fast healing. Who wouldn't want that?"

I gawked at her while she washed her hands. She really thought my eerie, superhuman healing was no biggie.

She tossed her paper towel into the trash can and wrapped her arm around mine. We walked out to meet Jaren at the car for another half-hour drive stuffed with break-up awkwardness.

* * *

The drive to Lynchburg was beautiful. Early November was perfect timing to take a road trip through the Shenandoah Mountains. The ash trees were in full display of their yellow and maroon garnishes. But, the most brilliant displays of color were given to us by the aspen and maple trees.

When we reached Lynchburg, Jaren steered the Land Rover along Ward's Road toward the small airport. I caught a glimpse of the runway as we drove past strip malls and big retailers. It appeared to be a small airport, and I feared the dinky, little plane we would be flying in. Garwin said we had to fly private because we couldn't risk my name coming up in the NSA or the airline's computer systems.

Garwin had told Jaren that Mirko would meet us in the airport's parking lot near the road. And that's where we sat, the

Land Rover idling for half an hour.

"Where's this Mirko guy?" Kaitlynn asked.

"Maybe we should call Garwin," Jaren said and pulled out his cell phone.

A guy walked up and knocked on Jaren's window. Jaren rolled it down.

"Brooke?" the guy asked, bending over a little so he could get a better look at me in the passenger seat.

"Who's asking?" Jaren replied.

"I'm Mirko." The guy spoke with a slight accent. He must have been only eighteen or nineteen, which surprised the crap out of me. I expected some middle-aged man, freshly retired from his stint as an army drill sergeant or something.

Mirko looked like he could've been military, but only because he was in lean, amazing shape, and his dark sable hair was cut short to his scalp. His ears stuck out a little, but in no way diminished his appearance. What struck me the most about him was his piercing, sienna brown eyes, which intensified under his straight, dark eyebrows—telling me he meant business.

"Do you mind getting out so I can see what I'm dealing with?" Mirko asked.

"Okay," I drawled. Weird request, but I complied. Garwin said to do as Mirko asked, and Mirko was asking. We got out. I walked around the front of the Land Rover. The heat off the warm engine felt nice against my legs, counteracting the fall chill.

Jaren and Mirko shook hands. Jaren stood taller than Mirko, and his arms were bigger, but Mirko's looked lean and chiseled.

Kaitlynn glanced over at me, and I knew we were thinking the same thing—Mirko's hot! We smiled.

"You're Brooke, and who's this?" Mirko asked, pointing at Kaitlynn.

"Kaitlynn," she said, looking happy that he noticed her.

Mirko turned back to Jaren. "First order of business: when

someone comes to your window, don't roll it down like that. Gives easy advantage to your attacker. Especially when you have a girl with you who's a target."

Jaren and Mirko both looked at me. Jaren blushed with embarrassment that he'd made such a mistake. Mirko's eyes raked over me, sizing me up and figuring me out with his penetrating gaze.

"Right then. Let's board the plane now." Mirko pointed toward the terminal entrance.

"We need to get our bags," I said.

We walked around to the back of the Land Rover and Jaren opened the rear door.

Mirko whistled. "Whoa, someone brought a lot more than the necessities."

I laughed. I hadn't expected this austere guy to have a sense of humor.

Kaitlynn blushed. "I had no idea what was going on, where we were going, or anything. I grabbed what I could."

"That's true. She didn't even know vampires existed until this morning," I said.

"Pijawikas or Zao Duhs. We don't like to be called vampires. 'Vampire' denotes a parasite or a leech. We consider ourselves above that." Mirko grabbed some of the bags from the pile.

"Wait," I said, dropping my bags back onto the trunk's floor board. "You're a Pijawika?" I didn't really want to be around any more of those things anytime soon.

"No, I'm a Zao Duh." Mirko smiled.

"What's a Tao Duh?" I asked.

He smirked at me as if I was born yesterday. "Zao Duh," he emphasized. "You really don't know anything about us?"

I responded with a blank stare. "Nothing comes to mind, no."

"They've really sheltered you."

My face soured.

"Wasn't trying to offend you. I'm shocked, is all. Let's get going, and I'll explain it to you."

I picked up my bags and followed Mirko and Jaren inside the terminal.

When we reached the desk for clearance onto the tarmac, a young man greeted us. "How can I help you folks?"

Mirko's eyes met with the clerk's, and the clerk's face went blank. "Do you have any expected flights leaving or coming in within the next twenty minutes?" Mirko asked.

"We have a Cessna departing shortly," the clerk responded, dry and clear.

"There's been a Gulfstream 650 parked out on the airstrip. It was never here, and you never saw us," Mirko commanded.

The clerk nodded his head.

"Great. Now delete the Gulfstream's flight plan in your system." The clerk typed on his keyboard with the same indifference he might have while browsing the Web.

What? Why was this guy listening to Mirko like that? "Isn't that a federal offense?" I whispered to Mirko.

"Only if he gets caught. Which he won't. I have people working on it. I'm just covering all the bases by having him delete it internally on their system."

Kaitlynn and Jaren appeared as stunned as I felt. Mirko's connections must have been deep.

The clerk looked up at Mirko, awaiting his next command.

Mirko stared into the clerk's eyes. "We were never here." He said as if he was burying it deep within the poor guy's mind.

The clerk replied with a single, slow nod.

Mirko turned on his heels, shoes squeaking on the linoleum, making his way to the runway door. Kaitlynn and I picked up our bags and followed.

"Whoa. How did you do that?" I whispered to Mirko.

"Sanjam. It's a form of hypnotism. Puts them in a dream state for mind control," he explained, walking toward some vehicles that looked like official airplane service trucks.

Kaitlynn leaned in closer to hear. "All you did was talk to him. No counting down, no snapping your fingers. How'd you do it?"

Mirko spun around so he was facing us and walked backward. "It comes with the territory." He flashed his fangs.

"Don't do that!" I shuddered, squinting my eyes to clear the visual.

Mirko chuckled.

"No, really," Jaren said, impatient. "How'd you do that? Did you do any permanent damage to him? How can you be sure he isn't going to remember us?"

"Well, let's see. How do you think Pijawikas and Zao Duhs get the substance we need?"

"You're talking about blood, right?" Kaitlynn asked, appearing nearly as squeamish as I felt.

"That would be our preference, yes."

Mirko walked up to a man near one of the vehicles. "Hey," he called. The man turned, and I could tell the moment Mirko's dream thing took effect.

"Drive us out to the planes," Mirko told him, strolling toward the front passenger seat. Mirko didn't hesitate. He knew the guy would do as he told him.

Creepy. Vampires could do a lot of crazy things with a power like that. It made me wonder if this was what the guy I killed was trying to do to me as he stood outside Jaren's door and told me I had to go with him. I had felt a strong pull to go with him, but I was able to deny it. The monster inside me must have saved me.

We tossed our bags into the back of the truck, and Jaren helped Kaitlynn and me up. I felt a flutter in my gut, similar to the one I felt every time Jaren touched me. My heart cracked a little more, remembering the way we were, and the way we could be right now if I wasn't a freak of nature.

He jumped into the truck's bed. The way he smiled at me reminded me of the wooded pond he'd taken me to last week.

Wow. It had only been a week ago when we stood near the waterfall and said we loved each other. I'd give up anything so I could go back in time and be like that with Jaren, even for one more moment.

His eyes remained on mine, and I wondered what he was thinking.

I ached to touch him and because I thought I shouldn't, my eyes burned with unshed tears. I turned my head and looked out at the blacktop behind us. It resembled my new life now: bleak, lonely, and fractured.

11
You'll Have to Earn It

When the truck stopped, I jumped out of the bed on my own. I couldn't keep myself composed much longer if Jaren's touch sent another thrill through me.

"You've been driving around, making your rounds of the airstrip," Mirko said, brainwashing our driver.

The plane faced the runway, already angled for takeoff. Its door opened, and the staircase unfolded, touching the ground. The plane was smaller than the commercial crafts I'd flown on before, but was bigger and looked sturdier than what I'd earlier imagined we'd be taking. At least something was going right.

A short, dark-haired man stood at the top of the metal staircase, just inside the cabin. Mirko climbed the stairs first and spoke to the man in another language. It made me wonder if the man was a vampire, too. Once inside, they turned toward the front.

Kaitlynn gasped as she stepped in.

I sped up, pushing Jaren against the railing so I could go around him.

I gasped, too. It was beautiful. White leather seats and a *couch*. Even a large flat screen stood on a polished mahogany cabinet. I walked along the aisle, touching the cabinet and the table across from it.

Jaren came in next. "What does Garwin do?" His fingers glided along the polished wood, same as mine had.

I smiled.

"Brooke!" Kaitlynn called. I followed her voice toward the back of the plane. I passed another flat screen and found Kaitlynn looking into her reflection in a stainless steel stove.

"Wow! This is nice!"

"I know, right? And we get to fly in it." She turned to me and grinned.

Jaren turned on the TV and sat down on the couch.

Mirko came out from behind a door that concealed the cockpit. "Nice, huh?" He relaxed on the couch next to Jaren and grabbed an iPod from the side table. "Check this out." He touched the iPod and the flat screen turned off.

"Sweet," Kaitlynn said.

"For sure. And we're about to take off, which should be smooth as butter." Mirko glided his hand through the air in imitation.

I felt a slight jerk and then speed. I knew when we left the ground, but it was absolutely smoother than any plane ride I've ever experienced.

"Impressive," Jaren said. "Have you flown on it a lot, then?"

"Some. It belongs to the Društvo. I do a lot of work for them, so I've used it here and there."

"Who's that?" Kaitlynn asked. I appreciated I wasn't the only one asking all the questions.

"Društvo?" Mirko asked.

Kaitlynn nodded.

"That's what we call the group of humans Garwin and Slatki's mother belong to," Mirko said, pointing to me.

I didn't know if Slatki was supposed to be an endearment or to grate on my nerves. "What's it mean?"

Mirko grinned. "You'll have to earn it."

Jaren opened his mouth, but I had more important details I needed to find out.

"So, what are you?" I asked and then blushed. "That came out wrong. I meant, please explain to me how being a Tao Sue makes you a different vampire than the Pijawikas."

Mirko laughed. "Zao Duh. Zao like 'Tao,' but with a 'Z,' and Duh as in 'do.' Zao Duhs are considered low-class Pijawikas. The difference is Pijawikas are born. Zao Duhs are made."

"Wait...my mom said you can't be bitten and turned into a vampire." Was he trying to confuse me?

"She's right," Mirko said. "The process is a lot more complicated than that. The point is there are two species. You are part Pijawikan, the vampires that are born. I'm Zao Duh. I was made." His eyes locked on mine as he spoke.

I felt awkward with his gaze on me, and my cheek twitched.

Mirko smiled. "I affect you, don't I?" He'd seen the minuscule movement from my jaw. It was as if he was attuned to me.

I didn't know what to say. He already knew he unsettled me. What else did he know about me?

"Right, we get how cool you are, but let's get back to vampires, please," Jaren said. I wiggled my toes within my sneakers, relieved he was taking Mirko's focus off of me.

"Not trying to be cool. It's just true," Mirko said. He gave me one last look, testing me, and then looked away.

"How is being a freak at all cool?" I murmured.

Mirko's hearing must have been exceptional because he replied, "Well, little Slatki, you're going to have to strengthen your *freak* side if you have any thread of hope you'll make it out of this situation alive." He stared at me, eyes piercing. They were firm and no longer held his teasing squint.

"What do you mean? Why do I have to do that? Aren't you supposed to keep me alive?" This sucked. What was the point of the whole running-across-country thing if he wasn't going to protect me? And no way was I going to become even more like that guy I killed. I shuddered thinking about it.

Kaitlynn grabbed my hand, giving me something to ground me.

"What I mean is that you are up against a Pijawika that has lived for hundreds of years longer then you have. Whoever it is, they're smart and desperate. Desperate—because they tried to take you when you weren't alone. This person also has an almost endless supply of money and lackeys to come after you. They're going to be smarter, older, stronger, richer, faster, and basically all around *more* in every area that counts in getting to you. So, maybe if you were a little bit more prepared," Mirko said putting his thumb and index finger about an inch apart, "your chances would make me feel a lot better."

Wow. If his aim was to scare me, he'd succeeded. I wanted to get up, walk down the aisle to the bathroom I'd noticed earlier, and lock myself in there for the rest of the flight. Maybe even forever because I was doomed to die. There was no way I would survive this. And if I did, it'd be by becoming one of those...*things*.

Kaitlynn's eyes grew hard when my face drained of all color. "You don't have to be such a jerk. She just had her life ripped out from under her, and here you are prancing in to supposedly save the day, but instead you're telling her she's going to die, anyway. What good is she going to be if she loses her mind?" She moved closer and linked her arm around mine to comfort me.

"Pardon me," Mirko retorted. "But we don't have time to tiptoe around Slatki's feelings. She has to buck up, and she has to buck up now. I'm not saying I'm going to stand aside and let somebody get to her. I told Garwin I would die protecting her, and I'm always good on my word. All I meant was that my job would be a hell of a lot easier if Slatki could kick some ass, too."

Jaren spoke. "I'm pretty sure she can handle her own if it comes down to it. She did take one of you out when she needed to, and I saw this dude. He was pretty wicked."

Mirko smiled. His eyes grazed over me.

Jaren shifted uncomfortably in his seat, and cleared his throat.

"Did the guy you took down say anything strange to you?" Mirko asked, getting back on track.

"What do you mean? The whole situation was strange." Did he expect me to be able to decipher what was strange in terms of a vampire? Yeah, not gonna happen. It was all strange.

"Well, what did he say to you?"

"He told me I had to go with him to his *Lady*. He also said something about a catalyst, but he pointed at me when he said it."

"So, it's definitely a Pijawikan woman in power. Lucky for you, there are only five of them, so that narrows things down. The catalyst part doesn't really give me much. We already know they want you for something or they would have killed you already."

"Oh, that makes me feel so much better," I sighed.

Mirko smirked at me. "It should. You're not dead."

* * *

We were quiet for a while after Mirko's serious conversation. Jaren turned on the flat screen and watched a movie.

Kaitlynn and I messed around with the powered seats until we finally left the controls alone to lie down and talk.

I laid my head against my chair's arm rest with my hair fanned out over the side. Kaitlynn ran her fingers through my hair—a usual for us when I was stressed.

"Do you guys mind if I turn some music on?" Mirko asked, glancing at me with an eyebrow raised.

"Depends on what you put on," Jaren said. Mirko kept stealing flirtatious glances at me, and I think Jaren didn't like it so much.

"Only the best album out right now." Mirko picked up the iPod and touched the screen to turn off the TV. He touched the screen again and music started playing.

I recognized it from the first chord. I didn't want to be all doom-and-gloom anymore. This was my favorite song, so I sat up, bobbing my head to the music, and laughed.

"Yep. I agree with Mirko. Florence + The Machine is, hands down, the best album I've heard in a long time." I clapped to the rhythm, and Kaitlynn and I started to groove our shoulders to *Dog Days Are Over*, slow at first, but we picked up our tempo with the first line of "Run fast for your mother, run fast for your father." By the time the third line started in the chorus and Florence sang, "Leave all your love and your loving behind you," Mirko stood in the aisle, dancing.

Kaitlynn and I laughed. She grabbed my hand and pulled me up to dance with her and Mirko in the aisle.

And Mirko could *dance*. He moved his hips like a viper climbed the air to the magic of a flute. Graceful, seductive. Dangerous.

I almost felt scandalized when the melody slowed down, and he smoothed a body roll from his ribs, through his abs, over his hips, and down to his knees. Then he brought it back up. I blushed, relieved when the drums started.

Mirko moved closer to me, head tilted down, a wicked grin across his mouth, heat simmering from his brown eyes. "Come here," he whispered.

Awkward. The guy I wanted more than anything to be with—who probably still wanted to be with me, if he was honest with himself—sat two feet away on the couch, while a guy who, I won't lie, looked very good and a part of me felt drawn to him, tried to get in my pants.

"You know what?" Jaren growled at Mirko, killing the music. "I draw the line with you hitting on my girlfriend." Anger flushed Jaren's cheeks.

"Oh, really? She's your girlfriend, huh? Because I wasn't getting that vibe at all. In fact, the vibes she's been putting off are saying she doesn't like you very much at all right now," Mirko said.

"Well, she is, so back off!" Jaren rose from the couch.

"Whoa, Jaren." I stepped in front of him. "You broke up with me. Remember? Either I'm your girlfriend, or I'm not. But you do *not* get to push me away and then stake a claim on me when another dog comes sniffing around."

Kaitlynn snorted. "Love the dog reference." She reached for a high five.

Mirko laughed. He raised his eyebrows at Jaren, challenging him for a response.

Jaren stood in silence.

Ouch. He couldn't even put things right between us when he was in a pissing contest with another guy over me. That sucked.

"Oh, it's like that, is it?" Mirko shook his head.

"Like what?" Jaren snarled. He'd made it apparent that he wanted to be with me. But he couldn't do it.

"Don't like your little girlfriend's fangies, do ya?" Mirko was good.

Jaren boiled with anger.

"I don't have fangs," I said. *Thank God.*

Mirko tsked me. "Yes, you do. You just haven't been shown how to extend them yet."

12
RUN

Fangs? Really? Why me? I needed to sit down. The zeal from my favorite song evaporated.

I grabbed Jaren by his arm and pulled him down as I sat. "Just sit. Please." I didn't want any more revelations today, so I sat in silence for the next hour and a half.

The pilot came over the intercom, "Prepare for landing."

"Already?" Kaitlynn asked, looking at Mirko for confirmation. The flight did seem short going from Virginia to Utah.

"This plane flies twice as fast as the commercial aircrafts," Mirko said.

I looked out the large window. "Hey, where are we?" We were at an airport, but it was a tiny one. I'd expected we'd land at Salt Lake International. This was not it.

"We're in Ogden. Figured we could remain a step ahead of whoever's after you if we went to a smaller airport. Plus, I can't use Sanjam on everyone. It would have been too risky."

"Garwin said we're going to your compound. How far away is it from here?" Jaren asked.

Mirko smiled. "I haven't heard it called that in a while. We call it The Base. We're about an hour away."

The plane bounced when the wheels hit the tarmac. It felt more like a Cadillac riding over a speed bump than it did a plane landing.

The pilot cut the plane's engine and opened the door for the stairs to unfold out onto the tarmac. Kaitlynn and I walked to the back by the oven, and grabbed our bags. Jaren followed; Kaitlynn had a lot of stuff, and Jaren was a gentleman.

Mirko was the first to descend the stairs. A black Chevy Tahoe drove toward our plane. It looked very official and governmental. My breath caught in my throat. I almost went into panic, thinking the clerk at the airport in Lynchburg ended up getting caught and sent the feds after us. But then Mirko waved at the driver.

A young guy got out. He looked to be about eighteen, and his light brown hair was cut similar to Mirko's.

"Ace, my man!" They slapped hands in some kind of handshake. "Have you been waiting here long?"

"Nah," Ace said. "I've been cruising around. They have a skydiving center down the road. Pricing's not bad. We should take your friends here and go for a ride," he said grinning and then grabbed one of Kaitlynn's bags to put into the trunk.

"That's going to have to wait until we get this situation with Slatki over here resolved." Mirko pointed back at me.

We introduced ourselves to Ace.

"Will you drive me up to the terminal? I'll get things situated, then we can leave," Mirko said. I knew when he said "situated" he meant that he was going to do some memory rearranging.

"Sure," Ace said, taking bags from Jaren and me to toss them, along with Kaitlynn's, into the back of the truck.

Mirko sat shotgun, and the rest of us got in the back seat. I sat in the middle because I wanted to sit by Kaitlynn, but I didn't want it to be too obvious that I was avoiding Jaren. So, I sucked it up.

Ace parked near the back doors of the terminal, and Mirko got out. "I'll be maybe ten minutes," he said before closing the door.

"Quite the adventure, huh?" Ace asked me in the rearview mirror.

"More like a nightmare."

"Even the G6?" Ace asked with wide eyes, pointing to the plane still on the runway.

"Oh, yeah," I smiled. "That part was nice. It's all the other parts that suck."

"Can you really control everything through the iPod?"

"Yeah," I said.

"Haven't you been on it?" Jaren asked.

"No. I can never get it to work out for me. Every time I need it, it's on the other side of the country. Mirko, the lucky punk, has flown on it a couple of times now. And every time he comes back, he tells me about the iPod."

"Well, the stairs are still down. I bet we could go back so you could check it out," Jaren suggested.

"Oh, that'd be sweet! But I can't take the Tahoe. Mirko would flip if he looked out and it was gone."

"You could probably jog over there real quick and then jog back," I said.

"True, but I don't want to surprise Pavao by having a stranger board his plane. Will you come with me?"

"Sure." Kaitlynn opened her door.

We climbed out of the truck, and Ace took the keys out of the ignition. We walked toward the airstrip.

When we stepped onto the road that lined the landing strip, I realized how much distance was left before we reached the plane. It didn't seem that far from the terminal when we drove away.

It seemed far now.

I grabbed Kaitlynn's arm. "Nah, you guys go ahead. We're going back to the car."

Ace and Jaren looked at me as if I was lazy. Maybe I was, but I was tired. Kaitlynn and I left to walk back.

With twenty yards left, a woman came into view from one of the side hills near the parking lot. Chills broke out on my arms. Why would a woman be out in the middle of nowhere hiding behind a hill, by herself? Something was off.

I looked back. Ace and Jaren were out of sight. I grabbed

Kaitlynn's arm. "Run!" I demanded, pushing her toward the terminal.

The woman sprinted for us at a speed unlike anything I had ever seen.

"Mirko! Help!" I hollered, picking up speed.

I turned back to make sure Kaitlynn ran beside me. She didn't. She was way back there, and the woman came up fast between us.

"Kaitlynn!" There was no way she'd make it past the lady and get to the truck.

If these bloodsucking monsters wanted me, they would have to work for it. I used my new found vampire speed and charged toward the woman. This would give Kaitlynn a chance to make it back.

The woman responded with a smirk on her face and charged at me. When we were close enough, I sidestepped, escaping her grasp, and ran down the hill on the other side of the parking lot.

She was faster. Her chilled fingers grasped around the back of my bare neck. I flew forward from the impact, hitting the ground. I rolled down the hill with the lady's limbs tangling with mine.

I struggled to keep her hands away from my vital organs.

This fight was different from the last one I had with a vampire. The intensity this woman used to try to take my life astonished me. I'm sure if she would have had a proper grip on my neck at the top of the hill, she would have ripped my head clean from my body.

Her fangs dripped menace and her eyes promised the death she was sure to deliver.

"Hey!" Mirko screamed from somewhere close by. I couldn't concentrate on his location and focus on saving my life all at once. He wouldn't make it in time. She was going to kill me.

She raised her claw-shaped hand, readying it to deliver the final death blow.

I struggled to get my arm unwrenched from behind me to stop

the attack.

The sun glinted off a charm she wore on a chain around her neck. The znak!

She hissed, swinging her arm inches from my face. And then I was free.

Mirko tackled her before she made contact.

I sat up, readying myself to help him. Mirko clawed and swiped at the woman's back as she fled. They flew all over the bottom of the hill. I could barely keep up with their location from one second to the next. I sat, stunned with the speed and ferocity with which he fought and she ran. It appeared to be a choreographed dance, if not for the violence and the blood spatter.

She spurred forward with a sudden burst of speed. It was clear Mirko wouldn't catch her.

When the woman disappeared from sight, Mirko dashed back to me with the same stunning speed he used in his attempt to catch her.

"Are you all right?" he asked, barely breaking a sweat.

"I...I really don't know. She didn't even try to take me. She started out wanting to kill me. Why?" I asked, looking up at him, desperate for him to make sense of it all.

"I'm sorry, but I really don't know yet. Something has changed, though." Mirko touched the small of my back, guiding me back to the truck. "We have to get out of here. Damn it! How'd she get away?"

"She was super fast," I said, lost in shocked delirium.

"You sure you're okay? Did you knock your head or something?" Mirko turned me by my shoulders, peering into my eyes.

"I dunno, but my knee hurts. My shoulder and elbow are tender, too." I rubbed my elbow.

Mirko released me. We jogged back to the car. At least as fast as

I could with my injured knee. "Now do you realize that you need to learn how to fight properly?" he asked as I worked to keep pace with him.

I scrunched my face. "Fine. But who's going to train me?"

"Me, of course."

* * *

Kaitlynn cried in Jaren's arms near the truck as I gimped up the hill. "I'm okay, guys!"

"Oh, thank God!" Kaitlynn ran to me, tears streaming down her flushed cheeks. "I thought you were dead. What was that?" She grabbed me, pulling me into the vise her arms created.

I gave her a pointed look. We'd been over this. "Vampire."

"Pijawika," Mirko corrected.

"Same diff," I retorted, pushing Kaitlynn off me to relieve my knee of the pressure.

"This is not cool. We need to get out of here." Kaitlynn sniffed and grabbed my hand, scurrying along beside me.

"Working on it."

"Faster," Mirko said, as he scooped me into his arms and booked it up the rest of the hill.

Jaren and Ace stood at the top. Jaren's face glowed with relief. His eyes revealed the tenderness he still felt for me. "Are you hurt?"

"My knee's a little jacked up. I can walk, even jog, but Mirko thought I wasn't fast enough."

Jaren's face soured at the sight of me in Mirko's arms.

"Save it." Mirko commanded. "We have bigger issues to worry about right now. What the hell, Ace?"

"That shouldn't have happened. I didn't tell anyone where I was going. No one knew when the plane was arriving. You were just over there, and I was just over here." Ace pointed to the plane.

"From now on," Mirko said, eyes stabbing Ace, "if I leave Slatki in your care, you better damn well care for her. You get me?"

Ace nodded his head, a frown on his face. "Yeah, man. I get you. It won't happen again. But I'm telling you, someone had inside information. And I mean *inside* because I hadn't said a thing to anybody."

"Oh! I saw her znak thingy," I said, pointing to my neck where a necklace would hang.

Mirko lowered his arms to release me to the ground. He looked into my eyes, and I felt as if he searched for a secret hidden deep within my soul. "What was it?"

"It was round and looked like a sun with rays coming out around it."

"A sun...," Mirko said. He stood so immobile, I was afraid to breathe.

"Yeah. I mean, I think that's what it was."

"Anything else? Any other details you can remember?"

"Um, the glare was red, like there was a red stone or a ruby in the middle," I said, swallowing.

Mirko smiled. "Good girl."

Ace's eyes grew wild and opened wide. "Jelena?"

"That's what it sounds like," Mirko answered, nostrils flaring.

"Who's Jelena, and what does this mean for us?" Jaren asked.

"Let's get her out of here first," Mirko said, hustling us toward the truck.

Jaren nodded and ran back, opening the back door to help me get in.

"I'm not handicapped, you guys. I can get in myself," I snapped.

Kaitlynn jumped in after me. Mirko turned the car around to take us out onto the road.

Kaitlynn started to cry again. "I'm sorry, but I seriously thought you were dead. That was the worst feeling I've ever had in my life. I know you only did it to make sure I was okay, but don't ever do that again. I couldn't live with myself."

Tears welled up in my eyes. "I couldn't let her have you," I said, voice cracking. "I'm so sorry. You were supposed to be safer coming with me, not in more danger."

Mirko cut into our tender moment. "If that lady would have gotten to you instead of Slatki, you'd be dead right now," he directed at Kaitlynn. She and I both shuddered and fell bawling into each other's arms.

"You're all rainbows and sunshine, aren't you?" Jaren asked, chastising Mirko.

"What do you want me to say? That next time they should stand there, doing rock-paper-scissors to see who takes on the bad guy? This is reality. Yes, it's a crappy one, but it's yours nonetheless. Slatki has good instincts, and you'd do right by her to encourage her to listen to them instead of making her ashamed and disgusted for being who she is."

"You don't understand. And it's none of your business anyway."

"Fair enough. But if you hinder her growth, we will continue this...*conversation*," Mirko threatened.

I didn't care enough about their argument to speak up. I had nearly died twice in as many days. I had almost gotten my boyfriend, and my best friend killed. I was a monster beyond measure, but at least my best friend didn't die today. She was alive and well, crying into my hair as my tears soaked into her sweater.

"I really can't lose you. You're the best friend I've ever had. I love you." I pulled myself back enough to look at the tears streaming down Kaitlynn's cheeks.

"I love you, too. Promise me that you'll do whatever Mirko says to stay alive." She found resistance on my face. "Please. I don't think you're a monster, and you're my soul sister. Do it for me. Please," she pleaded, breaking my heart enough that I had to give in to her.

I nodded.
Kaitlynn hugged me tight.

13
WE CAME HERE TOGETHER

Mirko sped over one hundred miles an hour, only slowing when a cop was near. I soon realized two things from this part of my journey: Mirko had excellent eyesight, and he was super perceptive. He could spot a cop car from a couple of miles away—in the dark—and from places you wouldn't even expect them to be hiding.

When we finally took the exit off the freeway, Mirko followed the road, then made a quick right, and then another quick right. The glow of the headlights reflected off a sign with threatening, red lettering:

No Trespassing
Government Property
Will Shoot on Sight

"Whoa! Where are you taking us?" I shrieked. I thought he was supposed to be keeping me alive.

"Oh, yeah. You mean the sign? That's for The Base. We can really shoot people if they get too close, too. The government says we can." Mirko's lip jerked up in the corner.

"What? Why would they allow that?" Jaren asked.

Mirko lowered his voice. "Well, as far as the people in Washington know, this is a government facility. They have real ones, like this. You know? The types of facilities that are so top secret that they get funding, but you'll never find the paperwork of where the funds are coming from or where they're being allocated."

Ace turned around, a grin on his face, and looked at Jaren. "We get the funding, too."

"That's disgusting," I said. Talk about leeches.

"Well, Slatki, it's not so easy for all of us to blend in as well as you have. It's not like we could all go out and get regular day jobs to financially support The Base, now could we? No, if we were ever found out, the government would be the first in line to do the most disturbing things imaginable to us. And that includes you, too. The best way for us to remain hidden from the government was to make them think they already knew what we were," Mirko said.

"Brilliant, actually," Ace said. "We do secret missions for the government when they need it. It hasn't been a strict 'they give and we take' relationship."

That helped me feel a bit better, but I didn't want to know what those secret missions were.

We followed the two-way road for a couple of minutes before a set of buildings, lit up with bright halogens, came into view.

"One thing you need to be aware of is to avoid Zack," Mirko said, eyes cast at me in the mirror.

"Why's that?" Kaitlynn asked.

"Yeah, and who's he?" That was all I needed; more people to avoid.

"He's a Pijawika," Mirko said. I scrunched my face. "But he's a nobody. He doesn't have any power or pull, but he is a creep. He knows not to do anything when I'm around because I'll kill him, but he might be stupid enough to try something with one of you girls while I'm not there. Just don't go anywhere by yourselves."

"Make sure you point out who this Zack is," Jaren said.

We pulled up to a security gate with a small building on the side of the road. The man standing post was dressed in military attire and held a rifle of some kind. "Who are your guests, Mirko?" the guy asked, leaning over to see inside the vehicle.

"They're part of an assignment, and they'll be staying here for a while." Mirko used a tone that warranted no questions should be asked.

The guard's forehead creased.

"I take responsibility for them," Mirko snapped.

The guard straightened his spine, but he went inside the building and released the gates. Mirko rolled up the window and drove through the opening. "You should be safe here, but don't go off saying anything about being a melez."

"A what?"

"A melez. A half-breed. A hybrid. Don't go spouting off that you have Pijawikan and human blood."

I snorted. "Oh, you don't have to worry about that." I preferred to think of myself as human. It was everybody else who wouldn't let me forget about the vampire side. And even better—they had a special name for what I was.

The Base consisted of only a couple of buildings. It looked similar to what I would assume any other military base would look like, but on a smaller scale. All of the buildings were angular, symmetrical, and nondescript. Mirko steered the truck between a couple of gray buildings and parked.

Ace was out first, striding to the back to unload our bags. "You guys are bunking in the same barracks we do. This will make it easier for us to keep tabs on you."

I followed behind Kaitlynn. My knee felt better, but it remained stiff. I hoped if I moved around on it, it would be good as new, thanks to my new super-healing.

Jaren shut the truck's back door and trailed behind us into the building. The industrial-grade carpet running along the hallway was a bland mixture of light and dark grays dulled from years of use. The light streamed down from the ceiling in rows of long light bulbs that no longer had covers over their fixtures.

Mirko led us down the hall and up a flight of stairs. "This is the girls' bathroom over here," he said, pointing to the hall down the right. "And the boys' bathroom is the same, but on the other end of the hall."

"Wait. We have to share? Like in college dorms?" Kaitlynn asked. She liked to take her time getting ready in the mornings. I bet she was now second-guessing her decision to come with me.

"There are some rooms that have their own bathrooms, but those are for the higher-ups. Like me." Mirko grinned.

"And me," Ace said.

"Well, why can't we have your rooms, and you take ours?" Kaitlynn asked.

"Because you're not higher-ups. Your bathroom is kept clean so you should be fine. And there are only a few girls that stay in this building, so sharing won't be much of a problem, anyway."

Ace turned over his shoulder, "You can use my bathroom if you'd like." The look he gave her suggested the offer involved a lot more.

Kaitlynn smiled. "Thanks, but I have a boyfriend. I'll stick with the communal."

Ace shrugged and then stopped in front of a large oak door and dropped the bags. He took out a key, slid it in the lock, and the door creaked open.

"It's not the Ritz Carlton, but you'll do just fine with it," Mirko said.

The room had a set of bunk beds and twin computer desks. A small window sat between the beds and the desks, and I was grateful for the natural light.

"This'll work," I told Kaitlynn, setting my bags on the top bunk.

She opened the door to the closet and noticed that it ran the length of the room, save for the area of the door.

"Yeah, we'll be fine," she said to Ace. He set her bags down on the bottom bed.

Mirko turned to Jaren. "You'll have the single across the hall." He pulled out a set of keys, took one off the key ring, and handed it to Jaren. Mirko spun around to me, a devious grin molding his lips. "We start training in the morning."

"Yippy," I said, rolling my eyes.

Mirko smirked harder. I had a feeling he was going to enjoy torturing me with whatever this "training" involved.

The guys lined up on their way out of our room and over to Jaren's. I stood against the door frame and watched Jaren open his door.

A tall blond girl in tight, black leather came strutting over to him. "Oh, looky here! What's your name, suga'?" she said, her accent sultry and southern. Not what I would have expected based on her get-up.

I perked up, away from the door frame. Her attention locked on Jaren. He looked at me surprised, and then turned back to the girl, his jaw hanging slightly open.

"I'm Jaren," he said, and I could hear the excitement and interest in his voice.

Anger coursed through me, hot as melted steel. I knew this girl was a vampire. And that he was attracted to her. This was wrong on so many levels. Something inside of me took over, and I stepped out into the hall.

"Hi, I'm Brooke." I pointed between Jaren and me. "We came here together." I couldn't exactly say that we were together, so that had to suffice.

Mirko looked from me, to Jaren, to the girl, and then back to me. He was clearly amused by the situation.

"Do tell," she said and set her focus back on Jaren. "I'm Holly Anne." She beamed, showing perfectly straight, white teeth, and offered her delicate hand to Jaren.

Oh, she did not expect him to kiss her hand. I twitched, on the verge of smacking it back, when Kaitlynn came around me, and grabbed Holly Anne's hand, shaking it. "And I'm Kaitlynn. Nice to meet you, Holly Anne. Now if you don't mind, we've had a long day and would like to get settled in. I'm sure there will be plenty of time tomorrow to do the whole meet-and-greet thing."

Holly Anne slid her hand out of Kaitlynn's grasp as if it were stuck in a pile of goo, a perfect southern smile plastered on her face the whole time. She opened her mouth, preparing to speak. I lifted my top lip in warning.

"We'll introduce you tomorrow," Mirko cut in, ebbing the fire that was sure to catch.

Holly Anne's smiling face flexed.

"I don't want to see you down this hall again tonight. Get me?" Mirko asked.

She closed her mouth, angled a genuine smile at Jaren, and then turned around, swishing her hair as she did, and strutted down the hall the way she came.

Kaitlynn relaxed her shoulders.

My eyes held daggers as they met Jaren's, and I let all the repugnance I felt flow through me and gather in the muscles of my face. As soon as I felt my message had been delivered, loud and clear, I turned my back on him and marched to my room.

If he thought he could shun me because my blood contained only half of what hers did and then get all excited like a dog in heat when she came around, he had another thing coming. And if little Ms. Georgia wanted to play games with me, I would knock her tiara off her head so fast, she'd get whiplash.

I threw the door shut behind me in case anyone still had any doubt of what kind of a mood I was in.

14
I'll Kill 'Em

I padded out of the bathroom the next morning to find Mirko propped up against the wall outside our door.

"I love the multicultural thing you have going on there," Mirko said pointing to the top of his head, indicating the towel I had wrapped around mine. "It's sexy."

"Oh, shut up." I pushed him aside so Kaitlynn and I could get into our room. "Just give me a few minutes to get dressed."

Mirko followed behind me into the room.

"No," I squealed. "You need to wait *outside!*" I pushed his chest, and shut and locked the door behind him.

"He's bad," Kaitlynn said, shaking her head.

I could hear his troublemaker's laughter through the door. "One of these days, Slatki, it'll be harder for you to push me out. And then one of these days, you won't even want to push me out."

Kaitlynn snorted, and I rolled my eyes. I dressed in the outfit I thought would be the most flexible and giving of the clothes I had packed. I had a pair of sweats and a pair of yoga pants, but I decided to go with the sweats. That ought to give Mirko less ammunition against me.

When Kaitlynn was ready, I pulled open the door. Mirko stood on the other side with his signature grin. "I was hoping you'd changed your mind about me not watching you change your clothes. But alas, here you are, dressed in your frumpies."

I laughed, my forehead creasing in amusement. "And your ribbed tank is so darn classy. You could take me to prom in that for sure."

"Ah. You'd like me to take you to prom, huh? I could arrange that."

I blanched. I didn't know if I'd ever be able to make it to prom now. All the things I had dreamed and hoped for would never be the same. And if I did make it out of this in one piece, would I even be able to go back to the same school? My mom would probably make us move again, so there went my life as I knew it.

"That bad?" Mirko said. He must've noticed the change in my demeanor.

"Let's get this over with." I stole a quick, regretful glance at Jaren's door across the hall and then swept my hand out for Mirko to lead me.

* * *

Mirko's idea of training was more like giving me a beatdown for fun. He was fast and could pack a punch. He knew all of the spots that hurt the body the most. The kidney, the throat, the temple, the back of my knees.

"You'll learn quicker once you've experienced it," Mirko said, kicking me on the meaty part of my forearm with his hard shin. "Keep your hands up."

I jumped back and held my arm close to my chest. "That hurt. You're just trying to justify beating me."

He grinned and bounced toward me.

I made sure to keep my hands up and noticed my focus increased with the pain in my arm. I was sure there were other ways he could have taught me those things, and I promised myself once I got strong and fast enough, I would make him pay for each one of my bruises.

Mirko bobbed in for a low jab, and I tried to connect my fist with his temple. He was too fast and danced back before I could touch him.

"Can we be done yet? I'm tired, and I'd like to do something else today other than collect bruises."

"Sure. Let's do some cool-down work, and then you can have the rest of the day."

I exhaled on a relieved breath. I couldn't handle one more attack or dodge. "When do we work with weapons?" Mirko had only talked about hand-to-hand combat and how things would change when I grew to be more advanced.

Mirko laughed. "We won't. We only fight with our hands. Weapons are made for the weak. If you can't win in a fair fight with your hands, then you don't deserve to live."

My jaw dropped. "That's terrible. What happens if you're not fighting a fair fight, and the other person is better than you? Then what?"

"You'd better hope that never happens, or if it does, you'd better hope someone more skilled than you is there to defend you."

We were working out our last stretches when Kaitlynn and Ace walked into the gym. "Oh, good," Kaitlynn said. "I was just coming to get you for some food."

"Oh, I love you. I'm starving."

I tied the laces on my sneakers and stood up. I couldn't care less what Mirko did with the rest of his day, so I didn't ask him. Ace remained in the gym when Kaitlynn and I left.

"Have you seen Jaren today?" I asked Kaitlynn as soon as I figured we were out of earshot. Way out of earshot.

"Yeah, I heard him when he came out of his room this morning, so I grabbed Ace, and I followed him."

"You sneaky little minx!" We snickered. "What'd you find out?"

"He didn't really do anything that interesting. He went to this little cafeteria they have. They call it the mess hall, same as they do in the army."

"Weird."

"I know. It's funny, but the food smells good."

"Did you see Holly Anne?" We strolled into the mess hall, and my stomach growled. Something smelled delicious.

"Yeah. When I came back, she was hovering in the hall a little ways down from our rooms. She was waiting for Jaren to get back, no doubt."

I clenched my jaw. "I hate females. You're about the only one I can stand right now."

"Aw, thanks," she said, kissing the air.

"So, did she find Jaren?" I grabbed a tray and started to fill it. An apple, some garlic bread, and spaghetti. That's what smelled so good.

"She didn't when I was on watch, but who knows now. Oh, and that's Zack." She pointed to a guy across the room. His back was to us, but he had dark hair. It was thin and scraggly from what I could see of him.

As if our looking alerted him that we were also talking about him, he turned back in his chair, an eerie glint in his eye. His cheeks sunk in a little, and his skin held a five o'clock shadow, from days ago, that suggested he wasn't friends with grooming. A slow, ominous smile spread across his lips.

I flashed him a wobbly smile in return and moved over to the drinks. "Can we eat this in our room?"

"I dunno, but we are." Kaitlynn snatched up napkins before we left.

We kept our heads down and hustled to our room.

"Yeah, thanks for the heads-up on Zack, Mirko," I said to Kaitlynn as she shut the door behind her and locked it.

"He's for sure a creeper. He didn't freak me out like that when I was with Ace, so we need to be careful around here."

I sighed and took a bite of my spaghetti. "Mmmmh. This is good."

She laughed and took a bite. "What I don't understand," she paused for a moment to finish chewing, "is why they have a mess hall in the first place. Don't they all eat blood?"

"Ew. Thanks," I said, not interested in my spaghetti anymore. "There are humans here, so that would explain why they need the food."

"Sorry. But don't you want to know how it all works?" she asked.

"No. I just want it all to go away. The more I know, the more realistic it will be that my life will never be the same. I mean, before Sunday night, I was finally realizing my dreams. I had Jaren. My best friend dated his best friend. We were becoming popular with the seniors. Jaren had his new place figured out. It was all going so good." I paused and looked at her. "I'm scared I won't be able to spend this summer with you, or go to prom, or graduate, or anything. *Everything* as I knew it is messed up." My lip quivered and tears welled up in my eyes.

"Oh, Brooke," Kaitlynn said. She put our trays on the desk and wrapped me in a much-needed best friend hug. "We'll stay together. No matter what happens."

"Not if my mom makes me move."

Kaitlynn pulled away and looked at me, her forehead creased and her brows raised.

"There's no way my mom's going to let me go back to normal if I make it out of this. She's a spaz. A move is almost guaranteed." Tears crowded on my lower lids and fell over, running down my cheeks.

Kaitlynn hugged me tighter. "We'll figure it out. I'll get expelled or something. I'll make my parents send me wherever you are."

My laugh got muffled in her shoulder. "You can't do that."

"Oh, trust me. If it will keep us together, I'll do it."

"Why do you even still wanna be friends with me?" I searched her face. I couldn't understand why she could accept it so easily.

"Just because you find out something's in your blood,

something that's been there the whole time, doesn't mean you're different all of a sudden. It doesn't make you automatically evil. I could find out my blood type is A negative tomorrow, and you know what? I look at it the same as you finding out what brand is in your blood."

I smiled, wanting to believe it and let my fears melt away. But they wouldn't. "Yeah, but A negative doesn't mean a whole species wants something from you, or wants to kill you."

She clasped my hands. "I can't blame you for any of those things."

I shook my head and wiped my face. "Jaren can."

"I don't think he *blames* you. I think he's not sure how to process it all."

I huffed. "He sure seemed to like the idea of processing Holly Anne."

Kaitlynn snorted. "I bet it was more that he was flattered. I don't believe anything will come of it. Oh sure, she'll try, but I doubt he'll go for it."

"Hmm. We'll see. His track record hasn't been that great."

A light tapping sounded on the door.

"Who is it?" Kaitlynn hollered.

"Jaren."

I rolled my eyes, and then checked myself in the mirror. I straightened my pony tail, cleaned up my eyes, and then nodded, sitting back down on the bed.

Kaitlynn hopped off the bed and unlocked the door. He strolled in, looking unsure about himself.

"I wanted to see how you were doing." He leaned up against one of the desks with forced ease.

I was mad at him, but he had a lot of guts and must've still cared or he wouldn't be here.

I sighed. "I guess as good as could be expected."

He nodded toward the sweat pants I wore. "Did you train with

Mirko this morning?"

I cracked a small smile. He knew very well that I did. "Yeah, it was brutal."

"Did he hurt you?"

"Lots." His posture swelled in anticipation of taking action. "It's alright, though, because I've already learned a lot. It's a part of the process."

His gaze held lingering questions.

"I promise. It's fine."

He nodded and then seemed to be gathering courage for what he wanted to say next. "Look, about Holly Anne. I didn't do anything. I was surprised, is all." A smile lit up his face. Such a hot, normal Jaren smile that it fractured some of the pieces in my heart. "You surprised me, too. Stepping up to her like that. Wow. That was big for you. I kind of liked it."

"Oh, stop. It was nothing." My face flushed. But it was a big deal. I never thought I'd have the courage to stand up to Tiffany that way, but now I was able to do it to a vampire.

"No, you were only ready to rip her head off," Kaitlynn clarified.

"Yeah, well...anyway, how have you been doing?" I asked Jaren, changing subjects.

"I'm doing all right. Mirko's driving me crazy, but other than that, things have been okay. As okay as can be expected." A nervous chuckle echoed between us. "What do you think of him?" Jaren rubbed his shoe against the carpet.

I watched him for a moment, not sure of what I should say or how honest of an answer he wanted.

"I think he's funny, but he's also cocky. He's a good fighter and knows what he's doing, so that's all that matters to me right now." I left out the parts that Kaitlynn and I thought he was a fine specimen of the male gender, and how I found pleasure in the way his muscles stretched and went taut when he fought.

Those things felt like too much information.

Jaren nodded in relief.

"What about Holly Anne? Have you seen her today?" I wanted to know, and I wasn't ashamed to ask.

"Um, yeah. I have. She approached me on my way back from lunch."

"What did she say?" I tried to keep my voice even. I didn't want him to be afraid to tell me things.

He scratched his nose. "She wanted to know my name and meet me."

"Did you kiss her hand?"

He laughed, relieved. "No, she tried, but I shook it instead."

Kaitlynn and I laughed.

I soured the moment with my next thought. "You know, she could make you. If she can do that dream, mind control thing, then she could make you do anything."

His eyes met mine for a horrified moment, and then he shook it away. "No. I think she has too much pride to try that on me."

"I hope so," I said.

"Me, too," Kaitlynn added. "We should ask Mirko or Ace about that."

"About what?" Mirko asked, inviting himself into our room.

"Your mind control...thing," I said, not sure what to call it.

"Sanjam. What about it?"

I tried to figure out how to phrase my thoughts without mentioning Holly Anne. "Well, there are humans here. And us. Do you guys have some sort of etiquette or rule that protects us from it?"

Mirko's lips curled. He tilted his head toward Jaren. "You guys scared?"

"No," Jaren defended. "Brooke brought it up. Not me." He pointed to himself in a gesture of innocence.

"Well, do I have to worry about it or not?" I barked at Mirko.

"That is one thing you do not need to worry about, Slatki. We have an unwritten code that it's disrespectful and rude to use it at The Base. It's similar to walking around naked...," he turned toward me and grinned. "Sure, you could do it, but it would make some of those around you feel squeamish."

"'Kay. Thanks. Now go away," I told him, flipping my arm in a shooing manner toward the door.

"Oh, spunky, too. Sexy," Mirko said, leaning back on his heels.

"We were having a conversation before you walked in." Jaren glared at Mirko.

Mirko chuckled. I didn't know why, but he seemed to enjoy the reactions he caused in other people. "I did come in here for a reason other than to hang out with you."

"Fine," I said.

Mirko's face fell into a serious scowl. "I've been checking with some of my contacts. Jelena has sent out lackeys to find you, and one line has been made aware that Jelena has a lackey here. At The Base."

I breathed in shallow, quick gasps. "What does that mean?"

Jaren's expression turned gloomy. "We've come all this way, only to be led directly to the person who's trying to take her? What a joke."

"She'll be safe here. All this means is that you all have to stick together and not go anywhere without Ace or me."

Jaren grunted. "We'd have been better off staying at Garwin's. You guys could have stayed there with us. It's a lot nicer there, too." I think the last line was spoken purely as a dig to Mirko.

"Garwin's property is in no way safer than it is here. There, you have to worry about an attack from many people. Yes, some*one* is here, but that is a single individual who will be dealt with. Big difference. And when I find the mole, because I will, I'll kill 'em."

Mirko spun around and left, not bothering to close the door behind him. I knew from the vicious glare on his face that another person would soon die because of me.

15
TRAINING, NOT FANGING

Ace walked with me to meet Mirko in the gym for the day's training. I was stuck wearing the yoga pants because I had yet to find where to do laundry here, and everybody's noses were keen enough to tell that I'd worn the sweats already.

I hesitated at the thought of being beat on for the second day in a row, but I was determined to bring some heat to Mirko today.

He was already in the gym, setting up floor mats, when we arrived.

"What are those for?" I hollered across the gym.

He looked up at me with a wicked grin and then finished placing the mats. He moved around shirtless, and I blushed at the reaction my body had while gazing upon his tanned, toned chest. "We're doing some ground work today. Plus, I figured you should learn how to extend your fangs, which will take a while, and I thought this would be a good place to sit."

Horror faded the blush from my face. "Un-uh. I agreed to training, not fanging." I turned around to head back to my room.

"Get over here," Mirko said, using his commander's tone with me, "and let me explain to you why you need them in a fight. If you still disagree, and honestly think they're not valuable, then you can skip today's training."

I stopped. I absolutely wanted to skip out on training today. I turned around and walked back with a victorious curve to my lips.

"Remember when you asked me about training with weapons?" Mirko asked, coaxing me into his explanation.

"Yep, and you told me we wouldn't be."

"That's true, but one of your best defenses in a close fight is your fangs. How would you stop someone when you have them held with both hands and no weapons? And you have yet to learn about your powers, let alone control them."

"Powers?" I asked.

"Yes," Mirko said. "All Pijawikas have some degree of power. Take Jelena, for example. Her power is starting and controlling fire with her mind. I guess people nowadays would say she's pyrokinetic."

My eyebrows raised and my jaw dropped. "But...how do you know she can do that?"

"Ace, can you shut the door, please?" Mirko asked, and then sat down on the mat.

He had my attention now, so I followed him to the floor and sat across from him.

He exhaled uncomfortably. "Let's just say that I have had a rocky relationship with Jelena."

"What? Like you dated her?" I was appalled.

"No," Mirko laughed. "I wish that's all it was. The story I'm about to tell you hasn't been told by me, except for a small number of times. Four before now, to be exact."

"So, why tell me?" I wanted to know what he knew about Jelena, but I didn't want to pry into his personal life.

"Because you need to really grasp who she is, and start taking training seriously."

I grew somber and tilted my head, waiting for him to continue.

"As you know, I was turned into a Zao Duh. I wasn't turned because I wanted into this life, nor did I want a chance at immortality. I didn't even change over because I wanted the strength, the speed, or the power. Yes, they're nice now that I know what to do with them. But I didn't choose this."

His eyes looked lost behind dark memories.

When he spoke again, his eyes were cloudy. "I was forced."

I raised my eyebrows. I hadn't expected that.

"I fought for Empress Maria Theresa of Austria in the War of Austrian Succession back in the 1740s."

"Whoa! That makes you...what? Over three hundred sixty years old." My jaw hung open.

"Give or take, yes." Mirko pressed his lips together and looked down at the mat.

"I'm sorry. It's just that you don't meet someone over three hundred years old, well...ever." I reached my arm out to rest my palm on his hand.

Mirko stared at me for a sorrowful moment and then continued. "Well, I fought among many warriors, but I soared above them all to the top of our ranks. I could see what my enemy would do as soon as he conceived it. Jelena saw this in me and wanted it for her own use. I didn't know there was such a thing as Pijawikas when she approached me."

"She had me followed to find what she could use against me. Well, she found it. In my little sister. She was barely five at the time."

He had a sister?

"Jelena told me that if I didn't change over she would do terrible things to Miska. She said that she would use fire to burn Miska, and then burn her in the same spot over and over again. I couldn't do that to Miska, so I changed."

I frowned. I would have changed, too.

"Jelena's purpose for me was to fight for her to keep the Pijawikas in power and the Zao Duhs and humans as slaves, or to slaughter them. I find it ironic that she changed me into a Zao Duh, for the sole purpose to fight against what would become my own people, and my freedom. When I look back on it now, the only thing I can relate it to is Hitler."

"That's terrible. I'm so sorry."

"It was terrible, and I was ruled by her until Zladislov became the new leader of the commission. He freed the humans, Zao Duhs, and me from Pijawikan slavery."

I stared into his sienna brown eyes and saw the pain he must have carried all this time. But he never showed any of it. He was playful and laughed often.

And I was drawn to him. I wanted to lean forward and touch my lips to his.

The urge snapped me out of my trance. "So, how is my learning to extend my fangs going to help me win a fight when the other person can start me on fire?"

Mirko grinned. "If you can slit their throat before they can do that, you win."

* * *

"Right then. Let's start with the fangs first, then we can focus on the fighting afterward."

I nodded reluctantly.

"Now, you know when you clench your jaw, you feel the muscles above your molars contract?" He pointed to his cheeks.

I nodded, my mouth too parched to answer. I couldn't believe I was doing this.

"Well, you want to create that same sensation, but with the front teeth." He looked at me expectantly, waiting for me to attempt it.

I stared at him.

"Just try it," Mirko coaxed.

I swallowed. "This is my worst fear," I spoke on a ragged breath.

"It's okay. Trust me."

I tried it, but I only succeeded at clenching my jaw.

"Again, but focus on the front muscles. Almost as if you're about to grind your teeth forward, but keep the focus on the muscles, not the teeth."

I let out a breath and shook my hands. "Ah! I hate this."

"I promise, you won't grow horns," Mirko teased.

I tried again and felt the muscles in the front of my face engage. My eyes widened because I thought I almost did it, but then they filled with fear.

"I can't do this," I said, shaking my head to rid the sensation from my memory.

"It's okay, Slatki. Remember what we talked about? This is life and death we're dealing with. I promise, as soon as you get it, we'll be done with that part for the day." He grabbed my hands, sliding my fingers into his soft palm. "Now, again."

I took a big breath, extending the exhale as long as I could. And tried again. I let go of the angst and focused on my task. I clenched the muscles in my jaw and thought of bringing the sensation forward. Tension flowed along the roots of my upper teeth as I ground the bottom ones underneath. When the muscles above my canines flexed, I felt tingles run through my gums, and then my fangs shot out.

"You did it!" Mirko congratulated me with glowing eyes and his head leaning forward in surprise.

I relaxed my muscles to retract my fangs, and covered my mouth with my hand, ashamed for succeeding. I was a true monster.

"Good job. I thought it would take a bit longer, but you did it. See? Wasn't so bad now, was it?"

"Other than letting me know I was more of a monster than I thought, yeah it was."

Mirko frowned. "Do you think I'm a monster?"

I looked at him. I'd never thought of him that way. "No, but that's different."

"Oh? Why's that?" He tilted his head.

"Well...I respect you, and you're Zao Duh, not Pijawikan."

Mirko laughed. "My experience has always been the opposite. I'm looked down on for not being born this way, and here you are, thinking better of me for it. We don't get to choose our lot in life, but what matters is how we deal with it." He stared at me for a moment. "Are lions evil because they hunt and eat meat to survive?"

"Well, no. It's nature," I said.

"Right, because they're predators. And so are we. Yes, some are crueler than others, but predators all the same."

I thought about what he said. It reminded me of the mountain lion and the way I'd felt standing against him. I figured I should ask Mirko about it, but I'd had enough surprises for the day. "Let's get on with training and be done, please?"

Mirko nodded, a grim smile on his face. He set me up in different positions on the mat. We started out slow as he showed me possible positions that I could be in during a fight. Then he showed me ways to get out of them, and ways to counteract them to be on the offensive.

We replayed the moves over and over again until I became comfortable with them. Eventually, we increased our speed, and there were times I got my arm or foot caught in a weird position. Mirko was extremely patient with me when I did so.

We intertwined and melded our bodies together in intimate ways. I tried not to think about that, but there were moments when his warm breath blew across my neck, or his leg stroked the inside of my thigh, which kept the thought fresh in my mind. I was grateful he kept focused on business and didn't try to hit on me when we were training.

When we finished, and Mirko rolled away from me, he said, "Good work today. You're getting much stronger and faster."

I sat on my knees, catching my breath. "I've been meaning to ask you that. Why is it that I was never this fast, or could see or smell as well as I can now?"

"You're becoming more attuned to your Pijawikan side. It's almost like an awakening. It sat dormant for years until you started to know about it."

"Yeah, but that doesn't explain how I was so fast and strong when that man attacked Jaren and me. Before we even knew I was a melez."

"You remembered the word 'melez.'" Mirko beamed at me. "But to answer your question, I think that could be explained by the level of adrenaline that you utilized at the time. You're Pijawikan side has always been there. And it knew what to do—naturally—when it needed to."

I really didn't know how to respond. I knew training would start to bring out this side of me, but now I had learned how to use my fangs. It felt like too much, too quick.

We finished our stretches in silence.

* * *

Mirko walked beside me on the way back to my room.

I heard them before I spotted them. "Jaren and Holly Anne. I like the ring to that." I heard in Holly Anne's southern drawl.

Mirko and I rounded the corner to find Jaren leaning against the soda machine, and Holly Anne standing way too close to him. He straightened up and took a step to the side when he noticed me, but before he did, I could see the interest in her on his face.

Fury curdled in my stomach. "Can I talk to you?" I said, grabbing Jaren by his shirt and dragging him toward our rooms.

"Hey." Holly Anne stepped in front of me.

Behind her, Zack stood outside of the mess hall doors. He watched me with his head tilted down and his eyes lifted. His lips arched up at the corners with a nefarious smirk.

Chills broke out on my arms, and I transferred my discomfort into rage. "Take care of her, Mirko. Or. I. Will."

Mirko came from behind her and pulled her arm back into an arm bar.

I stepped around her with Jaren following me. When we got to

124

my room, I flung the door open and pushed him inside. Kaitlynn lifted her head in shock, and I slammed the door shut. "What the hell were you thinking?"

"What? Everywhere I go, she's there."

"Man, you're such a hypocrite, you know that? Not only could she be the mole we're looking for, but you're just like your dad."

He flinched, then glared at me. "How so?"

"Your dad has always been too blind to see you in front of him instead of your cheating mother. And you're too blind to see me in front of you instead of the man who died on your living room floor." I realized I had done the same thing, but I was on a roll here and had to finish this.

He clenched his jaw. "I am not like him. At all."

"Really? Did you honestly push me away because I'm part vampire? You're not afraid of Mirko, Ace, or Holly Anne. So, what is it? Why did you throw me aside only to take up with the next vampire that looks your way?"

Silence.

I huffed. "Right." I opened the door. "Just leave."

Jaren took a few steps toward the door before he stopped in front of me. "I wasn't 'taking up with her.'"

"Whatever," I said, then turned my cheek away from him. As soon as he was clear of the door, I slammed it, rattling the hinges.

"What was that all about?" Kaitlynn asked.

"Only that Jaren was ogling Holly Anne again. Who knows what would have happened between them if I'd not shown up."

"Oh, I'm so sorry."

I shook my head, trying to keep the tears at bay. "You know, he told me that he loved me." The tears won. "And I still love him." I might have thought Mirko was hot, but I loved Jaren and wanted to be with him.

"Brooke." Kaitlynn came over to me as I slid to the floor.

"Why? Why did I have to fall for him? I want him to go home."

"Would he be safe there?"

"I dunno, but I *can't* take this anymore. It's killing me. He's supposed to be such a gentleman. And he still looks at me sometimes like he used to. It's so much back and forth with him. I know he wants me, at least I thought he did before right now, but then he does something so stupid. What if she is the mole? She could have killed him right there, and I'd have to live with that for the rest of my life."

"This is a lot for all of us. He just doesn't know what he's doing. He's an idiot." She pushed a loose strand of hair out of my face.

"Yeah," I said, wiping at the tears. "Then Mirko made me learn how to extend my fangs today."

"He did? Did you do it?"

"Yeah," I sighed.

"Can I see?" She continued to surprise me.

I looked at her for a second, knowing she deserved to see them, but really not feeling up to it. "Can I show you later, please?"

She nodded, lips held in a slightly regretful line, but she hugged me, anyway.

16
I'D RATHER DIE

I struggled to get up the next morning. My life as of late had taken a toll on me, and I was drained. I wanted it all to go away.

Mirko wasn't hearing it, though, when I asked for a day off. He wouldn't even budge to my pleas of postponing our training until later in the day. He kept going on about having other stuff to do, so I'd better get with the program.

In the gym, Mirko punched me in the shoulder hard enough to knock me down.

I jumped up and counterattacked. I hit his jaw as hard as I could without tapping into my vampire strength.

"Oh, come on! You're not even trying!" Mirko scowled at me.

That infuriated me. "I am, too! It's not like I enjoy getting bruised, Mirko," I panted, swiping a stream of sweat off my forehead. "I wouldn't exactly consider this fun."

"It's not supposed to be fun. The whole point in doing these exercises is to strengthen your Pijawikan side, to bring out the predator within you." Mirko used the tone one would use with a child.

"I don't want to strengthen that side! The last time I fully tapped into it, I killed somebody." The man I'd killed was about to strangle Jaren, but I still had a point. "What makes you think I would be all gung-ho about doing it again?"

"Did you forget you almost died at the airport? If I hadn't been there, you would have been killed, and your friends would have been slaughtered. Or worse. And until we can figure out how to stop Jelena, nothing is going to change."

I felt depleted. "I didn't ask for this. I never wanted any of it. The only things that have come my way from being a dear, blessed Pijawika, or more accurately, a cursed abomination, is that I lost my home, my school, my friends, who knows when I'll get to see my mom again, and my boyfriend broke up with me. You think dying is going to be a good motivation for me to tap into my other side? Well, you've got another thing coming, buddy. I would rather die than continue on this way, or worse, strengthen the good ol' lucky charm that is my Pijawikan side."

I grabbed my shoes and turned toward the door. I had enough for the day. Maybe for the rest of my life. What I was giving now was going to have to be enough. There was no way I was going to embrace my other side fully and risk losing myself in the process. I could already feel it happening.

"We're not done here."

"Tootles." I reached the doors and made a sharp right turn down the hall to my room.

* * *

I hoofed it along the carpet, thinking of ways to get home. I wanted to be done with this place.

The lights above me flickered, and I halted. "Stupid government building."

I started walking again, and Zack stalked around the corner. "Well, aren't you good enough to eat," he said, pushing me up against the wall, causing me to drop my sneakers.

"Don't mess with me."

"I have something important to tell you," he breathed into my face. His breath was hot and sour, like decaying flesh might be.

I fought back the bile rising in my throat.

"Jelena has plans for you." My eyes stretched wide. "You're her catalyst. She has everything set up. All she needs is you." He brushed his thumb over my lip, and I jerked away.

"Set up for what?" There was that word again: catalyst.

He smirked at me. "Jelena's going to get the old ways back. We'll be out from under the humans and we won't have to hide anymore. We'll have all the food and power we could ever want." He tucked a loose strand of hair behind my ear, and I cringed. "Did you know that the Mafia makes more money every year than Microsoft? And that's not even a fraction of what's capable for the Pijawikas when Jelena takes over. And...," he gripped my chin and jerked my face up to look at him, "if you come with me, we'll have a comfortable position right beside her."

"What are you talking about? I'm not going anywhere." I pushed at his chest to get him off me, with no success. Panic quickened my pulse. How could I not push him off? Everything else in my life had already been taken out of my control.

"Oh, you're coming. Or things are going to get real uncomfortable for you and those you care about." He looked at me for a moment, dark eyes brooding as he rested his cheek against mine and sniffed the hair that fell back over my face.

I struggled to get my chin out of his grip, and he backed his face away slightly. He smiled, and then smashed his lips against mine.

His lips moved like worms after a soggy rain, trying to force their way into my mouth. I gagged, but he didn't stop and even slid his tongue inside my mouth.

Molten lava exploded within me. Fever coursed through my veins, and out toward my fingertips. "I said stop!"

I focused every cell of my being to ensure his pain. My mind assaulted his, and I triggered every nerve ending within his body, setting them ablaze. He released me and stood there, struck with what I was doing mentally to him.

It wasn't enough. My anger boiled beyond the place I could rein it back.

I concentrated on the area within him that controlled his breathing, and I paralyzed it. Warm liquid fell from my nostril, running over my lip. I stood against the wall, eyes locked on Zack, watching him turn blue. His pain was great and he suffocated, but it still wasn't enough.

"Brooke!" I heard a muffled scream from not far away. It sounded like Mirko, but I was too busy to care.

Zack fell to the ground, petrified. Satisfaction tingled through me, and liquid now dripped out of both nostrils.

"Please...stop." It sounded like Mirko was choking. He grabbed my arm, and only then did I look over to him. His tanned face had gone pale.

I released Zack, and he and Mirko both gasped for air. I wiped at my nose and came away with bloody hands.

"Ace!" Mirko yelled when he could speak.

Zack remained huddled on the ground coughing and keening between ragged breaths.

Ace turned the corner at vampire speed and made an immediate stop in front of us. "Whoa. What did you do to her?" he yelled at Zack.

"She did it to him," Mirko said, standing up straighter. "He's the mole. Get him out of here."

Ace hefted Zack up by his arm and dragged him away.

Mirko peered at me in a way he'd never done before. It was fear. He was afraid of me.

All of my energy evaporated, and I slid to the floor, sniffing and wiping at my face.

"You have to be careful," Mirko said, bending at his knees. "You possess a lot more power than I'd ever imagined was possible. We have to train you."

"No," I said. I was done, and I most certainly was not going to start training this power that reared its ugly head.

"You have to. It's too dangerous if you don't know how to control it."

"You." I glared at him. "It's because of you I have this problem to begin with." I thrust my bloody hands in front of him. "Just flash your fangs, Brooke. Come on. Trust me," I said, mocking his words. "None of this would have happened if you hadn't forced it out of me."

Mirko ignored me. "A few seconds longer and your brain would've been mush." When I didn't concede, he tried again. "Think of Jaren or Kaitlynn. What if they were the ones to come down this hall and not me? They'd be dead. Simple as that. You broadcasted too much, too far. I'd be surprised if a couple of humans hadn't felt that throughout the building."

I squared my shoulders. "Fine," I said between gritted teeth. I never wanted to hurt Kaitlynn or Jaren. I wanted their safety more than I wanted to be done with everything. I'd suck it up for them.

17
I FELT THAT

"Great. We leave now," Mirko said, standing and pulling me up by my arm.

"Why do we have to leave?" I planted my feet.

"Because I'm taking you to someone who will train you properly."

"Uh-uh. First, I clean up." I pointed to the mess that had dried on my face. "Then you're going to tell me every little detail about where we're going, what we're doing, my training—everything from here on out. You get me?"

The corner of Mirko's lip curled, and he raised his hands in surrender. "Whatever you say, Slatki."

I turned around and advanced toward the bathroom.

"Nope." Mirko pulled me by my waist. "You'll use mine. Let's try to keep this contained as much as possible, huh?" He steered me by my hip and strange things happened in the pit of my stomach.

We turned down the hall that led to the men's bathroom. Mirko stopped in front of his door and unlocked it, pushing the door open. He turned on the light, soaking the room with an ambient glow.

"Whoa." Mirko's room differed from anywhere else in the building. They must have knocked down walls because his room was cavernous. He'd decorated it with soothing, rich burgundies and inky blacks. The colossal bed rested in the corner and was covered with a comforter so buoyant, I ached to lie down on it.

"No wonder you didn't want to trade rooms," I said, following him toward the back.

He chuckled and turned on the bathroom light. Bright rays flooded the room. "You don't have time for a shower, so just wipe yourself down," he said, handing me a dark towel.

I took the towel to the sink and put it under a stream of warm water from the faucet.

"Aww!" I screamed, bending over the sink from a pain so fierce, I almost blacked out.

"What is it?" Mirko asked, easing me to the floor.

I couldn't speak. All I knew was the pummeling torrent inside my head. It engulfed me, drowning me. I felt something cool touch the back of my neck, and then I felt nothing.

* * *

When I woke up, I was lying in the back of the Tahoe. The pain was gone, but we were moving. I looked in the front, and the passenger seat was empty. Mirko drove, but he looked back at me. "How are you feeling?"

I sat up, wondering where everyone else was. "Where's Kaitlynn? And Jaren?"

"They're staying at The Base. So, much better, I presume?"

"Why didn't she come with me?" I was torn about wanting Jaren to come, but I was set on taking Kaitlynn.

"You can't have her around while you're trying to hone in your ability," he said matter of fact.

"You don't understand." I tried to calm down. "I *have* to have her with me." She was the last thing that tied me to who I was before my life as I knew it had ended.

"Slatki, it's just not possible. You want her safe, and right now, you are more harm to her than you're aware of."

I breathed in short, ragged puffs of air.

"She understood. She'll be there when you get back."

He couldn't know that for sure. Especially if this took longer than what her mom would allow for her to help me with my *grandma's death*. "I need to call her."

Mirko pulled out a sat phone and dialed. "Ace. Yes, she's awake. Put her on." He handed the phone back to me.

"Kait—"

"Brooke? Are you all right?" Kaitlynn said, concern in her voice.

"I feel better. But you stayed." I tried not to, but I sounded wounded.

"I know. Mirko explained what happened in the hall. Brooke, I felt it. What you did to Zack, I felt that."

Guilt sliced through me. I knew in explicit detail what I was doing to Zack. Hearing that an ounce of what he felt had touched Kaitlynn made my stomach sour. No, it went deeper than that. It tore at my soul. "I'm so sorry." I knew right then she shouldn't be anywhere near the monster I'd become.

"It's okay. You didn't know. Mirko's going to help you learn to control it, so listen to him, please?"

Listening to him got me separated from her. "Mm-hm. Are you going to be okay staying there?"

"Yeah. I think so. Some guys came and took Zack away, so we don't need to worry about him anymore."

"What about Jaren? What does he think about all of this?" I had to ask. I still cared for him.

"He wasn't too happy about not going with you, and he didn't like the idea of you going alone with Mirko, either. But they didn't really give him a choice."

I looked at my palms and noticed they had been cleaned. "What about the other stuff? What did he say about that?"

"Oh, he was furious with them for not taking the proper precautions with your power. He said that they should've known since they know a lot more about this vampire stuff than we do."

"Oh, God," I said, wiping hair away from my face. I didn't even want to know what he thought about me now.

"And I'm on Jaren duty, so you focus while you're at...wherever it is you're going." I didn't know whether I should tell her thanks or to not worry about watching him. He broke up with me, and I already told him everything I thought about it, anyway.

"Thanks," I said because I would probably be wondering about it regardless.

"Hey, Slatki," Mirko said, cutting into my conversation. "We're almost there, and I'd like a chance to talk to you before we arrive."

I sighed. "Well, Mirko needs to talk to me, so I'll call you as soon as I can."

"All right, and try okay? Really try to get your power thing in control."

"I will. I'm so sorry about that. Honestly, it makes me sick."

"I'm fine. I love you, so take care."

"Love you, too, and be safe."

"Bye." And the only sound left was of the car's tires spinning on the freeway.

"What did you need to tell me?" I handed Mirko's sat phone back to him.

"First of all, how do you feel?"

"Tired. Sad that Kaitlynn felt what I did to Zack."

"It was nowhere near what Zack felt. She felt aches throughout her body, and she had a hard time breathing."

"Hmmm." Still, that was too much for me. "What about Zack? Does Jelena know you're helping me?"

"I don't think so. We're lucky he's prideful. He planned on bringing you in and being the big hero. He didn't want to take any chances Jelena would send someone else in for you."

"Well, that's good." I looked down at my palms again. "Did I finish cleaning my hands?" I looked in the rearview mirror at my reflection. "And my face?"

Mirko's eyes flickered with an emotion he hid too well for me to get a read on. "No, I did that before I grabbed the others."

I couldn't remember any of that. "How did you get the pain to stop?"

"I knocked you unconscious," he said, curling his lip.

My eyes widened. "You punched me in the head?"

"No. Pressure point," he said, pointing to the back of his neck.

Ah. The cool pressure I'd felt. "Well, thanks. But where are you taking me and why?"

"I'm taking you to Lijepa. She's what I guess you'd call a savant when it comes to powers."

I tilted my head.

"She can sense them. She explained it to me at one time that she can taste what someone's power is. They each have a flavor, I suppose."

"And how's that gonna help me control it?"

"Lijepa's very old. She's trained many Pijawikas in their power."

I scrunched my nose. "She's Pijawikan?" I wasn't having very good luck with those.

"Yes, but the ones you've met so far haven't been good ambassadors. I think you'll like Lijepa. Plus, she'll be able to tell you the degree of your power, and if anyone can teach you how to control it, it would be her."

I nodded, hoping he was right.

18
The Man of Your Dreams

I sat up against the leather in the back seat, nervous about meeting Lijepa. I didn't have much time to stir about it, though, because before I knew it, we were driving into the mouth of a canyon. The trees weren't as vibrant here as the ones in Virginia. These leaves *looked* like they were dying. Brown and brittle.

Mirko followed the narrow road and soon turned down what looked like a service road. It was small, meant to only fit one car's width at a time. When the trees opened up, I spotted a cottage up ahead. It appeared old, like it belonged to the mountain. Stones made up its siding, and the roof matched the earth's tones. Twigs and brown stems lined the front and probably made for a beautiful garden in warmer weather.

Our tires crunched against the gravel road as Mirko drove up alongside the cottage and parked. I climbed out after he did. He reached behind the driver's seat and pulled something up from the floor.

"My bag! Thank you," I said, reaching for it. I couldn't believe he'd remembered to bring it.

"Well, I am the man of your dreams. You just don't know it yet."

I rolled my eyes. "Can we get this over with?"

He grinned and then led me to the front door. He knocked, and we stood outside for a minute. I was about to ask him if he called this lady beforehand, when the door creaked open.

A beautiful woman stood on the other side. She had blond hair and high cheekbones. Her skin was flawless, not a wrinkle or crease on her face. She looked...ageless. But then I noticed it in her eyes. They gleamed with an intelligence that spoke of many lifetimes.

"Come in. Come in," she said, stepping aside. Her home was stunning. She'd decorated it with porcelain knickknacks that had the same faded topcoat found on many antiques. She had placed many of these porcelain gems on white shelves hanging from the light green walls. A rich mahogany armoire slumbered against the side wall, its doors gone, and books with spines reminiscent of the earliest in print sat on the shelves. It was evident that Lijepa had placed everything with great care.

She shut the door behind us. "I'm Lijepa, and you must be Brooke." She said my name with reverence.

"Uh, yeah. Nice to meet you." I stuck my hand out, and she pulled me in for a hug. I stood in her embrace, stunned, but I quickly relaxed. She smelled like chamomile tea and comfort.

"It's very nice to meet you," she said, pulling away from me. She had an accent similar to Mirko's, but it sounded more refined. "Please, have a seat." She pointed to a striped Victorian sofa.

I followed Mirko and sat down, placing my bag on the floor beside my feet. "Thank you for taking us in like this." I wasn't sure of the arrangement Mirko had made with her, but it seemed like the proper thing to say.

She replied with a graceful nod and a smile. "Would either of you like some tea?"

"No, thank you," Mirko said and turned to me.

"I'm good. Thanks." Vampires could drink stuff other than blood? Interesting.

She sat down on a chair across from us, modern in design, but it complemented the sofa.

She crossed her feet at her ankles and angled toward me. "I understand you're nervous, but I also understand you are very limited on time." She raised her eyebrows for my confirmation.

"Uh, yeah." I looked at Mirko. "I just really don't know what to expect."

"I see. How about we start by me telling you something about myself first? Would that make you feel a touch better?"

I nodded.

"Well, dear. I am very old, as I am sure Mirko has told you," she said, tilting her head toward Mirko. "I generally prefer to stick to myself up here, in my woods. It's beautiful and peaceful, and I've paid my dues in politics. This is sort of my version of a retirement." She smiled.

I smiled, too. She didn't look old enough to retire.

"Mirko told me about what happened back at The Base, so I understand if you're tired, but I'd like to hear from you about what happened."

I wasn't sure that I wanted to tell anyone about it, but Mirko thought she could help me, and she seemed nice enough.

"Well, there was a vampire, a Pijawika," I corrected. I didn't want to offend her already, and I was nervous about what I did, so I had a hard time finding the words. "He pushed me up against the wall, trapping me, with his arms on both sides of me. He told me that Jelena, she's the lady that's after me. Well, that she was going to set things back to the old ways, and that I would be her catalyst." Lijepa's eyes grew sharp, and I continued. "He said something about money, and the Mafia and Microsoft. And that if I went with him, we'd be in a good position with her, and if I didn't, things would be bad for me and those I cared about. Then he kissed me—"

Mirko grunted his disgust.

"And I snapped, I guess."

Her eyes remained on me, and held no judgment in them, so I continued. "I imagined him in great pain because he wouldn't let me go, and I found a way to reach his mind. It was open to me, and I connected to what seemed like pathways, or networks within the maze, and I set them on fire." I paused to see her reaction, but there wasn't one.

"It didn't seem like it was enough." I adjusted on the couch, ashamed at myself for what I did. "I snapped, and I wanted more. So, I found a pathway that I knew controlled his breathing, and I blocked it. That's when Mirko stopped me." I turned to Mirko for him to add anything.

They both sat silent for a moment that felt much too long.

When Mirko spoke, he sounded jolted. "Can Jelena really bring back the old ways?"

She smiled, but it was grim. "I think she can." She set her eyes on me. "And she'll use you to do it."

"What do you mean?" I asked. Whatever it was, it wasn't good.

Lijepa frowned. "It was only over three hundred years ago, when Pijawikas controlled the humans and even the Zao Duhs. Slavery is what it was."

"That's so terrible." I glanced at Mirko. He slouched over, his arms resting on his knees, his head hung low. He'd lived through it. "Well, how did it change? How did they get free?"

"Lots of fighting and dying," Lijepa said. "But it really didn't take effect until the old ruler of the commission—that's the governing body of all the Pijawikas in the world—died, and Zladislov took over."

Right. Mirko said something about that guy freeing everyone.

Lijepa continued. "He made the treaty and regained peace around the world. A lot of people were mad at him for it, and many still are. Jelena would have to have allies to achieve this."

"But how is she going to use me to do it?" This wasn't good at all. A lot worse than I could've imagined.

Lijepa peered at Mirko. Did he know?

"You're a melez, which is already bad." She looked to me, and I nodded. "It's forbidden for humans and Pijawikas to pro-create.

So, not only does this put your life at risk but also your mother's and your father's."

"Yeah, but that still doesn't explain how she's going to use me to enslave everyone."

Lijepa's eyes softened. "Zladislov is your father."

19
THE FIGHT OF YOUR LIFE

I struggled to speak. "You mean the same Zladislov who freed everyone? The ruler guy?"

"Yes," Lijepa said. That single word carried a weight so heavy, it smashed against my lungs, and I couldn't breathe.

When I could finally speak, I asked, "So, I'm like the president's, or the big, world Mafia boss's daughter?"

"From what I was able to gather, yes," Lijepa said.

"Wow." I huffed and fell back against the couch. "And because he made me with my mom, because she's a human, Jelena can use me as proof to discredit my father, have him killed, whatever, so she can step up?"

"Right," Mirko said. "And once he's out of her way, she's free to rile the masses and push her agenda."

I turned to him, my eyebrows drawn together. "Did you know about this?"

He sat up straighter. "I had no idea what Jelena wanted from you. I knew it had to be bad, though. And I thought it was possible Zladislov could be your father because your mother fed him, but it could have been someone else, too. Garwin never spoke of who your father was. I just didn't think Zladislov would have been so careless."

"Well, is he going to want to kill me now? I mean, if he could be brought down by me simply existing, would he want me dead? And there has to be many others who would want me dead, too, if they found out, right?"

"Yes, not everyone wants war again, so they would," Mirko said, then glanced at Lijepa. "How readily available was this information? About who her father is?"

"Extremely difficult to come by," Lijepa answered. I didn't know if I should feel relieved by this or nervous because it was still out there.

I glanced back and forth between Mirko and Lijepa. "So, what do we do?"

Mirko answered. "We train you for the fight of your life."

This was way past worst-case scenario. It exhausted me thinking about dealing with it.

"Well, let me show you to your rooms," Lijepa said. "I'll give you the rest of the day and night to let everything soak in." She led us through a hallway and then down some stairs.

We followed her down a corridor, and she opened a large, heavy door to reveal more than a simple basement below her cottage. It opened up to a lair. A hallway spanned in front of me further than Lijepa's cottage reached. The underground hallway opened into a large den on the right and doors dotting the hallway that continued on the left. Maybe Utah really did have some cool vampire hideouts.

Lijepa showed us to Mirko's room first and then took us to mine. It was beautiful. An elegant canopy bed rested against the far wall. A chandelier hung from the center of the ceiling, reflecting rainbowed streams of light that shimmered over the woven silk, draped around the bed's frame.

This was way better than my room at The Base. I wished Kaitlynn was here with me.

"Thank you," I said to Lijepa.

"You're welcome." She smiled at me, and then stepped further into the room. "I know you're frightened, dear, but you're strong and very powerful. I can feel it."

I offered her a dismal smile. I didn't think my chances looked too great at the moment.

"I'll let you two be, then." She strolled out of the room, closing the door behind her.

"Are you wishing you would have never gotten involved with me?" I asked Mirko.

"No. I've lived through worse." The shadows in his eyes let me know he spoke the truth.

"I'll wake you in the morning to start training," he said, and then reached for the door.

"Mirko," he turned over his shoulder. "I won't let her."

He faced me, questions in his eyes.

"Jelena. I won't let her use me to take over." I meant it, too.

He flashed me a proud smile, the same one he gave me when I remembered the word "melez". It made the weight on my shoulders a little easier to bear.

He turned around and stepped out of the room, pulling the door shut when he left. I stared at the door for a while after that.

When I didn't find any solutions to my problems in the wood's grain, I moved over to the bed and lay down. I was beat, but my mind raced.

I didn't know how I'd do it, but I knew I needed to keep my promise to Mirko.

Eventually, I drifted off to sleep and fangs, blood, chains, and fire met me in my nightmares.

* * *

When Mirko woke me from my nightmares the next morning, it was before the sun had risen. I didn't complain because I now understood why Jelena wanted me, and I had to do whatever I could to avoid it.

When I met Mirko in the gym—yes, Lijepa even had a gym in her lair—he told me that I would train with him from seven thirty in the morning until twelve thirty. Then I could take an hour lunch, but I only got an hour, and then the rest of the time would be spent training my powers with Lijepa until she released me for the day.

"No, bend the tips in more like this," Mirko said, showing me how to hold my hands properly in the clawlike position I'd seen used by the vampires I'd fought. "And move your pinky out more."

I spread my pinky away from my other fingers.

"Good," Mirko praised. "See how your little fingers bend in like that? It's an adaptation Pijawikas have to protect their pinkies from breaking in a fight."

I looked at them now. I could see how that little defect could be useful when I applied force to them while in this position. "I always thought it was a glitch."

He chuckled. "No, a much-intended evolutionary enhancement."

"Hmmm." I did a practice swipe at him.

"The face is a good place to make contact with, but stay away from the mouth. If your attacker bites you, they'll take your finger clean off."

I pounced at him and he danced back. He swept to my side and caught me in an arm bar. "Do it again, but this time sweep out with your foot."

I repeated my attack, he moved back, and then came at me from the side again. I dropped low and stretched my leg out. He jumped over it, but I came up with an uppercut, grazing him against his jaw.

He beamed. "You're learning. And you've gotten so much faster, too."

"Well, you ticked me off. I thought I was supposed to sweep your feet out from under you. I was looking forward to dropping you on your butt."

He laughed deep from within his throat. "So, that's the trick? I just need to piss you off, and you'll give me what I want."

I huffed air out my nostrils and flew at him with a roundhouse kick, snapping my foot out at the last second. He blocked me, slid his arm around my shin, lifting me from my foot, and flung me on my back, coming down on top of me.

"You're cute when you're mad."

He still had a hold on my leg so I flung it around his body, pushing him to the floor, and used my momentum to wrap my other leg around him, while grasping one of his arms and pulling it behind him.

I laughed. I didn't know how he thought he'd get out of this one.

He lurched his free arm up and clasped his hand around my windpipe. I relaxed my legs.

He didn't squeeze, but he kept his hand there for emphasis. "You need to be aware of where *all* my limbs are at all times."

"Yeah," I panted. He released me, and we stood up.

"I know it's a lot to think about, but that's why we practice. Soon, it will all feel natural."

I bowed my head, and waited for him to advance at me this time. He did, and when I weaved away from him, his hand swung out and grazed along my hip.

It sent my heart fluttering. I turned to Mirko, my lips parted. I stared at him, fighting with myself from stepping forward and kissing him.

His pupils dilated as he stared back at me.

"Lunch is ready," Lijepa said, stepping into the gym and then leaving.

I dropped my eyes. "Wow, twelve thirty already? That was quick." I inhaled deep, trying to slow my heart rate.

"Time flies when you're having fun," Mirko said, grinning at me with a knowing glint in his eye. "Let's stretch, then you can eat."

I followed Mirko's movements, but I kept my eyes away from his. I was confused. I knew I still loved Jaren, but Mirko had succeeded in drawing me in to him. And what made it worse was sometimes I was furious at Mirko, and then other times I was enticed by him.

* * *

"Wow, Lijepa. You didn't have to do all this," I said. She had made BLTs that smelled delicious.

She smiled, and I was stunned by her beauty. "It was no trouble, dear. I like to cook. I don't do it very often anymore, so it's a pleasure to have company here to share it with."

I sat down at the table and noticed she had three plates set out. She placed a BLT on each plate and then sat down after Mirko did.

"So, you guys can eat? Food, I mean."

Mirko chuckled. "Of course we can eat. What'd you think? We sat around all day wishing we could bite your neck?"

My cheeks burned. "I didn't know. When you think 'vampire,' you just don't think they can eat."

Lijepa finished chewing the bite she took. "Yes, we can still eat food. It doesn't provide the nutrition or strength like it does for humans. Our bodies process it much too quickly and our metabolism burns at a much higher rate. Thus, the need for blood. We do, however, continue to eat it for the pleasure and taste."

Ew. Thinking about drinking blood made me wish I could push my sandwich away. But my stomach growled. I'd been fighting with Mirko for the past five hours, and my appetite wouldn't be squelched. I bit into my sandwich. It was divine. "Wow." I wiped mayo off my lip. "This is so good."

"Well, when you've lived as long as I have, you get a knack for some things. How's your training coming along?"

"Okay. I think." I glanced over at Mirko sitting in the chair next to me.

He finished chewing and then swallowed. "She's coming along great. Much stronger and faster than we'd have ever predicted she could be. Which surprises me. She's stronger than some full-blooded Pijawikas I've trained with."

Lijepa regarded me for a moment before she spoke, and when she did, she sounded proud. "She's born of one of the strongest Pijawikan lines in our history. Having the mother she does doesn't diminish this fact. It only offers her a humanity that would have been hard to obtain otherwise."

I sat stunned for a moment, not because of what she said about my vampire side, but because of what she said about my humanity. "So, Pijawikas are inherently evil?" I had presumed as much.

"Oh, no, dear, I wouldn't go that far," she said, giving me a delicate smile. "Most of it comes from their life experiences, and most of them have been raised to believe they can take what they want. It runs in the culture, and it takes something introduced to the person to change those beliefs."

Mirko took another bite into his sandwich.

"And your father," she said with a smile that lit up her face, "he's the exception. Don't be mistaken. He can be swift and steadfast in dealing justice, but he's a fair man. Very bright, too." He must be where her fondness for me stemmed from. "But enough of that. You need to eat up if you intend to finish before your break is over."

I wanted to call Kaitlynn on my lunch, so I ate as fast as I could without causing my stomach to cramp.

Mirko gave me his sat phone again and had Ace put Kaitlynn on for me. I didn't know if I should tell her about all the new details I had learned, but lying had never worked for us before now, so I told her everything.

"Wow," Kaitlynn said on an overwhelmed breath. "So, what does this mean for you? Once you take care of this Jelena lady and we go home?"

I slumped my shoulders. "I dunno. I haven't really thought that far ahead. But you're right. Once my father finds out about me, will he want to get to know me, forget I was born, or want to kill me?"

"Well, that lady, Lijepa, seems to think highly of him, right? Maybe she could say something to him or make sure he doesn't hurt you."

"True, but that means she'd have to contact him and tell him about me, and I prefer to deal with one thing at a time." I glanced up at the clock above the entry into the kitchen. I had only a few moments left. "I gotta go soon, so tell me what's been going on with you."

"Nothing much here. Jaren's been minding his p's and q's, and Ace has been showing me around a bit."

Lijepa came into the kitchen. She didn't say anything, but I knew I needed to hang up. When I did, I set the sat phone on the table for Mirko to find.

Lijepa left the kitchen, so I followed her out and down a hall that led to a small room on the main floor. It was a cozy small den with soft whites and bright blues.

She sat on a sofa and patted the seat next to her. "Have a seat, dear. Let's try to help you figure out what to do with your power. Or powers. I sense you have many of them."

I sat with my eyes bulging. "As in more than one?" I was afraid of the one, and now she was telling me I might have many?

Lijepa patted my knee. "You have great strength, my child. As I said in the kitchen, you descended from one of the most powerful lines in the history of Pijawikas. You must embrace this strength."

I twisted my hands together. "Can you understand where my resistance is coming from? Why I don't want to embrace something that I feel might turn me into a monster?"

"Oh, my dear child. I do, and I won't lie to you and tell you that embracing your Pijawikan side will not change you in ways you may not like. Many people who have changed over become someone they never would have foreseen. The power, the strength, the virtual immortality that comes with it—it does something to the mind, something to the soul, that corrupts it. So, your conflict with this is justified. However, you do not have the luxury to remain as you are."

I took what she said as a loss. I could feel things would never be the same for me, but I still hoped they could be.

"Don't despair, dear. You can surrender to your enemies and allow them to use you in a way that I am sure would be harmful for mankind. Or, you can embrace your Pijawikan side with your determination to remain good, and use that to uphold justice, maybe not peace because war is inevitable, but justice and freedom for all races."

"And how exactly do I do that?"

"You have to embrace your Pijawikan side. You have to become someone the race would feel is a shame to be without."

"Or if I embrace it, those who would have remained neutral will pick a side. And I fear it won't be mine. I'm not supposed to be this strong, am I?"

She shook her head.

"They'll think, 'How is it that the melez gets such strength and power?' They might want me dead even more, because of that," I said.

"You're right. Many will fall to the side that does not benefit you. But it is your job to obtain as many of them as you can. Pijawikas might be resistant to change, but we have had to adapt in order to survive and stay hidden for so long. Eventually, it will come down to surviving once again. Things are going to change, my dear, and it is up to you, if you would like to be weak during the upheaval, or be strong and help usher in the kind of change that you would like to see and live with."

She was right. Things were going to change for me whether I

wanted them to or not, like fall giving way to winter. And apparently, I was going to have a major role in this change. I could sit back and let others decide what role I would take, or I could carve it out for myself.

I decided in that moment that I wanted a choice in how things changed. And I wanted things to be the best they could be for me and those I cared for. If it meant I had to do things I was afraid of to keep Kaitlynn, Jaren, Mirko, and my mom safe, I would do those things.

I squared my shoulders. "All right. Tell me what I have to do."

20
UNTIL I'M DEAD

Lijepa began our training by telling me about one of my powers. "It tastes similar to the chameleon, but it's a little different, and I can't figure out why."

"Well, what is the chameleon power?" I asked not sure how this was supposed to help me.

"It's not really called that. That's what I have come to call it. The technical term is *nestati*, or to disappear. You should be able to hide yourself from the sight of others."

I straightened my spine and pulled my feet up under me on the couch. "So, what does that mean? Do I change colors to match my surroundings, or what?"

Her shoulders bounced with her hearty laugh. "No, dear, you change your vibration to a pitch that is unseen by the eye. Even the Pijawikan eye."

My jaw dropped. "That's possible?"

She nodded.

"And you're going to teach me this?"

"It will be difficult for you to learn, but I will do what I can to teach you."

"Wow." That actually sounded kind of cool. Like a superpower you only see done in the movies and think it'd be cool if you could do it in real life. And I actually could.

"But, I can't figure out what exactly is different. It tastes different on you."

"How so?" Maybe it was all screwed up, and I'd never be able to do it.

"Well, it's hard to explain, but chameleon tastes salty and

sharp at the back of my throat. And I taste that on you, but it has a bitter undertone that sticks to the roof of my mouth."

I didn't know how to interpret that, but "bitter" was never good.

"I wouldn't worry about it, except I've never tasted that last part before. On anyone. I think the approach we should take is to try to train the chameleon power and hope the other part reveals itself."

"Okay. What do I need to do?"

She tilted her head and stared at me. "I think we need to get you in control of Sanjam first."

"Oh." I wasn't as excited about that one.

"Getting control of this first will strengthen any other power you have. As you probably know, every Pijawika and Zao Duh have some degree of Sanjam. And humans are more vulnerable to it than we are because their minds are weaker."

I furrowed my eyebrows. "I was able to do it to a Pijawika, though."

"Yes, dear, that's because you are very strong." She grinned.

"Well, how did I even know how to do it in the first place? No one ever taught me. I saw Mirko use it twice and then I could just...do it." I rubbed my arms. It was starting to get chilly in here. I looked out the den's window.

"It's snowing!" It never snowed this early in Virginia. And these were large flakes, too. "They're the size of cotton balls."

"Oh, yes, I get a great deal of snow up here. It's a bit early still, so it should be melted soon if it doesn't continue on like this much longer."

I beamed. The way the snow fell made me happy. It seemed almost ethereal. Something heavenly in my world of chaos. A sign that there could be beauty in discomforting change.

"Here you are, dear," Lijepa said, reaching behind the couch and pulling out a blanket. She handed it to me and tucked it in around me.

"Thanks." I snuggled into the blanket.

"You're welcome. Now, back to Sanjam. Have you ever heard that humans only use ten percent of their brains?"

"Yeah, and how we're supposed to be able to do marvelous things if we were to use more of it."

"That's right. Well, Pijawikas use more than just the ten percent," she said, tapping the side of her head. "This is where our powers, Sanjam, all of it, comes from."

"Mirko said I was going through a sort of awakening. That my Pijawikan side was only showing now because I was allowing it to."

"He's right. And the more you allow it to come through, the more you'll be able to do and quicker, too."

Could she feel my lingering resistance to all this? I tried to be open to it, but the fear remained deep rooted within me. Who knew what I was actually capable of? Who knew what degree of pain I could cause, intentional or not? "What kinds of powers does my dad have?"

Her teeth gleamed in the light. "He's probably one of the strongest Pijawikas with Sanjam I've ever known of. I'm sure that's where you get your strength from. He can stop an ancient Pijawika, midattack."

That reminded me. "I stopped a mountain lion midattack once."

Her eyes glittered. "Really?" she asked. "Tell me."

I did.

"Yes. You are definitely Zladislov's daughter. Some people have the power to communicate with animals and suggest or ask them to do things, which I think is what that fellow did when the lion came after you. But from what you just described, you did something different. You controlled the animal. This is rare. An animal's brain functions differently than ours or that of a humans. Animals are a lot more stubborn and less malleable, so being able to do what you did is something very special indeed, my dear."

I liked Lijepa. She reminded me of Kaitlynn in the way she accepted me and thought highly of me. There was no judgment from Mirko, but I felt forced to accept things from him. But with Kaitlynn and Lijepa, I felt extraordinary and a small amount of my fear about who I was flaked away. I looked forward to introducing Kaitlynn to her. She'd like Lijepa.

"Oh, look at that," Lijepa said, glancing up at the clock. "I need to teach you something before we're finished here."

I was under the impression she'd taught me about a lot today.

"First things first," she said and then put her feet up on the couch, mirroring me. "I want you to focus in on my mind like you did with Zack. I don't want you to do anything once you're inside there. I only want you to try to find the pathways."

I gulped. I doubted I could do that.

"Just look at me, and try to find them."

I looked at her and shook my hands out. I exhaled a deep breath and cleared my mind. Then, I focused on her mind and tried to reach into it the way I did with Zack's. Nothing. "It's blocked. It's not open like his was."

"Very good, dear. Yes, I'm stronger than he was, so it's going to be harder to reach mine. I want you to focus on finding an opening. Everyone has one; you just have to find it."

I had no clue what she meant. I've never done that before, but I tried to mentally find a place that didn't block me. I thought of different areas and tried to wiggle from different angles, but failed to find it.

"I can't do it," I said, growing weary.

"In time, you will. I'm sure of it. You're new to this, so it will take a while for you to pinpoint those areas or to break through others. You did a fine job today. You're free to go."

"Thank you. And thanks for all your help with the other stuff, too. About making me feel better about who I am."

She smiled. "You're welcome, dear." She leaned forward and embraced me. "Same time tomorrow."

I nodded and folded the blanket I'd used, placing it on the back of the couch as I left the den.

On my way back downstairs, I stopped in the kitchen. I was ravenous. I pulled one of the BLTs out of the fridge that Lijepa stashed away in there from lunch. I didn't even bother to warm it up. I just ate. It was still good, too. I grabbed a string cheese out of the fridge's door, and I padded my way down to the lair.

Mirko sat in his room when I came down. I strolled in, putting the last strip of string cheese in my mouth.

"How'd it go?" Mirko asked.

"Not bad. Pretty good, actually," I said, sitting next to him on his bed.

His lip curled. "Oh, really? Do tell."

"Well, Lijepa? She's cool. And I really like her. She made me feel as if I could actually use this part of me that I've hated for good. I dunno. Usually, I despise myself and feel disgusted when I think about my Pijawikan side. And I don't feel that so much right now."

His cheeks lifted with a proud smile. "That's good, Slatki. What'd you learn from her?"

"Oh. So, she said I have this power similar to a chameleon." His eyes bugged. "Yeah, I can go invisible. Well, we don't know until I do it, but the probability is there. So, I was thinking. If I could get close to Jelena, I could use my chameleon thing and sneak up on her to kill her."

His smile turned sour.

"What?" I asked. I thought it was a great idea.

He sighed. "Honestly? A couple of things."

"What do you mean?"

"She's pyrokinetic, remember? Even if you could get close enough to her, you'd have to kill her as soon as you touched her, or she could start you on fire."

"Well, that's what I'll do, then." I'd have to be quick, but I could do it.

"Right, but it gets even more complicated than that."

"How?" What else could there be? I couldn't imagine a way for it to get worse than her burning me alive.

"You *can't* kill her."

"I know I'm new at this, but if we trained longer, and I worked really hard—"

"No," Mirko said, cutting me off. "It's not that you're not physically able. You know how the Mafia built itself off the structure of the Pijawikas?"

"Yeah, but what do they have to do with it?"

He shook his head. "They don't. You're getting ahead of me. Anyway, are you familiar with the term 'Made Man'?"

"Yeah, David, that's Kaitlynn's boyfriend. He has that game Mafia, and you could become a Made Man, where they can't kill you." I paused. It hit me so hard, I felt faint. "I can't kill her. Others will come after me in retribution."

"Yes. They will."

I flopped down on the bed, covering my head with my arm. "So, what do I do? How am I ever going to get my life back? She'll keep coming after me. Until I'm dead."

"She might," Mirko said, lying down beside me.

I turned over to him, resting my head on my hand. "No, she will."

"We'll find someone who's willing to risk it." His face lit up like he knew who this person was.

"How do we do that?"

"Already found him. It's me."

21
TASTE YOUR TEMPTATION

"No," I said, sitting up. "Not you."

"Why? I can do it. And I would rather die than go back to the way things were. It wasn't good for me, Brooke."

The moment was thick, almost as if he were crying in front of me. He'd called me by my name, and the way he stared at me caused my heart to ache and my flesh to burn. "I know, but they're not even aware you have any part in this right now. I should be the one to do it."

He sat up and leaned forward, cupping me by the side of my head and rubbing his thumb against my cheek. His eyes moved back and forth, searching mine. It was so intimate, and he was so exposed. "But you're just getting started," he said and kissed me. His full lips caressed mine, but grew firm and urgent when I parted my lips.

Something stirred within me. Almost a flutter in my gut, but less gentle, like a lion stretching and flexing its claws into the earth. I didn't want to push him away, so I didn't. When my urgency matched his, he pulled me to him, laying us down on the bed and embracing me in both of his arms.

Everything about him was different than Jaren. He was hard where Jaren was soft. He even smelled wild and tasted distinctly wholesome where Jaren was sweet. My reasons for being drawn to him were contrary to the reasons I was lured by Jaren. But I was here with Mirko, and I wanted to be here with him like this. So, I let Jaren slip from my mind and filled it with Mirko.

He bit my bottom lip, and I made a sound that set his hands in motion. They wandered under my shirt, along my belly, and then his fingers hooked the hem of my shirt to pull it off.

I withdrew my lips from his.

His hands froze in place. His eyes raked mine, raw and open. "Will you mess up my bed with me?" he asked.

I sat up, pulling my body away from him. This was too much, too fast. And my hands shook because I wanted to.

I didn't say anything. I didn't know how to respond to that.

Mirko's face hardened. "One of these days, you're going to be over that punk and realize you've wanted me all along."

I glared at him. "Well, it's a bit early to assume today is that day, don't ya think?" I didn't wait for his response. I slid off the bed and stood up, pulling my shirt down. I didn't look back as I marched out.

I slammed my door shut when I got into my room.

How could he be so callous? So much had happened and changed in such a short amount of time. And he acted as if I had no right to be confused, like I should've jumped into bed with him from our first kiss.

At least Jaren wasn't pushy when it came to that. And I had a lot more to be conflicted about than my feelings with Jaren.

The only thing that remained constant through all of this was Kaitlynn. She had been my rock. Everybody else I knew had turned out to be different than who I thought they were, and everyone I'd met had so much more to them then they let me at first believe.

Mirko had started to let me in. He told me about his past with Jelena and his fear of going back into slavery. But he was so cocky. I couldn't refuse him because I didn't want to be with him in that way. Oh, no. It had to be explained by my messed-up emotions over Jaren, which upset me even more because that was exactly why I'd pulled away from Mirko.

I grabbed my bag and stomped into my bathroom. I turned on the shower as hot as I could stand it and stood on the warming tile, imagining my frustration and pain evaporating with the steam.

When I finally relaxed enough that I knew I could get some sleep, I got out and dressed into some comfy sleep clothes. I wrung my hair out and put it up into a messy bun.

I came out of the bathroom, stepping into my room, and jumped when I saw Mirko sitting on my bed. "What do you want?"

"I'm not big on apologies, so hear me out, please?"

I strode up next to him by the bed and leaned against the canopy's frame. "I'm listening."

"Look, Slatki. I'm sorry." He squirmed a little.

I held firm. He also owed me an explanation.

"I shouldn't have pushed you like that. I shouldn't have said those things, either. It's just that I've bared my soul to you, which is rare for me. And I could taste your temptation." He flashed me a seductive grin and my legs trembled. I sat next to him on the bed.

He continued. "Regardless, I shouldn't have treated you like that, and I'm sorry."

"You're right. You shouldn't have treated me that way. I mean, how cold would I be if I could turn my feelings for Jaren off so quickly? I'm not going to lie to you. He was basically my first love. We didn't have a lot of time to kindle it, but it was there for me, and it ran deep. So, the only thing I ask of you is that you try to keep that in mind. Because I'm seriously confused. And not only about him, or about you. But everything. I don't really know who I am right now, or the world that I've been thrown into. So, if I don't know how to respond to one guy not wanting me, and then another guy who does, don't be too surprised."

He sighed. "All right. I'll give you time, because I'm confident you'll end up with me. Plus you're cute, so that helps."

I laughed and relaxed against his shoulder. "I appreciate your apology and that you gave it to me now instead of in the morning. I probably would've been cursing you all night if you hadn't."

He wrapped his arm around me and held my face in his palm. "Just make sure that whatever you decide, it's what all of you wants, not just the torn part of you that speaks louder." He brushed his lips against my temple then rose. "Sleep well, Slatki. Training bright and early." And then he left, clicking the door shut behind him.

22
YOUR BODY WILL REQUIRE BLOOD

The nightmares stayed away. In fact, I slept better than I had since finding out vampires existed, and that I descended from one.

By the time I strolled into the gym, Mirko was already there. His eyes gleamed, and he gave me a crooked smile. "Nice of you to finally show up. I was beginning to wonder if you were thinking of calling in sick."

I laughed, then sobered. "There's no time for sick days."

He responded with a terse nod. "Right. Let's get to work."

And we did. For the span of five hours, Mirko pushed me harder than before, and I pushed back. Again, I was faster than I was yesterday, but I still didn't think it was fast enough to avoid shooting flames. There had to be another way to stop Jelena without either Mirko or I dying in the process.

Practice had also improved my claw swipe. Mirko charged at me with a left hook. When I dodged, he used his momentum to swing his body around, trying to clock his right fist up against my head.

I anticipated it, so when his back was to me, I swiped out my hand and scored it across his back. His shirt shred beneath my fingers.

"Aaahhh," he growled.

"I'm sorry!" I flinched in regret. I stepped toward him and inhaled the spice of copper tang absorbing into his shirt, and my stomach rumbled.

I froze. My eyes bulged, and Mirko's flickered with recognition. "What does it mean?" I asked, voice trembling.

"That was actually a great move," Mirko said, ignoring my question and wiping at his back to catch the dripping blood.

"Don't mess with me," I snarled. "What does it mean?"

"It's natural, Slatki." When I wouldn't yield, he rubbed his hand through his hair and shook his head. "It means that if you keep going at this pace, your body will require blood."

That was a place I was not willing to go. I squared my shoulders. "And what if I deny it?"

"You'll get weaker and grow feeble until you give in."

"Well, we better hurry and kill Jelena then."

"If you let it go too long, it becomes painful. Let it go long enough, and you could end up harming someone." Always thinking ahead. That was Mirko.

"I'll worry about it then. It's lunch time. I'm going upstairs." I grabbed my sneakers and shuffled toward the door.

"You should stretch," Mirko hollered.

"I should do a lot of things," I said and thought about eating real food, which was cooked and prepared for me by Lijepa.

I opened the door to the first floor, and cinnamon enveloped me with small wafts of vanilla lingering below. My stomach rumbled again, and this time, I welcomed it.

"Breakfast for lunch?" I asked Lijepa. I wasn't complaining. It smelled delicious.

"Yes, dear, I realized the time, but since this is your first meal of the day, it remained appropriate. I hope you like palacinke," she said, and I worried about what she was rolling into the dough.

Alarm filled my eyes, and she laughed. "They're pancakes, dear. Same thing as crepes, as the French call them, but better."

"Oh, well, what are you stuffing them with?" It smelled amazing, but I couldn't be too sure.

"It's a secret recipe, but there are yams and ham in it. You'll like it. Where's Mirko?" she asked, bending over to look into the hall.

I shrugged my shoulders and leaked a noncommittal sound.

She inclined her head. "Did training go all right today?"

"Yeah," I exhaled. "I dunno. I sliced his back open with my claw thing," I said, imitating the claw slashing movement. "And I'm not sure how to feel about my response."

She rolled the last crepe. "Why? What did you do?" She put it on a plate and took it to the table.

I hopped off the stool and went to the drawer to grab the forks. "I didn't do anything, but my stomach growled when I smelled the blood." I stopped with the forks in my hand. "Let's eat first and discuss this later."

She offered me a comforting smile. "That's fine."

Mirko sauntered into the kitchen with a new shirt on and only the smell of *dried* blood clinging to him, which didn't have the same effect on me as the fresh. He mumbled something in another language.

I creased my forehead. It was rude to talk in another language when someone present couldn't understand it.

Lijepa laughed at my scowl. "He was merely showing me an honor by complimenting me in Croatian."

"Oh. What did you say?" I asked Mirko.

He repeated it in Croatian, and he and Lijepa bubbled with laughter.

"Fine, don't tell me."

"I told her that her food is divine."

"Oh, yeah, it is," I said, looking to Lijepa.

"I haven't had any good palacinke in a long time. Thank you for this."

"My pleasure," she said, eyes sparkling.

My teeth scraped against the fork, pulling a bite of palacinke into my mouth. My taste buds exploded with sweet and sweeter. "Mmmm, Lijepa. This is so good. You could package this stuff and make a fortune," I said as soon as my tongue was free.

"There's no fun in cooking for someone you don't know or when you can't see them enjoy it," she said.

None of us said much after that. We were too busy enjoying our food. Mirko kept peering at me, and soon I forgot I was mad at him for trying to avoid the blood episode. I allowed my gaze to loiter on him. Usually, I squirmed, or tried to hide my anxiousness about his gazing at me, but now that I'd acknowledged my attraction for him, I enjoyed the grin he gave me when he knew I was staring. I could now read it for more than just the "Aha! I caught you!" I recognized that it also said, "And I like it." Which made my insides clench.

Mirko cleaned up our plates, and I followed Lijepa into her den. "It's melting," I said, referring to the white blanket covering the ground outside. The only snow remaining lay in the pine tree's shade.

"Yes, but we'll get plenty here soon enough. Have a seat, dear."

We took up the same position on the couch that we did yesterday. "What's on the agenda?" I asked Lijepa, curious as to what she'd reveal to me in today's training session.

She inspected me for a moment before she spoke. "I think we should work through a few things before we go any further."

Lijepa was taking up a role in my life of many positions; she was a mentor, a friend, a nurturer, my teacher, and apparently, my shrink. It didn't bother me, though, because she didn't ask me questions in the same doctor/scrutinize/you're messed up sort of way.

"All right," I drawled, unsure of where she was going to focus on first. I had a lot of issues burdening me at the moment.

"Your reaction to Mirko's bleeding. Why does it upset you so much?" Her face creased with concern.

"I dunno. I've been unsettled about the thought ever since I found out that vampires exist. And I'm trying to take all of this in and accept myself for who I am, but these are big changes, and drinking blood seems so taboo and dramatic."

"I see. Humans have become very detached from nature. Things that made sense and were understood many years ago have now become unacceptable and frowned upon. However, there are many things now that people of the past would have fallen to their graves over if they knew of such things. It's all relative. But are you aware that there are still humans, such as tribes in Africa, where the people still drink blood?"

I shook my head.

"They drink it for nourishment. Many of the tribes over there measure wealth by the number of animals they own, so they don't slaughter them for their meat. Instead they drain some of the animal's blood and drink it."

I was glad we saved this conversation for when I was done eating. "Still. That's animal blood they're drinking. Not from other people."

"It is only because the human digestive system is weaker than ours. If the human body were more tolerant, I am sure they would drink the blood from others instead of animals. Human blood contains proteins and peptides that animal blood does not. And it is within these molecules where true strength lies." Her smile spoke of experience.

"I understand the why, but I don't see myself wanting to do that anytime soon." Which wasn't entirely accurate, because a part of me already recognized it did want in on that action. I wasn't willing to listen to that side. Ew.

"Just keep in mind that people try a lot of crazier, unnatural methods to get their bodies to do certain things—starve themselves to lose weight and inject steroids to become strong."

"True," I said.

"Now, let's do a little work with Sanjam, and then we can move forward and touch on chameleon."

I tried to touch the pathways in her mind, but I still couldn't breach her walls. "Maybe it's because I'm thinking about it, or because I'm not mad enough." It always seemed like I could do crazy stuff when I was mad.

"That's the idea of these exercises. You need to learn to be able to do it on command and to control the level of power you exert. You're in the stage I like to call the 'baby rattlesnake'. Young rattlers have yet to learn about the dose of venom to deliver with each bite, so they release a full dosage," Lijepa said. She glanced up at the clock. "Let's try for a little longer. Again."

Instead of focusing on her mind, I focused on mine and that I had the ability to be inside hers. I thought of my awareness wandering around hers as a cloud might coast across the sky.

That was when I sensed it. An area that was pliable and bent when I tapped it. I pushed forward and a steel wall came crashing down.

I huffed in frustration.

"That was excellent! Sometimes, force is not the best method. I'm sure you could have succeeded had you continued with a gentle advance."

I swiped at my face and pushed my hair back.

"Let's move to chameleon. Now that I know where you're going to go with Sanjam, I'm going to resist harder, and I want you to have some strength for this exercise."

"All right," I said, standing up and straightening my pant legs. I bent to sit back down.

"No, we'll stand." Lijepa stood and faced me. "Now, you know the warm feeling you get when you tap into your Pijawikan side?"

I grunted. "So, that's what that was?"

"Yes. I want to you think about how you felt and what you were thinking during those times you felt it."

I pondered for a moment. "Well, it's usually when I'm really ticked off or when I'm about to die." Yep, that pretty much covered it.

"Good," Lijepa said, grabbing my shoulders. "I want you to focus on that and what instinct you called forward."

I had no idea how to do that, but I closed my eyes and tried to replay the images of the mountain lion bounding toward me, the moment when the lady came between Kaitlynn and me at the airport, Zack's slimy tongue penetrating my mouth. I thought I grasped it, so I nodded, keeping my eyes closed in fear of losing it.

"Think of it spreading out through your limbs," Lijepa whispered. "Warming the back of your thighs and the inside of your forearms."

I did, and it felt as if I stood too close to a flame. My wrists burned and then my fingers relieved them, taking some of the miasma inside them.

"Great. Try bringing it back up."

I opened my eyes. "That's possible?" I had never done that before. All the other times, the heat faded. As it did now.

She released my shoulders. "Yes, and when you do, you will be able to tune into your vibrations. And eventually, you will be able to adjust them."

I shook my arms out and shimmied my shoulders. "Let's try again, please."

Lijepa tilted her head down and then placed her palms on my shoulders again.

This time I only focused on the image of Kaitlynn trailing behind me at the airport. Her legs switching beneath her in sluggish torture. The look on the lady's face when she blocked my view of Kaitlynn.

Fever branded through me in half the time it did a moment ago. When it reached my nail beds, I held it there, calling the fire to cook my cuticles. Then I commanded it to follow my breaths as I inhaled. Again, I felt the blaze underneath my translucent wrists, this time flickering toward the creases in my elbows.

Awareness opened up within my mind. I felt my vibration, and it was beautiful. My cells rippled like the top of a pond during a steady rain, vibrant colors pulsing outward in ever-bigger circles.

I was doing it. I shuddered on exhale because of my excitement, and I could feel my flesh break out in bumps from the rapid temperature change as the fire cooled.

I tried to call it back, but the furnace died.

"Hmph." I opened my eyes. "I lost it."

Lijepa flashed me her sparkling teeth. "You did it, dear. You became invisible for a moment. That was excellent. You continue to baffle me. Hopefully, we can discover soon what the bitter taste woven within your power means."

I smiled, elated. I enjoyed making Lijepa proud of me. Although, I wasn't excited about finding out the source of her bitter taste. I was sure it was bad.

Fatigue made my eyes flutter, and I was frustrated with myself, sure that I could have succeeded today if I wouldn't have lost my focus.

"You can go rest now. We'll continue this tomorrow," Lijepa said.

"Thanks." I nodded and then lumbered into the kitchen to find something to eat.

Mirko sat on the stool and leaned over the counter. The moon reflected a purple glow in the tiny strands of his dark hair. I craved to touch it but resisted.

I turned on the light, then perched on the stool next to him. "What're you doing?"

He lifted his head and looked at me. "Thinking." His forehead creased, and his eyebrows furrowed. He didn't even smile when he glanced up at me. I'd never seen him look this gloomy before.

"Why? About what?"

"I have a team trying to find Jelena. We don't know where she is, and on top of that, I can't think of a way to stop her without being the one to do it."

"Oh." I slouched. That really was bad. "So, what do we do? Well, I mean..." Of course he didn't know what to do this time. That's why he looked so hopeless. "Isn't there someone we can go to? I don't know, a higher-up who would help us?"

"That would be Lijepa," he said, pointing to the den. "Most anyone else wouldn't want to get their hands dirty in this."

Right. Neither would I. "What about if we both took her on? At the same time. I come in with my invisible stuff and grab her, while you come in with your cracked-out Bruce Lee?" I beamed.

He smiled weakly. "Sounds good. In theory. But I don't want you that close to her. It'd backfire, and she'd use you against me. You're too cute to risk being damaged." He stroked his finger down my cheek. At least he appeared to be cheering up.

I thought about it, trying to strategize a way for this to work. "Well, do you have any special powers?"

"You mean other than looking this good? It's voodoo on the ladies."

I laughed. It was. I didn't see it coming. That was for sure.

"No," Mirko said, leaning his elbow on the counter and his head in his palm. "Zao Duhs only get the strength, speed, and Sanjam."

I guess that limited our options. I got up and pulled out the leftover yam stuffing from lunch. "Want any?" I asked, popping the lid off the container.

"What's your plan after you eat?" Mirko asked, wiggling his eyebrows.

I snorted. "Not that."

"Your loss, Slatki." He lifted from the stool. "Nah, I'm good. Don't stay up too late. Training. Bright and early."

"Can I call Kaitlynn?" I asked, pleading with my eyes.

"Yes. Just a second." He turned toward the basement.

When he came back with the phone, I sat at the table eating my own piece of heaven. Even as leftovers, Lijepa's food was gourmet.

"I need to call another contact in about fifteen minutes," Mirko said.

I nodded. He called Ace and handed me the phone.

I told Kaitlynn about the blood situation while training with Mirko today.

"I feel for you on that one. I'm not grossed out by it, but I wouldn't want to have to drink the stuff any more than you would," Kaitlynn said.

"See, it's too weird."

She asked me about my training, and I shared my progress with her.

"Has it been good for you to be by yourself and not have to worry about what Jaren, or anybody else, is thinking of you?" she asked.

I hadn't really thought about that, but maybe that was why I was finally able to sort of accept these changes. "I think it has. But I really miss you, and I can't wait to introduce you to Lijepa. You'll love her."

"I'd like to meet her. She sounds cool. At least you've gotten to meet one good Pijawika. Oh, and Jaren's been ignoring Holly Anne."

I smirked. "I bet she hasn't liked that too much."

"Not. At. All. But what is she going to do? She's not supposed to use Sanjam on him, so she'll just have to deal."

I laughed.

"How are things with Mirko?" Kaitlynn asked when we quit laughing.

Oh, I should probably tell her about the kiss. I stood up from my chair at the table and went to see where Mirko had gone. I checked downstairs. I didn't see him, so I hollered, "Mirko?"

"Yes, Slatki?" he replied from down in the lair.

"Never mind."

"What's that all about?" Kaitlynn asked.

"Oh my God, Kaitlynn. We totally kissed last night," I said, walking back into the kitchen.

"What? What about Jaren?"

I sighed. "I know. I'm way confused. Jaren doesn't even want me, though, and I keep thinking about him. And then Mirko's here, he accepts me and he's hot, and he wiggled his way in there."

She chuckled. "I can see that. So, what are you gonna do?"

"Nothing right now," I said. "I'm way too confused, and there is so much other stuff going on. You have to go home soon too, right?"

"Yeah, but Ace is working on that, so don't worry about it."

Mirko came out of the basement, and I was glad Kaitlynn and I changed the subject before he came in.

"I'll try. But Mirko needs the phone, so I'll call you tomorrow."

I offered the phone to Mirko, and Lijepa came in.

"Shall we have a few small slices of pie before bed?" she asked.

Anything Lijepa made was good. "Sure."

"Cut me one," Mirko said. "I'll be back in a minute." He left the kitchen.

"It seems you two get on all right," Lijepa said, grabbing from the drawer a beautiful silver knife, with what looked like rubies and emeralds on the handle.

My cheeks flushed. "Yeah, we do, I guess."

"Ah, I sense more than that," she teased. "Come on. You can tell me."

I smiled and shook my head. Might as well. "I like him, but I'm confused."

"I got that as well."

"What do you mean?" I asked her. She brought the pie and the knife to the table.

"I know you look upon Mirko, but there is another as well."

"Yeah, but he doesn't want me," I said, looking down.

"Well, Mirko sure does," she said, grinning.

"I know. He doesn't try to hide it, either."

Her gaze turned serious. "It's deeper than I expected."

"How so?" I asked. I grabbed the plates and forks and set them on the table.

"Mirko opens up with you. He's dropped some of his walls he carries with him when associating with others. I think he cares for you a great deal. But shhh," she said, picking up the knife, "he's coming back."

I sat straighter, thinking my posture would give me away if I was bent over the table.

Lijepa placed the first piece of pie on a plate and cut the next.

Mirko's face was grave when he walked in. "My contact found Jelena. She's in Utah."

23

A Lair within a Lair

Lijepa set the knife down next to the pie platter. "Do you know where she is or where she's heading?"

"No. She was last seen in Salt Lake earlier today," Mirko said.

Not good. "Are Kaitlynn and Jaren safe at The Base?" I asked. They were my first concern.

"We're not sure who else she's brought with her, but it would take a lot to breach The Base."

Lijepa's eyes widened, and she grasped the edge of the table so hard her knuckles turned white.

"What is it?" I asked, staring at her with trepidation sinking in my stomach.

"They're here. I smell them. Jelena's here."

I rose, knocking my chair over as I stood.

Car doors slammed, lots of them, coming from the front of the house.

"You need to leave now," Lijepa demanded.

I shook my head. "We're not leaving you."

Mirko grabbed my arm and pulled me toward the basement.

I trembled, dreading what would happen to Lijepa if we left her. "No. I can't leave her," I said, tugging out of Mirko's grasp.

"You have to," Lijepa said, pushing me to the basement door with Mirko. "There's too many of them, and it is better for all of us to die than for them to get a hold of you. You need to leave *now*."

Fear won, and I ran with Mirko down the steps. He flew into his room, ripping his quilt off the bed and tearing back down the hallway. I followed beside him, his free hand clutching my arm to spur me onward.

When we reached the edge of the hall, he opened a closet and tore out the shelving. Towels and blankets flew to the floor. He tapped the wall, and it opened.

"A lair within a lair?" I asked. "But they'll know we came this way." I looked at the obvious mess on the floor.

"Go," Mirko growled and pushed me inside. "It leads outside. Run." He pushed me forward. Frigid air assaulted me. Darkness filled the space, but I ran.

"Get in front of me," I told Mirko and pulled him around me to take the lead. I clutched the back of his shirt and pushed myself as hard as I could to match his speed.

We turned left down a corridor when it split in two directions. Our feet echoed along the concrete floor. A growl vibrated off the walls from the direction we just fled. I gripped Mirko's shirt tighter and propelled forward faster. My heart beat so forcefully, I thought it would crack my ribs.

"We're not going to make it," I huffed.

"We will. Run faster."

I was already running as fast as I could, but his words gave me the strength to keep pushing. We turned down another tunnel and then another where water flowed up to my ankles. My feet splashed, but I tried not to let it slow me down.

We reached the end of the tunnel, and Mirko punched the ceiling. Moonlight flooded into the concrete waterway on a rush of cold air. Mirko threw the blanket up and then jumped, and he stood over the tunnel. "Come on," he said, reaching his hand down toward me.

I grabbed it and jumped. Mirko pulled me up to adjust for the distance that I missed in my leap.

"Oh my God," I said, once outside. I'd jumped out of the tunnel and into an ice box. Mirko grabbed the blanket, wrapping it around me, and then we ran up the mountain.

"Avoid the patches of snow," Mirko whispered back to me. I grabbed the back of his shirt again and kept my eyes on the ground to watch where I landed my feet.

We ran for what felt like an hour. Mirko led us up the mountain and then down again. I had no idea where we were, and I had a feeling Mirko ran us the way he did to keep Jelena's people confused about our location.

"Through here," Mirko said. He bent down to crawl into a small opening in the mountain.

I kneeled and then crawled in behind him. The echo revealed a cave. And a very dark one, too. "I can't see anything. Can you?" I asked, grabbing his shirt again and mirroring him when he stood.

"Not really. Hold onto me and stay close." We walked slowly as we wound deeper inside.

"Here," Mirko said, grabbing the blanket and easing me to sit down beside him against the rocky wall. He wrapped the blanket around us when we leaned up against each other. "Are you comfortable?"

"Yeah, but I'm cold and my feet are wet," I said, wiggling my toes in my damp socks.

"Take your shoes and socks off." He reached down and the blanket dropped from my shoulders. He took off his shoes, as well.

"Are you sure there's not a bear in here?"

"No, but I'm more worried about Jelena and her men than I am about a bear. A bear would be a welcome challenge."

Right. Worry about the larger threat.

"Come here," Mirko said. He pulled me down so I was lying on my side between the wall and him. He flung the blanket out over us and must have hooked the far end with his foot because it went taut. He scooted closer to me and tucked my feet between his with his heel.

I cringed when his cold toes touched the sensitive underside of my foot.

"I know they're cold, but we'll warm up in a few minutes. Put your arms in front of you."

I folded my arms across my chest, and Mirko wrapped his around me, pulling me closer to him and then pushing my back further against the wall.

Within a few minutes my jaw relaxed, and my teeth quit chattering. My shivers grew further apart. "Feeling better?" Mirko whispered.

"Yeah, I'm warm now. Thanks."

"Sure. Try to get some sleep. I'll keep watch."

I lay there for a moment. I was too wound up for sleep. "I can't believe we left Lijepa." Guilt stirred within my unsettled stomach.

"It's what she wanted," Mirko whispered.

"Well, what are they going to do to her? She must have thought they might kill her if she said it would be better for all of us to die than for them to take me." We should have stayed.

"She's strong, so I'm sure they'll be careful not to try anything to hurt her. Plus, she's old, and a lot of very important people would be upset if they harmed her."

That made me feel better, but if Jelena was as evil as they told me, I wasn't so sure. I hoped that some of her allies thought highly of Lijepa.

Mirko held me in silence. I tried to imagine how we were going to solve this Jelena problem when I had an idea. I cleared my mind and let it tiptoe over Mirko's. He was strong, and I knew I wouldn't be able to breach him easily. I glided over his mind to try to find his weak spot instead. I searched for the same sensation I'd had when I found Lijepa's opening.

I tried to regulate my breathing, so Mirko would think I was asleep and not feel me when I found his weak spot. I wandered for a few minutes, but when I found it, I was gentle in my approach.

And it worked. I was inside. His pathways were networked in ways that Zack's weren't, but I also sensed different streams among them: dignity, honor, honesty. I experienced these qualities in my dealings with Mirko, so it was nice to know that they were genuine. His mind was a lot more pleasant to be inside than Zack's.

I roamed deeper, and stumbled upon a section that concerned me. Lijepa was right. His feelings for me went way beyond being attracted to me or wanting to get into my pants. The pathways surrounding his feelings for me were empty, and I wondered if he ever felt this way for anyone else. I decided to see if I could find out, so I moseyed a little deeper.

I startled when I saw an undertone of darkness in one of the corners. I moved in a way that could be compared to a flinch, but within my mind, and then I was shoved out of his and locked out.

"That is unacceptable," he barked, pulling slightly away from me. I felt the biting chill as air came between us.

"I was only trying to see if I could. And where does the darkness come from? What's that about?"

"You shouldn't have even been in there. If you weren't new to all of this, I would have killed you for it."

"No. You wouldn't have. I saw how much you care for me." I unfolded my arms and draped my left arm over him, pulling him back to me. He didn't resist.

"I could have. Anyone else and I would have. It's warranted with something like that. Had you done it to someone else, they could have killed you for it. Don't ever do it again, unless you are sure you would win in a fight." His tone altered from anger to concern.

"All right. I promise, but tell me about the darkness."

He sighed, and his breath fluffed the hairs on my forehead. "I'm not used to telling someone else these intimate details about myself."

"Well, you've seen me at my worst, and it's not like I'll judge you."

"Right. Because you only see yourself in the harshest light and everyone else's wrongs can be explained away," he said.

I kneaded into his back with my knuckles. "Tell me. Please?"

He lay silent for a moment before he spoke. "I already told you how I was Jelena's slave. Let's just say she wasn't a good property owner, and I'm not too pleased with the things I did for her, either."

I rubbed his back. "You can't blame yourself for that. You had no choice."

"You always have a choice." His voice stern in his belief. "I could have died fighting for what was right, but instead I was weak and allowed her to break me."

I pulled him closer to me. He lifted his arm and wrapped it over mine, tucking my head into the crook of his neck with the palm of his hand. I tilted my face up so I could speak. "Had you done so, I wouldn't have met you, and I would probably be dead right now."

He lifted his head in what I thought might have been an effort to look at me. Then his hand grasped my chin and lifted my face toward his. His lips were warm, but his mouth was warmer. His movements were slower and more controlled than they were the last time we kissed, but they remained as intense.

Mirko didn't try to progress things any further, which I was glad for. I wasn't sure if I was strong enough this time to stop things from going at least a little bit further than kissing.

He pulled away from me and cupped my head, stroking my outer ear lobe with his thumb. "Please choose me," he pleaded.

I grunted and began to pull away.

"No," he said, clutching me to him. "You're right. I said I'd give you time to figure it out. I won't push you." He turned so he lay more on his back and slid his hand up, guiding my head down to lay on his chest.

"I wish I could be with you and be done with all of these conflicting emotions. I really do care for you, you know, with all your voodoo magic and all."

His chest rumbled with his laughter.

"But I can't choose yet."

"I know," Mirko said, stroking my chilled hair. "I'm not going to push you, but I won't back down. You wanna make out, we'll make out. If you allow me to hold you, I'm going to hold you. And don't think I'll hide my feelings for you in front of Jaren. He brought it on himself by pushing you away, so if he doesn't like it, it's his own fault."

"Yeah, but you don't have to prod him. I swear some of the stuff you said at The Base was to piss him off."

He laughed, "Or to make you squirm. You're cute when you do. I couldn't help it."

I snorted. "You're a brat."

We were quiet for a moment before Mirko asked, "What if he decides he wants you back?" He didn't sound scared when he asked it, more as if he wanted to know where I stood.

"I don't know," I said. "I wouldn't jump right back in with him, though. It's messy, so that's all I can say."

Seriously considering who I should be with brought up a bunch of questions. "What about me being with you? Are there rules against that like there are with humans being with Pijawikas?"

"Yes, but it's not the same. Sure, Pijawikas say that we're not supposed to, but it happens more often with us than it does with humans and Pijawikas. Plus, we're already looked down upon, so it's more of the attitude that it's expected than it is a fall from grace. Also, if I answered to only one Pijawika, and depending on who it was, it could be bad, but I'm more of a free agent, I guess you'd call it."

"So, what is it that you do? I mean, when you're not trying to keep me alive?"

He chuckled. "I hire out to whomever needs me. Sometimes it's to the commission, or to Pijawikas, or the Društvo. As long as they can pay, and I agree to the work, I'll do it. But at least now, I get to choose who I work for."

I smiled. "That's good."

"It is. You should try to get some sleep. We're going to have to hike all over this mountain to get back, so get some rest."

I snuggled in closer and relaxed. His heartbeat was a lullaby that eased me enough I could doze off. Despite our predicament, I fell asleep feeling comfortable and safe.

24
I DON'T GIVE SECOND CHANCES

Mirko woke me with a warm kiss to my cold forehead. "Slatki, we need to get going."

A stream of light allowed me to see the cave more clearly than I had last night. It was huge and had tunnels everywhere. I hoped Mirko would be able to get us out of here. "Did you sleep at all?" I asked, sitting up. Oh, it was cold.

"No, but I'm rested."

I grabbed my shoes. "They're still wet," I said, scrunching my nose.

"It will be uncomfortable, but better than nothing." He grabbed his shoes and began to put them on.

I dusted my socks off and tried to straighten them out. I pulled the first one over my toes and sucked in a deep breath at the bitter cold.

I didn't hesitate with the other one. It was similar to ripping off a Band-Aid. The faster, the better.

Mirko stood. "You can have the blanket again. You ready?"

I rose and stood on my toes to stretch the fold in my shoes that had become stiff from the water. "Let's get this over with." I was also getting anxious to see Lijepa.

He came over to me and hugged me. "We're going to run most of the time because we came a long way, and it's cold." He kissed me on the lips, then pulled away with a grin on his face. "For the road," he explained.

He grabbed my hand, turned around, and started to lead us out.

"You know where you're going?" I looked at the maze that

loomed before us.

"Do you doubt me?" Mirko asked, with a cocky smirk.

"I wouldn't be able to do it. That's all I'm saying."

"Fine. If I get us out of here, I get you booty shorts and you wear them to our next training," he proposed with devious amusement.

I punched his arm. "You wish. And you better get us out of here. I need to make sure that Lijepa's okay."

His eyes grew dark. "She better be." He picked up the pace. We went left, then right, and made a whole bunch of other turns I couldn't keep up with until we got to the opening we crawled through last night.

Mirko dropped to his knees and crawled out. I handed him the blanket through the hole, and crawled toward the light. The sun shone bright enough to hurt my eyes, but it was still so frigid. Mirko wrapped me in the blanket when I stood, and then we took off.

We ran until I could tell that we were getting close to Lijepa's cottage. It always seemed like the trip back was quicker than the trip away.

I ran faster and passed Mirko. He grabbed my waist. "No, we can't go running up there. We need to scope the place out and make sure no one is lingering behind to snatch you."

Good point, but it still took some self-control not to bound off after Lijepa.

We crouched low and stepped with light foot falls as we approached the cottage. We wound around the hill to enter the property from the side. And that was when my nose crinkled with the smell of burnt rubber.

I dropped the blanket and ran the rest of the way down the hill. "Lijepa! Lijepa!"

"Shhh," Mirko hissed at me. He grabbed me from behind, but I pushed him off. I cleared the trees and saw our truck on the other side. The tires were flat, and it had been set on fire, but only the driver's side from what I could see from this angle.

The door to the cottage sat wide open, and lingering smoke wafted out toward the sky. Fury boiled within me. Something terrible happened here.

"Lijepa!" I screamed and leaped through the front entry. I slid to a stop in shock. All of her furniture and decorations that had been placed with such precision and care had either been broken or burned. There wasn't any evidence the fire had licked up the walls, so I knew this was all Jelena's handy work. "Lijepa!"

Mirko halted behind me. He grabbed my shoulders and motioned for me to go outside.

"No." I shrugged him off and glared at him. "This was because of me. I better damn well see it!"

"You don't need to see it," Mirko said, using an authoritative voice with me. "At least stay right here."

I didn't respond. I clenched my jaw and turned around, stomping toward the kitchen. "Lijepa," I hollered. I reached the kitchen then dropped to my knees. "Oh, no. No, no, no, no, no, no, no."

"Shit," Mirko said.

Lijepa was here. Her prone body lay on the cold floor among the ash and debris. Her beautiful, unmarred face had been burned to a crisp, with not even a blister on her neck. I reached out to touch her, but couldn't stand the thought that her skin might feel cold, so I withdrew my hand. My stomach turned, and my mouth flooded with saliva. I bent to the side and vomited. Tears streamed down my face as my stomach clenched on each spew.

Within moments I'd expelled everything and began to dry heave. When the reflex abated, I sat down on my heels and wiped at my mouth, tears spurring down my cheeks.

"What the...?" Mirko said, but I wasn't really paying attention to him.

I had caused this. Lijepa died an evil, terrible death because of me, and I couldn't even muster the courage to touch the hand that had been so gentle with me.

It's because I was a coward that this happened to her. No more. I reached out and clutched her hand. "Oh, Lijepa." It was cold. I brought it to my chest and fell forward over her waist and sobbed. The pain cut so deep, like a sharp knife immersed in acid, plunged and twisted into my heart, filleting any life that fought to come forth.

"Brooke," Mirko said. I ignored him. He grabbed me by my shoulder. "You need to see this."

I tried to shrug him off. I wanted to lie down and die next to Lijepa.

He pulled my shoulder harder and stuck something in front of my face. "Read it," he demanded.

I whimpered the same way a child does after they have cried too long and inhaled a ragged breath. I wiped my eyes, trying to clear them enough to make out the words. The tears kept coming. It took me a minute before I could finally read the fine calligraphy.

Brooke,

I left you a present, just in case you thought I wasn't serious before. The same comes to those who aid you in defying me. I am weary of chasing after you. You will come to me this time. If not, your family and anyone that you have ever loved, known, or passed by on the street will die a much more excruciating death than poor Lijepa did.

I don't give second chances.

Aunty Jelena

"It was stuck to the frame here," Mirko said, pointing to the wall, "with this." He stuck out the knife Lijepa had used to cut up our pie last night.

I dropped the letter. "Aunty Jelena?"

He nodded. "She's Zladislov's sister."

Betrayal fought with anger inside me. "How could you not tell me?"

He didn't even look regretful. "Would it have made any difference? You weren't close to her. Your father's not close with her. You don't even know her."

"It doesn't matter. The fact remains that it's a pretty big piece of information, and you hid it from me," I growled. Now, I was furious. "Did Lijepa know as well?"

"Yes, but it would have stunted your growth. Our goal was the opposite."

I closed my eyes. Everyone. Everyone had now lied to me. Except for Kaitlynn. I stood. I couldn't do anything more here for Lijepa. My opportunity to help her had passed.

"I need to get to Kaitlynn." I stepped on Jelena's note because I didn't have the energy or care to step over it. I walked through the living room, toward the door. My wet sneakers crunched against pieces of porcelain and burnt wood.

Mirko trailed behind me. "Wait. Let me go see if I can find the sat phone."

I snubbed him and kept walking. I walked down the steps and down the dirt road in front of the cottage. Mirko hadn't grabbed me, or come after me, and I didn't care to find out why. My mind was set on one thing. Kaitlynn. I would hitchhike and force the first person I came across to take me there.

I made it all the way to the main road before Mirko reached me. "We're going to have to catch a ride back."

I didn't look at him.

He stepped in front of me, halting me. "Look Slatki, don't you dare give me this attitude. I have risked my life for you and your friends, and I won't put up with it."

I pierced him with my gaze. "You. Lied. To. Me."

"I did, and I did it for your own good. If you'd known Jelena was your aunt, you would have used it for more ammunition to hate yourself. 'Oh, I'm such a monster.' You would have been more determined to hide away and let everyone else take care of the bad guy."

He was mocking me.

I clenched my jaw. "Didn't I come to you and tell you the other night that I wanted to go after Jelena myself? And don't lie to me because I know I did."

He grunted. "Yes, but that was only after Lijepa had shown you that you weren't a monster and you had opened up a little bit to your powers. You think you would have had the balls to even consider going after her when you were in your scared, denial state? I don't think so."

"I'm on my way to Kaitlynn. You can follow or not. I don't care." I stepped around him and onto the asphalt.

He spoke to my back, "I'm coming, but you better start appreciating that your precious little Kaitlynn is safe right now because Ace has been taking care of her. At my base. Because I ordered him to. Chew on that with all your other crap." And he stepped around me, hiking down the road, his back to me.

25
I Intend to Keep You

Mirko flagged a car coming down the mountain with a young couple driving it, but when they stopped, I stepped in front of him to use my Sanjam. I did it to make a point—I could do things myself.

Mirko grinned at me. But once we got in the car and it came time to direct them, I remembered that I'd been asleep the last time I left The Base; and the time before that, it had been dark. I couldn't remember how to get back.

Mirko had to take over their minds from there. I was glad he didn't rub it in when he did so. He did smirk before I gave them to him, though.

The roads were clear on our way to The Base, but it still took us almost an hour to get there. When we pulled up to the gates, Mirko instructed the couple, and they left. He walked up to the small security building and grabbed keys to the Hummer parked beside it. "I'll have someone bring it back," he told the guy. The guy opened the gates, and Mirko drove us to the barracks.

I hopped out of the Hummer before Mirko killed the engine. I took the steps two at a time and ran down the hall. "Kaitlynn," I yelled. I fled up the stairs and made it to our hall before I yelled again, "Kaitlynn."

She came out of our room. "Brooke?"

I slowed down before I plowed into her. I wrapped my arms around her and cried on her shoulder. She pulled away enough to look at me, "What's going on? What are you doing back already?" She grabbed me and steered me into our room, then shut the door.

Three seconds later, there was a knock on the door, and Jaren peeked in. "Brooke? Are you all right?" He sounded worried.

"Yeah," I said, wiping at my eyes. "Can I talk to Kaitlynn for a bit?" He looked slighted, so I added, "I'll talk to you in a minute, okay?"

He nodded and closed the door behind him.

I reached down and snatched and yanked at my shoelaces to get my feet out of the soggy socks. As soon as I did, I realized I didn't have a stitch of clothing to my name right now. Everything had been left behind at Lijepa's. "Can I borrow a pair of socks?" I asked, my bottom lip quivering.

"Sure." Kaitlynn walked over to the closet. "Where's your bag? And you didn't say anything about coming back today when I spoke with you last night."

"Let me get these on first." I reached for the clean pair of warm cotton socks she handed to me.

I slipped them over my feet and wiggled my toes, savoring the tickles caused by the lint balls inside.

I exhaled a deep, long breath. "All right," I started, and then told her the whole story, beginning with the moment I hung up the phone with her. She cried with me over Lijepa's murder. We cried together for a long time before I finished telling her the rest of the details and about how Mirko and Lijepa had lied to me and why Mirko said they did it.

"They were right," she said.

I frowned. "You think they were right by lying to me? Everyone has lied to me except you." I raised my eyebrows. "At least that I know of."

She gave me a weak snort in reply. "I've never lied to you, but Mirko was right. If they had told you Jelena was your aunt, would it have blocked all the progress you were making?"

I thought about it and really wanted to say no, but couldn't. "If I had known, I would have pushed harder against the changes." I slouched my shoulders. "But how do I reconcile that he lied to me over something so big, but then not be mad at him because he made the right decision? What if it didn't turn out so great? Forgiving him would give him free range to lie to me about anything, as long as he thought it was for the right reasons."

Kaitlynn squeezed my hand. "Yeah, I don't know what to tell you. Do you think he would ever lie to you for selfish reasons?"

I pondered if that would be something Mirko would do. I recalled how I felt while wandering the pathways in his brain and how honesty had been prominent. It must have worn heavily on him to keep my relation to Jelena hidden. "I don't think he ever would."

Kaitlynn looked pleased with my reply. "Well, that's something." I agreed with her, but still didn't know how to keep Mirko from lying to me again if he thought it was best.

We wound down our conversation by going over what she'd been through while here. It wasn't nearly as eventful as my time away had been, but hearing her talk offered a moment of normalcy.

When we finished, I asked, "Do you know what Jaren wants to talk to me about?"

"No, but he's probably worried. You ran in here bawling and hollering for me like a crazy person."

I laughed. "I did, didn't I?" She nodded. "Great, add that to the long list of baggage. Now, I'm embarrassed for making a scene."

Kaitlynn laughed and shook her head.

"Can you tell Jaren to come in here? Or do you want me to go to him? I don't want to come back and then kick you out." Man, that sounded terrible of me.

She smiled and rose from the bed. "It's no biggie. I'll go get him."

"Thanks." I smiled.

* * *

It wasn't long before Jaren knocked.

"Come in," I replied.

"Hey," Jaren said, walking into the room. "How are you doing?"

I smiled weakly. "It's been really rough. Things were going great until today. Did anyone tell you what happened with Lijepa?"

He knit his brow. "Yeah, Mirko told me while you were talking with Kaitlynn. I'm really sorry to hear that. I can tell Lijepa had come to mean a lot to you."

"Thank you. How about you? How've you been?"

He sat next to me on the bed. "Okay, I guess. I've been doing a lot of thinking while you were gone, well, more like ever since you told me off." He chuckled.

I smiled, but didn't say anything.

"Well, I realized that you were right. I transferred my fear of the guy who attacked us at my apartment onto you. And frankly, I was attracted to Holly Anne. I couldn't figure out why I was fine with her being a vampire, but hesitant about it with you, until you mentioned what I was doing. I finally understood that you're still the same girl. You run with a bit of a different crowd now, but you're still you. I'm sorry. I wasn't fair to you, and I miss you. I'd like to be with you again, if you're willing to forgive me."

I sat in stunned silence. I thought he would be coming in here to check on me. When I'd dreamed of his apology, I always envisioned it with me having more time to sort out my feelings for him. I focused on his last sentence and didn't know what to say, but then I processed everything else he said before it.

I smiled, but it didn't reach my eyes. "I've wanted to hear those words ever since the night I found out I was a vampire, and you tossed me aside like damaged goods. And now, here I am, hearing these words, and I'm not sure they mean what I thought they would." I frowned and met his gaze. "I'm not the same girl. I've changed. Whether I am a monster, or whether I'm not, is irrelevant at this point. There's so much more going on than my feelings for you or your feelings for me, or who I am, or what my DNA is made of. I need to get this figured out with Jelena. If I don't, you, Kaitlynn, and those around me will always be in danger. And I can't be the person that's the cause of any more deaths or suffering. What Jelena did to Lijepa was terrible. And I'm going to feel responsible for that for the rest of my life because I was too much of a coward to step forward or sacrifice myself so she wouldn't have to."

He shook his head in protest, but I continued.

"It's changed me. I'm not the same girl, and you need to know that. I'm not even sure that being with you is right anymore. I still love you, care for you, and want the best for you, but I'm not sure that's me anymore."

Jaren cleared his throat, but when he spoke his voice broke, anyway. "This was not how I thought this would go." His face was dismal, and he blinked hard. Then anger replaced the sorrow on his face and he pursed his lips. "It's Mirko, isn't it? He got to you."

He was right. If I didn't have these feelings for Mirko, I would have taken Jaren back right now.

"Honestly, I have feelings for Mirko, and I have to contend with those, too."

Jaren squinted his eyes. "I knew that's what he had planned when he wouldn't let me go with you."

"Did you not feel what I did to Zack? Because Kaitlynn did."

He nodded. "Yeah, but it was nothing serious. I bet they could have managed it while we were there. But he didn't *want* us there."

"Jaren, please," I pleaded, pinching the bridge of my nose. "This needs to stop between you two. I need you to work together until this is over and stop stressing me out."

He got up from the bed. "Fine. I'll be civil with him until Jelena is taken care of, but this is not over for him. I may have been stupid before by not fighting to keep you, but I won't make that mistake twice. You loved me first, and I intend to keep you." He walked toward the door. When he opened it, he paused and looked over his shoulder. "I really am glad you're okay." Then he turned so that he faced me. "I love you, Brooke." My jaw dropped, and he stepped outside the door and closed it.

26
ENJOY THE LITTLE THINGS

Sleep evaded me. My body shut down, but my mind reeled. I knew some of it stemmed from having too much to solve, but mostly, I feared seeing Lijepa's charred flesh when I closed my eyes.

I hadn't talked to anyone else, other than Kaitlynn, after Jaren left. I wished she'd been able to tell me what to do with everything.

Someone knocked on the door as the sun began to peek between our curtains. I jumped off the bed, landing softly on the floor so as to not wake Kaitlynn. I turned the knob, and Mirko stood on the other side of the door, appearing too cheerful for this time of day.

"Morning, Slatki," he said and then recoiled. "You don't look so cute this morning. If you couldn't sleep, you should have come down to my room."

Who tells a girl she looks like crap? I pushed the door to slam it in his face, but he stopped it with his foot. "Regardless," he said, holding up a plastic bag, "we have training to do. Get dressed and meet me in the gym."

I snatched the bag and pushed the door shut. This time he didn't resist. I looked inside the sack and found he had bought clothes for me to wear. I grabbed a clean towel and ambled down to the bathroom.

When I slid the tight pants on and looked in the mirror, I grumbled to myself, "Mirko. No wonder you were so chipper this morning." I would've asked to borrow something from Kaitlynn, but she had a long night, too. I decided to suck it up and went to the gym.

Mirko stretched as I came in. "Mirko," I chided. "What's this?" I pointed to my pants.

He grinned. "What? I like to see the way your body moves."

"You're such a brat," I tried not to smile but failed. "I'm still mad at you for lying to me." I tried to regain my resolve.

He moved toward me with his steady swagger. "It was either this," he said, pulling on the tight material covering my thigh, "or booty shorts. I preferred the booty shorts, but I thought you'd prefer these."

Figures. Jaren wants to buy me lilies, and Mirko wants to buy me booty shorts.

I punched his shoulder. "Stop. I'm serious. I'm still mad at you. I viewed you as one of the few people I could trust, and you polluted it." I stepped back from him.

He scowled at me and closed the distance. "You never asked me if Jelena was your aunt, and I never lied to you, saying that she wasn't. What I did could be more accurately described as a partial truth. And you have no idea how much it ate at me that I couldn't tell you."

I'd suspected he had a hard time with it. Good, he should have, but my anger softened, anyway.

He stepped forward and kissed me on the cheek. "I promise it'll never happen again."

I held him with my eyes. "It better not. You're already on shaky ground." I sobered. "Now tell me, what are we doing to take care of Jelena?"

"I have a meeting planned after this where we'll go over strategies to address it."

"Well, we should be focusing on that. Why not meet now?"

"Because not everyone is here yet, and until then, you're mine. So, start stretching."

I rolled my eyes and walked away from him.

"Wow," Mirko said, then sucked air in through his teeth. "Those pants look better on you than I'd imagined."

I turned around to face him and started stretching. "We have more important things for you to concentrate on right now than my butt."

He joined in stretching with me. "There's always a crisis going on, Slatki. You'd do well to start enjoying the small things when they're given to you."

I studied him. "Even with what happened to Lijepa?"

He nodded. "I've lost many people throughout my life. That's why you have to enjoy the little things. You'll go crazy if you don't."

I agreed. I hoped I never lost anyone else, but I could see how I might go crazy if I did. Then, I realized that I would end up losing someone. Eventually, I'd have to choose between Jaren and Mirko. How do you give up one to gain the other when you might love them both?

Things had turned out to be awfully messy. I wished no one else close to me died anytime soon. I started to hope that I would be the first to die so I wouldn't have to watch any of my loved ones go before me.

Mirko stunned me out of my morbid comfort zone when he lunged at me. I escaped his advance and counterattacked, striking him with my foot in his thigh. I fought him with more ferocity than I ever had before, and I relished in it. My muscles welcomed the strenuous crusade I sent them on, and my bones found penance in the reverberations of Mirko's pounding against them.

When I thought I couldn't fight anymore, I pushed harder, and my skin buzzed with adrenaline. Mirko finally called a truce, and I smirked at him. "I totally kicked your trash," I said, breathing hard.

He bent over to catch his breath. "I wouldn't say that," he straightened, "but there is no doubt that you're good. Really good."

"Thanks," I said, satisfied.

He stepped up to me and wrapped one arm around my waist. The muscles along the outside of my abs quivered from his touch. "I wasn't giving the credit to you, Slatki. Skill like that is gifted by the teacher." He kissed me on the lips.

I pushed on his chest and laughed, letting my head fall back. "My teacher is more arrogant than he is skilled," I lied—he was both in equal measure.

Someone cleared their throat. I turned my head and found Jaren standing in the gym's doorway, his lips pursed in anger.

I stepped away from Mirko.

"Ace is ready for you two," Jaren growled between clenched teeth.

Mirko nodded and walked toward the door. I followed, but I fell behind him. He turned back at me, grinned, then exited the gym, leaving me to deal with a furious Jaren.

"So, you chose him, then?" Jaren asked. The rough planes of his face melted.

"No," I said, wrinkling my forehead. "I haven't chosen anyone. I'm still as confused as ever."

His sky blue eyes blazed into mine just how I remembered. Comfort subdued the adrenaline rushing through me like returning home after a perilous journey. I wanted to touch him, and I guess the words he spoke last night did matter. They'd lifted a barrier between us.

I raised my hand and placed my palm against his cheek. My eyelids fluttered closed. It eased something inside me, the same way a balm would after being rubbed into a long-endured wound.

I recalled sitting in the back of the service truck at the airport when we left Virginia and how I ached to touch him. It was like I yearned silently for this sensation from that moment to now, and I had been carrying a thirst I didn't know needed quenching. I opened my eyes, and a tear fell from one of them.

He blinked hard, wiped my tear away, and then clasped my hand. "I didn't kiss anyone when I was confused. I might have been drawn into Holly Anne's advances, but I never kissed her in the hall that day."

He did with Tiffany, though. I had never felt so conflicted before, except maybe when I left Lijepa behind to run with Mirko to safety. I dropped my hand. "I didn't mean for you to witness that. I'm sorry you had to see it and for the way it makes you feel, but any of us could die at any moment. Things change too quickly to deny those you love of knowing it."

His jaw dropped. "You're in love with him?"

"I didn't say that. I don't know what it is. With you, things were simple. I had a crush on you forever, and then it grew and blossomed into something deeper, and there were no perplexing feelings to hamper it. With him...it's messy."

He sighed and slid his hands along the sides of his head, combing his fingers roughly through his hair as he did. "What have I done?" He dropped his arms to his sides. "You were mine. I had you, but not only did I let you go, I pushed you away." He bit the inside of his dimpled cheek. "Is this how it felt?"

"How what felt?" I asked, not sure what part he meant.

"To want to be with someone, but you *can't*."

I nodded, and more tears leaked from my eyes. "Yeah."

He shook his head. "I'm sorry. I never looked at what I did as losing you. I still loved you, I just needed to distance myself from you, but I was still here physically."

"Brooke," Ace said, poking his head into the gym, "we're about to get started, and we need you there."

I replied with an exaggerated nod, keeping my head facing Jaren. I didn't want Ace to know tears streamed down my cheeks.

A moment after I thought Ace stepped back out, I moved toward Jaren and hugged him. "I'm still in love with you. And the few times I wished I weren't hasn't changed that." I wanted to ask him not to give up on me because I might still choose him, but I didn't think that was fair.

Then I realized how fast things had changed with everything else, and I wanted to be selfish. I didn't want to hold back words that felt this strong anymore.

I pulled away enough to stare into Jaren's eyes. "Please don't give up on me. I still love you, and I don't know how this is going to end, but a large part of me still wants it to end with you."

He dropped his forehead, resting it against mine. "I won't this time. I love you."

I licked my tear-soaked lips and tilted my head up to meet his. He tasted salty, but the same. I wasn't sure why I thought I might forget how it felt to kiss him, but I believed it was only fair, after I'd spoken my selfish request, that I give myself something to remember him by as he competed with Mirko.

I pulled away and wiped my eyes. "Ready?"

"Yeah," he said, grabbing my hand and squeezing it.

27
I'LL GO

Mirko held the strategizing meeting in a large, sterile room. It reminded me of a classroom with its chalkboard and the way the tables sat positioned to face the front. Mirko had asked me to sit in the front next to Ace on the end, and Jaren took a seat in the back.

The amount of people that had packed into this tight space awed me. They were all here to help me fight Jelena. My heart filled with gratitude.

Mirko began the meeting. "I'd like to thank all of you for coming out here on such short notice. You all should have been briefed on the situation." Heads bobbed. "Good. Yesterday we lost an amazing asset to all races. Lijepa will be mourned, but she will not be forgotten." Somber agreements pulsed within the room. I had never seen Mirko in his commander duties, but seeing him now, I felt lucky that he was the one protecting me. The Zao Duhs respected him, and he stood tall with practiced power.

"We'll begin with the note." Mirko held up the paper on which Jelena had written her message to me. "Jelena demanded that Brooke," Mirko looked at me, and the sea of heads turned to me as well, "come to her this time."

"Do we even know where she is?" One of the men in the center of the room asked.

"We do. Ace?"

Ace stood. "Jelena's stražar called The Base this morning and gave us the meeting place."

I jerked my head to look at Mirko. "She knows that you're involved in helping me?" My heart sped up, and my hands felt clammy.

"It appears she does," he said, holding his facial muscles steady. He had a lot more practice schooling his emotions than I did.

I must have reeked with fear. I recalled Jelena's threat from the note:

The same comes to those who aid you in defying me.

I pictured Mirko's smooth cheeks and chiseled jaw line marred with blisters and blackened with ash where the skin had charred. Mirko had already been traumatized by this woman, I was sure of it. And here he stood, willing to defend me against her, anyway.

"I'll go," I said, keeping my eyes locked on his. It was time to end this.

"No," he said, without looking away.

I stared at him. I wouldn't back down. "I'm going. I'm sick of being the sniveling little girl hiding in the corner. I have powers."

He smirked as if he'd already won the argument. "Have you used nestati yet?"

"Not completely, but I can get it. I almost had it the night Lijepa was murdered," I said, reminding him that I knew how terrible Jelena could be, and I still wanted to help.

"No," Mirko said, unmoving.

"Then what's your plan? How do you solve this without me?" I cocked my head to the side and raised my eyebrows. I knew I was right.

Ace spoke. "The simplified version is that we take a team to the meeting place, and we kill her."

I faced forward, piercing Ace with my eyes. "And what if that doesn't work? What if Jelena doesn't even go to the meeting? Many of you will die. For nothing."

Ace turned to Mirko. Guessing by the way their eyes locked onto each other now, they had been over this scenario.

Mirko looked back to me. "I'll force one of her men into giving up her location. I'll handle it," he said, clipped.

A young guy from within my row stood. "Jelena would most likely send her men to pick up Brooke. She'd probably have a team stay behind to ensure that we don't follow, and another team to take Brooke to her. I doubt any of her men would give up her location."

"Couldn't you guys follow me based on the signature of my brain waves or something?" I asked.

"Not from a distance. No," Mirko said.

Another guy further in the back added, "Couldn't we give her some kind of tracking device to keep tabs on her whereabouts?" He had a thick British accent.

"Yeah, there has to be some way you can track me. You're gonna need me to get to her."

"We do have the new RDIF chips," Ace said. "We could probably have one flown in by the morning. That would give us enough time to implant it into Brooke and still make the meeting in time."

I wondered how large this device would be and how invasive the procedure would be to get it *implanted*, but I hid my hesitation.

Mirko sat, still as a stone. The whole room seemed to be waiting on the same held breath.

"She's right," Ace said, breaking the silence.

Mirko glared at Ace. "Would you be willing to give up your girl to play bait to that woman? You know what she's capable of if we don't get her back."

Ace squared his shoulders. "If she were as competent and willing as Brooke is, yes, I would."

Mirko looked, for the first time since the meeting started, that he might be considering my involvement.

"She obviously doesn't want to kill me. She needs me," I said, hoping to sway him. His face softened. Then I remembered that a woman had attacked me at the airport, and she had clearly wanted me dead. I couldn't figure out why or how that fit into all of this, but right now didn't seem like the right time to bring it up to Mirko.

"She should have a say in this," Jaren said from the back of the room. Mirko tilted his head at Jaren, and Jaren continued. "This woman has turned Brooke's life upside down, killed her mentor, and who knows what she'll do next. If Brooke feels that she can do what her part requires of her, and she has the faith in you to do yours, she should be given the opportunity to end this."

I beamed at Jaren. He believed in me. He loved me, and I'm sure this plan terrified him, but he still wanted to give me the choice. "Thank you," I mouthed.

Mirko stared at Jaren, but Jaren didn't falter. "Get the tracking device ordered," Mirko said, turning to Ace.

I sighed and my shoulders sagged in relief, but then my stomach clenched in fear. I would soon be face to face with Lijepa's murderer. I hoped to get justice for Lijepa. If the other Pijawikas came after me for retribution, then so be it. Jelena would be mine.

28
I'll Kill You for This

The following morning, Mirko drove the Hummer to take Jaren and Kaitlynn to the airport. With Jelena somewhere in Utah, it was safer for them to go home. As a precaution, Ace had arranged for a team of three Zao Duhs to go back to Virginia with Kaitlynn and Jaren. My nerves buzzed with fear and anticipation of meeting Jelena later today, and I was grateful I didn't have to also worry about sending Kaitlynn and Jaren home without any protection. Their security detail drove in the Hummer behind us.

All the other Zao Duhs that had attended Mirko's strategizing meeting had been broken up into two teams: a "secret follow me once I go with Jelena's men" team, and a "stay behind to act as my drop off" team. These teams were now in transit to the meeting place to take up their positions.

The plane had been scheduled to land at a different airport than the one we landed at when arriving. This time we drove west across the salt flats and toward the Utah-Nevada border. Mirko suggested I stay behind, to prepare for the day's events, but I wanted to see Kaitlynn and Jaren leave on that plane in safety.

I knew what would be waiting for me once we returned to The Base. Ace had told me that the tracking device was about the size of a grain of rice and it would only be as painful as a pin prick when they implanted it.

Mirko pulled the Hummer into a parking spot at the Wendover Airport and killed the engine. A few cars and a van littered the lot, but it appeared to be a quiet day for the airport. Kaitlynn's team pulled into the slot a couple of spaces over from us.

Everyone unloaded from the Hummers and came around back to help carry the bags. Ace opened the back when I heard the scuffle of sneakers against the asphalt and then saw a group of men jump out from their hiding places behind the parked cars in the lot. Seven fanged men ran toward us at vampire speed.

Fighting broke out around me. Snarls erupted, and grunts mixed with the echoes of fists and knuckles slapping against flesh.

Mirko jumped into the fray with an intensity I had never seen. His fangs sprang from his mouth and he sliced them against his attacker's throat. Blood erupted, jetting into Mirko's face as his attacker bounded back, clutching his neck.

I pushed Kaitlynn and Jaren behind me and to the side of the Hummer, keeping them out of the fray. A Pijawika with bleached-white hair stormed toward us. I dropped low and swiped my leg out to knock him off of his feet, but he jumped over my sweep, exposing the tender flesh along his Achilles tendon, above the back of his sneaker. I stretched my hand into my practiced claw and swiped, tearing into muscle and snagging against bone.

The Pijawika crashed to the ground, landing hard on his shoulder. He grabbed his ankle and spewed words in another language that I had no doubt translated into vulgar cuss words. He rolled onto his back, and the sun glinted off his chest. When he shifted to his side, I glimpsed the znak that moments ago had mirrored the sun's rays. The ruby sat snug in the center, the same as the one on my prior attacker upon our arrival days earlier. However, the bronze-gold metal of this symbol arched in ways the other znak had not.

This znak resembled a true sun with rays beaming from the center, shooting away from the ruby, different from the one that I described to Mirko at the airport. This was the one Mirko thought I saw. This was Jelena's.

"Stop!" a woman ordered, stepping out from behind a van. She was gorgeous, and moved with regal authority. Most of the fighting seized, and my train of thought transferred to this woman. She faced me, and my knees lost their strength. I leaned against the back of the Hummer to catch myself.

Her appearance mirrored mine. My jaw arched at a wider angle than hers, and her eyes were bigger and sparkled brown where mine were blue, but the relation between us became clear. Jelena.

A whimper sounded behind me, and I turned.

Kaitlynn stood in the clutches of a Pijawika that must have snuck around the other side of the Hummer while I was fighting.

"Dikan," Mirko said with hatred thick in his voice, a sign of bad blood between the two.

Dikan's arms imprisoned Kaitlynn, while his hand craned her head to the side, fangs extended and hovering above the delicate, pulsing skin of her neck. Tart whiffs of ammonia wafted toward me. My eyes followed the scent and found a trail soaking down Kaitlynn's pant leg as she wet herself.

Heat coursed through my body so intense the only thing comparable would be the time I stood with the mountain lion. This time, however, the heat burned hotter. Fire licked my veins, driving from my heart and tearing toward my fingers and toes.

I extended my fangs and opened my mind, readying it to hit the Pijawika with so much force he would have fallen dead from the onslaught. But my rage was a wild beast, and I didn't trust it to keeping the strike limited to her captor.

"Nestati," Jelena purred with a thick accent. "So much better than I thought you would be, darling."

I peered down and found that my legs and feet blinked in and out of sight. My fury had been so great that the flames within me activated the chameleon, but because I held myself back, it must have caused it to flicker.

"Dikan." Jelena laughed. Her giggle reminded me of wind chimes. Such a disparity from the way I viewed her. "Merely hold her still for now."

Mirko moved to lunge at Dikan.

"No," I screamed. Their numbers were close to matching ours with their wounded incapacitated, so it would have been a fair fight, but I couldn't risk Kaitlynn. One slight move in the wrong direction, and he'd slit her throat.

"Come to me, niece, and I'll let your human live," Jelena said.

Rage boiled within me, but doubt never crept into my mind. I would go. I took a step closer to Jelena.

Mirko roared. "I'll kill you for this, Jelena."

She laughed, clanking wind chimes ricocheted around me. "Mirko, I've missed you."

"I'll go," I promised. "Let her go now, and I'll leave with you."

"No. You come to me now, and your human goes free," Jelena said.

I walked on shaking legs toward her. I passed Mirko.

"You don't have to do this," he growled, wiping blood off his face.

I looked back at Kaitlynn to remind myself why I had to do this. "Would you do the same for me?" I whispered.

He squinted, and that was enough of an answer. "Get her to safety, and then come find me."

Jaren stood to the side, mouth set in a tight line of anger, his eyes wide in fear.

I marched toward Jelena, covering the distance in seconds. She grabbed my arm, crushing my tendons into my bones.

"Release her, Dikan," Jelena said, keeping her word.

He released her. "As you wish, My Lady," he said and bowed.

Kaitlynn stumbled over to Ace with retching sobs rising from her throat, and he clutched her to him. Relief filled me and mixed with the adrenaline and rage. I struggled not to cry.

I tried to focus my efforts to Jelena's mind, to any of my enemies' minds, but my strength had been weakened with holding it back until Kaitlynn's release, and their minds were too strong.

"It's about time you got acquainted with your family," Jelena said, nails digging into my arm, causing blood to well around her fingertips as she dragged me into the van.

29
LET. ME. GO.

Dikan jumped into the van before we drove off. Jelena sat to my left and he sat to my right. I wandered their minds, trying to find any breach I could to get out of here.

Jelena had recognized the tickle of my probing and had cackled at how much stronger I was than she'd anticipated. I decided at that point to allow myself to rest and recharge before I tried to hijack their minds again.

She talked with me, sweet at first, and then bordering on aggressive in her attempt to persuade me to tell her of any other powers I possessed. I clenched my jaw to show her I wouldn't provide her with any such information. I couldn't have revealed anything to her, even if I did know of any other powers. Lijepa had said that I had many, but Jelena killed her before Lijepa and I were able to uncover them all. Animosity rose on acidic bile within my throat, but I smothered it. I needed my strength to get out of this. If I could kill Jelena on my way out, I would attempt it, but I doubted the opportunity to do both would arise.

I wondered why Jelena wanted to change things. Did she want power? Money? Unlimited resources to food? What exactly drove her to all this trouble in using me?

As we pulled up to her property—I assumed she owned it because she called it home—I knew the purpose couldn't be to obtain more money. Her house resembled a castle, but without the stains and wear that collected on the older structures. It stood bigger and grander than even Garwin's did.

Dikan pulled me up the stairs and through a large doorway that opened into the modern-day castle. We entered a foyer with opulence so magnificent, millionaires would be living in squander in comparison.

I faced Jelena in awe. "What do you hope to gain from me?"

She smirked, beauty queen teeth twinkling in the light. "You can bring me nothing by yourself. As my catalyst, you will elevate me to a power unknown to any other woman in Pijawikan history."

"So, that's all this is? Destroying so many? Lijepa, me, and anyone else who has gotten in your way? All because you're power hungry? You make me sick," I said, disgusted.

"You're so feeble minded, niece. Never before has a woman held a position within the commission. Sure, some have been more powerful than our male counterparts, but we have been denied regardless. I'm creating history. It will be because of a woman that my race will no longer be denied its birthright. Zao Duhs and humans have been running wild long enough." She glided toward me and held my chin, locking her eyes on mine. "We will always be weak under Zladislov's oversight. I am merely doing what is right for my people."

I spit in her face. She backhanded me, causing me to bite my tongue. Blood trickled down my throat. I sucked it forward and shot it out onto her pristine marble floor.

"I'm feeble minded? You're ignorant. We've tasted freedom for far too long. You think we'll be molded by you so easily? We won't. We'll fight, and we will not go down quietly. You want war, we'll give you one, and you'll have to kill us all to get to the top." A smile spread across my face. "And you'd better hope we don't kill you in the process."

"Stražar, take her to her room," Jelena order, and Dikan pushed me forward. "You two," Jelena pointed, "guard her door. No one goes in or out unless I authorize it."

Dikan shoved me up three flights of stairs as I trailed behind the two Pijawikas assigned to guard my door. All three of them wore the same znak as the Pijawika who I'd fought not even an hour earlier. And these znaks were definitely different from the one my attacker wore at the airport. Someone else wanted me dead. But who?

Before I figured it out, Dikan opened a door and pushed me inside. He slammed the door shut and a lock jarred into place on the other side of the steel frame.

I kicked the door. "You're gonna die, too, Dikan," I cursed at the door. I promised myself I'd kill Jelena, but if I couldn't, I would at least make sure I took out Dikan.

His chuckle faded as he walked away.

* * *

I plopped down on the mattress that rested above an iron bed frame. I hoped Mirko got Jaren and Kaitlynn home safely. I also wondered how close he was to finding out where I had been taken. Too bad The Base hadn't been stocked with that stupid tracking device and I'd been able to get it implanted last night. Jelena's men hadn't even patted me down or run an RDIF reader over me like Mirko and Ace had thought they might. Ace said that the RDIF frequencies would be unique enough that a scanner shouldn't pick it up, but Mirko still worried.

My brain floated in a fog, but I tested the walls built around my guards' minds regardless. Blocked, just as I'd suspected. I relaxed, hoping I could recharge to a level that would allow me to get out of here later.

I examined the room for anything that would help me. My prison had a small window nestled into one of the walls. I could probably squeeze through, but it would be a long tumble to the ground. I rose from the bed and walked over. I shook my head, staring down the bare brick wall. In movies, the building where captives were held always had a trellis or a drain pipe that served as a convenient escape route. Just my luck that I'd get neither. If I magically wiggled through the tight spot between the window's seals, I'd have to jump, or fall.

I strolled back over to the bed. I had no clue as to how long Jelena would hold me in this room before she moved forward with her plan, but I also couldn't fathom how close Mirko had come to finding me. I decided to wait it out for a while, my knee bouncing in anxiety.

After waiting for what felt like hours, I resolved to take my chances with the three-story drop. I pulled the quilt off of the bed and dragged it over to the window. I lingered until I thought my guards were deep enough in conversation that they wouldn't hear me breaking the window. I folded the quilt until I thought the layers would muffle the sound of shattering glass, but not enough that it would pad the force needed to smash the pane.

Nerves curdled in my stomach, and my heart beat to crescendo almost to the point of exploding. I only had this one chance, and I'd better not screw it up. I raised my shaking arms, holding the quilt up to the window with one hand. I punched the window as hard as I could.

The glass broke, but the crash boomed through the room. I knocked out the shards hanging from the top of the seal, and made haste laying the blanket over the pieces stabbing out of the bottom.

Metal groaned as the guards fiddled with the lock on the door. Shouting broke out in the hallway.

I hopped up, grasping the sides of the window frame, and propelled forward. My momentum faltered when my hips caught in the small frame. I pushed against the grainy brick and wiggled my legs to give me the force needed to squeeze through.

The door crashed against the inside wall of the bedroom, and footsteps pounded toward me. I pushed against the brick, its rough surface stabbing into my palms, and then I flung into the air, free falling toward the ground.

I shrieked. I knew that landing head first from a three-story fall would surely slow down my escape, so I arched my back and neck, hoping the weight of my head would cause the pull of gravity to spin me around. I flung my feet forward and started to fall parallel to the ground. I used the drag, flipping in the air and landed on my feet. My knee jammed upon impact, and I let myself roll with the momentum. I hadn't rolled early enough and pain shot up my thigh.

I lay on the cold, dead grass, cursing Mirko for not teaching me how to fall and roll properly in our training. That was definitely a skill I could have used right now.

Boots drumming across the concrete echoed toward me from the side of the house. I pushed myself up and rose to my feet. I tuned into my vibrations to use my chameleon power, but I realized I only had enough strength to use it or run. Not both. I wobbled forward on my hurt knee, clenching my teeth in pain.

I peered over my shoulder to find men barreling toward me faster than I ran away. I sucked in a ragged breath and fled, forgetting the pain in my leg and focusing on my escape. I might not be able to kill Dikan or Jelena at this point, but at least she wouldn't be able to use me to enslave mankind.

I drove onward, tapping my stored energy and calling forth my Pijawikan side. It roared within me and reveled in its release. I shot forward with speed that I had seen others use, but doubted I possessed.

I swiveled my head back and found that the men were still fast approaching. One of them lunged into the air and tackled me to the ground. I struck my hand out as we rolled in the dirt, swiping my claw along his stomach. He spun off of me and three more men landed on me. My arms wrenched out from their sockets as they pulled me to my feet. I lashed out with my legs, snapping bone with my heels wherever they connected.

More men grabbed me, sweeping me off my legs, and I swung from their arms, vertical to the ground as they carried me back toward the house by my wrists and ankles. "Let. Me. Go," I growled, arching my back and pulling at my arms and legs, but found no give in their hold.

One of the men punched me in the gut. I folded up as much as I could, which wasn't much with the way my captors held me. I coughed, trying to catch my breath. "Give it up, little girl. Your half-blood is no match for us," he said, revolt emphasizing each word.

My attempts had been futile. All it brought me were bruises and an almost losing battle with tears. I sagged in defeat as they carried me back into the house and up the stairs.

Dikan stood on the landing of the third floor, a symbol of my failure at all things today, and his smirk rubbed it in. "In here," he said, creaking open a door to another room. The men threw me in, and I landed hard on my hip. I gasped in pain and tears burned my eyes. I kept my face just above the floor so they couldn't see the tears spilling over.

The door slammed behind me, and I wished I had jumped out of the window, landed on my head, and broken my neck, ending this nightmare once and for all.

30
RESISTANCE ENDS NOW

I lay huddled on the frigid floor because this room didn't have a bed. Nor did it have a window. The room also seemed to be barren of a vent for any heat to flow through. The temperatures had fallen sharply in Utah, and all I had to cover my arms was the light jacket Kaitlynn lent me to cover my spandex top Mirko had purchased for me.

Hours passed, and I hadn't so much as moved across the room. When Jelena swung the door open, in what I assumed would have been the next morning, my arms had gone passed the tingly stage onto the dead-weight stage.

"Put this on," she said, throwing a gown of amethyst silk toward me.

I sat up and scowled at her.

"You do it, or I get Dikan in here to dress you." She looked serious, so I picked up the dress and tried to figure out how to put it on. Sharp needles stabbed at my fingertips as proper circulation returned.

"Dikan will be in here in five minutes. You may want to be dressed by then." She pulled the door shut with a bang.

"Yes, evil stepmother," I said, gathering the silk. This would be it; she would dress me in a Cinderella gown and march me toward those who would bring the Zao Duhs and humans back into slavery.

The way to avoid it evaded me, but I knew I couldn't be the coward I had been when I sat by in English class while Carley ridiculed Miss Andersen about her chalk marks, nor could I be the deserter that I had been when Lijepa lost her life. My time to step forward had come.

I looked at the high-end gown that would be my battle uniform and sighed.

I slid the jacket off my shoulders and then pulled the spandex shirt over my head. I picked up the silk dress and searched the sea of material for the top of the zipper.

Bunching the silk, I tucked my head through the hole, then released the fabric and let it flow around me. The glitter woven into the material was evidence that I had been given a dress more expensive than I'd ever worn before. This surely would be a special occasion for somebody.

I reached my arm back to snatch a hold of the zipper in order to close the back of the dress, but dropped my hand in pain. My shoulder ached, reminding me of my weaknesses, that I would never possess the strength needed to escape Jelena's tyranny.

The thought that Dikan would be coming soon, and he would most likely touch me to get the zipper closed, spurred me forward. I reached behind my back again, sucking cool air in between my teeth, and clasped the zipper, guiding it closed.

A moment later, the door opened to Dikan standing on the other side. "Kako si lijepa," he said, eyes alight with desire.

I pursed my lips. He'd called me beautiful. Lijepa told me her name translated to *beautiful*. "Jelena's waiting," I said, giving him an evil smile. If he tried to touch me, I'd do my best to rip his arm off.

* * *

We drove in an Escalade for almost thirty minutes toward what I guessed must have been Salt Lake City's downtown; the buildings grew taller, and parking became sparse.

The driver pulled the Escalade into an underground parking tunnel nestled below a lavish marble hotel. This must be where we would meet the other Pijawikas—the start of my father's demise.

My heart beat like a jackhammer in my chest, and my palms grew sweaty as I gathered my resolve to fight the vampires. When I couldn't wait any longer, I tested my mental strength by roaming it over the minds in the vehicle. All of them, save for the driver's, were secure. I wiggled inside his mind, and when I grew confident I had landed on the right pathway, I set it ablaze.

He screamed, turning the wheel sharply, and smashed into a concrete wall. I held onto his mind as Jelena grabbed me by my arm and dragged me out of the vehicle. She threw me to the ground, and I hit my head, teeth chattering. I lost the link to the driver's mind, and the screaming stopped.

Men in fine, tailored suits sped toward us. Their speed gave them away as Pijawikas. "Is the catalyst still alive?" one of the men asked.

"Yes, Commissioner Abdul-Hakeen. She's fine." Jelena clipped. "Get up," she said, kicking me in my shin.

"We need her intact. Everyone is seated and waiting for the reveal," said an Asian man dressed similar to the commissioner. He must be in the commission, too. These men ruled their part of the world under my father, and they were her allies.

"She has been more than an annoyance ever since I found her. This resistance ends now. Get. Up," Jelena growled.

I pushed up on my arms, tucking the pleats of my dress under me as I stood. My eyes bore into Jelena's. They had everyone here, the witnesses who would find my father unworthy to serve them any longer. They would throw me down in front of them as evidence to be used in turning humans and Zao Duhs into slaves.

I couldn't allow that.

People die for their country, and people die for their loved ones, but rarely is someone given the opportunity to die for mankind. I would fight Jelena, and I would try to kill her, but I felt confident that I would be the one to die.

Pijawikas surrounded me. I jerked my head to the right,

immediately to my left, and then I slowly raised it up to match Jelena's eyes. I stood, calm and elegant, staring at her.

I lunged for her throat, fangs extended to spill her blood.

She spun, avoiding me. Her men moved to contain me. "I'll handle this," Jelena ordered with a confident smirk on her stunning face, and her men backed away.

"You had better," said Commissioner Abdul-Hakeem in a Middle Eastern accent. Everyone backed away.

I attacked Jelena again, but I dropped low, sliding my feet out to knock her off of hers. She jumped, eluding my sweep.

Before I could rise, she pounced on me, landing heavy blows to my jaw and eye sockets. Blood gushed into my eye and blurred half of my vision.

I flung my leg up and captured her by her shoulder, pulling her weight off of me enough that I could use the momentum to swing forward and up.

"Impressive," she said and lunged at me again.

I bounded back, blood from the cut above my eye running down the side of my mouth and then inside as I inhaled. The copper tang tingled on my tongue and my rage demanded that I draw hers. When I considered her to be at the right angle, I thrust my fist out and landed it in the center of her throat.

She coughed, glaring at me, her nostrils flared. Her eyes held her promise to teach me a lesson. She charged and pushed me up against the concrete wall, trapping me between the crashed Escalade and her pounding fists.

My skull bounced against the cold, solid slab, and I tried to guess how many more punches it would take to end my life, but they kept coming without any reprieve.

"No more in the face!" one of the commissioners yelled.

Pain registered throughout my body as Jelena struck everywhere, save for the face. I couldn't focus. All I could think about was pain and the sweet smell of leaking antifreeze mixing with the concrete dust from the crash.

It made me wonder if Lijepa could smell the burning flesh as Jelena fried her face. That sent a fire of my own through my veins. I used the tension of the wall and drew my legs up, shredding the material on the back of my dress. Once I connected the bottoms of my feet with Jelena's gut, I pushed.

She flew back and across the parking lot.

I ran after her, jumping onto the bumper of a car and over the hood. I spun my arms around and over as I jumped off, twisting my legs together and barrel rolling toward Jelena. My dress flowed out around me as I spun.

Blood from my split brow dripped, discoloring the cement as I landed on the other side of Jelena. I grabbed her by her neck and squeezed, drawing blood as I formed my fingers into claws around her windpipe.

Arrogance swelled within me, and I peered into her eyes, assured this would end here and now.

Her lip lifted, and she grabbed my hair, torquing my head back in brutal agony.

I released her throat and clawed at her grip on my hair. I knew I should have been willing to die today, but I wasn't ready for it. Fear paralyzed me as chunks of hair ripped from my scalp.

"That's enough!" the Asian commissioner said.

Jelena ignored him. Her eyes were maniacal. She'd finally reached beyond the point of breaking me to now wanting me dead. She brought her free hand up in front of my face, showing me that her palm held a small ball of blue flames. It floated above her hand and shot toward me.

I closed my eyes, longing to be somewhere else and dreading the promised pain before death would free me.

When I opened my eyes, I stood on the other side of the parking lot. Jelena's fire splashed onto the windshield of a car that, just a second earlier, had been behind me. The fire flickered and sizzled out.

Everyone in the parking garage stared at the car in stunned silence. I had moved from one place to another without physically moving. I hadn't gone invisible and ran over here.

I had teleported.

31
THIS IS FOR LIJEPA

Jelena broke the stillness in the garage by shooting another flame at me. I thought of the wall where we crashed, and then I stood on the other side of the Escalade.

I giggled. Who knew fighting to the death could be this fun?

"This ends now," one of the commissioners yelled.

Jelena and I continued to fight.

She flung another flame at me, and I disappeared again. I landed on her back with my legs wrapped around her and my hands clasped on the sides of her head. I called forth all the anxiety I'd felt when Jaren hung from her lackey's hand—gasping for air—and I summoned all the rage I'd buried when I found Lijepa burned and murdered on her kitchen floor, all of the horror I'd felt when Kaitlynn wet herself in fear, and every other emotion I'd avoided handling since the moment Jelena's lackey arrived at Jaren's house that horrific night.

Lijepa had been right; power comes to you when you accept yourself. "This is for Lijepa."

I twisted Jelena's skull, snapping her neck. A loud echo danced along the concrete walls. I dropped to the ground with her lifeless body as it fell into a limp mass on the cold stone floor. Fitting that my nightmare ended the way it began.

I stood up and looked around. Pijawikas gawked at me, some of them in horror and some of them in fury.

Colorful rays reflected off the commissioner's znaks. Beams of emerald, sapphire, and topaz sparkled in front of me, but none of them resembled the znak my attacker wore at the airport.

Some of the Pijawikas stalked toward me. I'd understood that some would come after me in retribution for Jelena's death, but I had thought I would have more time between then and now.

Guess not. I wiped the blood away from my eye and crouched low, readying for another battle.

"I'm Pijawikan, too, but I've got nothing to lose," I said and raised my hands up defensively like Mirko showed me.

Tires screeched as a white Mercedes with blacked-out windows swung around the corner and sped toward us. Some of the Pijawikas scattered, but I remained.

Brakes squealed as the sedan stopped in front of me. The back doors opened, and I recognized the dark fuzzy hair that peeked over the top of the roof.

"Mirko?" I gasped. Tears filled my eyes and a relieved sob escaped my throat. I didn't pay any attention to the other man who stepped out of the back of the car and onto the concrete, or the men who moments ago, had prepared to attack me.

Mirko sped toward me, jumping up and sliding his hip along the trunk of the car to get to me. He caught me under my arms and lifted me in the air, spinning me in a tight embrace. The ruffles in my gown expanded, encircling us in an amethyst river of silk.

He dropped me enough that my feet touched the ground, but he didn't release me. He pressed his lips to mine, saying everything that words did not: fear, excitement, passion, and power.

When he withdrew, his eyes blazed with flecks of copper, and his lips curled. "I love you," he said and linked his lips to mine again.

At that moment, I knew I felt the same way for him.

32
WHAT IS IT?

A man's voice broke through my haze, and it held a force and authority within that caused me to remember my surroundings. "You will not seek retribution," the man said. He had been the one to step out of the Mercedes along with Mirko and another gentleman.

Mirko grabbed me by my waist and tucked me behind him.

I snorted. I had just killed Jelena, and he still thought I needed to hide behind him.

Commissioner Abdul-Hakeem swore. "She did not have our permission to kill Jelena. It is our right to seek revenge."

"And it should also be my right to kill each of you for your scheme against me. Jelena belonged to my blood, and I am calling for a cease in your vengeance," the man said.

I sucked in a deep breath, and my eyes widened. This man before me was Zladislov, the ruler of the vampire world.

My father.

At first, I felt fear and wanted to run, but then it dawned on me that he ordered these men off me. Did he care for me? Did he know his daughter waited anxiously behind him? He must have known something if he'd driven here with Mirko.

My father, the man who I had wondered about for the past sixteen years, stood an arm's reach in front of me. I wanted him to turn around so I could see if I had his blue eyes.

"You may be correct about that right now, but that is your abomination," Commissioner Abdul-Hakeem said, pointing to me, "and it will not go unanswered."

My father growled, a formidable and menacing rumble from

deep within his chest. "Get out of here before I change my mind about sparing your lives."

Pijawikas began to disperse, but the commissioners remained for a few seconds in angry reluctance. When they had finally walked far enough away that they appeared to be leaving, my father turned to Mirko and I.

"Hello, Brooke," my father said, with a grin on his face brighter than the glare from the sun.

Joy filled my heart. I did have his blue eyes. The outer corners of my eyelids even curved the same when I smiled.

"Hi," I said sheepishly. What do you say to a man you've wanted to talk to your whole life? And I looked like a mess, too. I had blood smeared all over my face and my dress was dirty and torn.

"I'm very pleased to meet you, but I need to go take care of this," my father said, pointing to the doors that led into the hotel.

I nodded, sad that our first meeting was cut short.

He locked his gaze on Mirko. "Take her home, and keep her safe." He put his hand out and the gentleman standing beside him placed a set of keys inside my father's palm. They clanked and jingled as my father passed them to Mirko.

"Let's go," Mirko said, and he stood by the driver's side door, watching me over the rooftop until I had gotten into the passenger side and closed the door behind me.

* * *

"Kaitlynn and Jaren?" I asked Mirko as soon as he pulled the car up the ramp and out into the sunlight on the road.

"Kaitlynn left on the plane with her guards, but Jaren wouldn't budge. Part of the deal we made was that he couldn't come on the actual rescue mission when we found you. He's waiting at Zladislov's," he said, shaking his head. "He's a persistent little punk."

Mirko gazed at me, fierce emotion in his eyes. "I'm proud of you, Slatki. You actually did it. You took Jelena down all by yourself. Banged up a little bit, but no burn marks. I almost can't believe it."

I smiled, big headed. "I told you I was hard core." I laughed. "But I had to use a new power to do it."

"Oh, really?" Mirko grinned and raised an eyebrow. "And what was that?"

"I teleported."

Mirko stared at me, his eyes wide.

"Yeah, I disappeared and ended up somewhere else. Instantaneously."

He shook his head. "I got that part. I'm stunned only because there hasn't been anyone who could do that in generations."

"Really?"

"Yes. I've heard of people having that power in the past, but they're all long gone now."

"Hmm. That must be why Lijepa couldn't figure out why my power tasted so funny." I smiled, knowing Lijepa would be proud of me.

"I always knew you were a special one, Slatki," Mirko said, grabbing my hand.

He held it until just before we arrived, and I was too anxious to sit still. I'd had my chance to hold Mirko and see his face again, and I was excited to do the same with Jaren.

When Mirko parked the car, I shot out of my seat and darted toward the door. I slowed down and turned back, hesitation on my face, my shoulders sagging. I loved Mirko, but I also loved Jaren, and I couldn't wait to see him.

Mirko shook his head. "Go ahead. He's been as worried for you as I have."

My heart swelled for Mirko at that moment. He wasn't handing me over to Jaren, but he could accept the fact that I loved each of them and needed them both, but in different ways. I'm not sure he'd always be this understanding, but right now, I was grateful for it.

"Thank you," I said and turned around, dashing toward the door.

I flung the bulky oak door aside and ran down a large hall. The house wasn't as massive or affluent as Jelena's had been, but my father's decor screamed esoteric.

"Jaren?" My excitement echoed along the walls.

"Brooke?" Jaren asked, ratcheting up my excitement further.

I ran faster toward the sound, passing paintings and adornments hanging from the walls.

I recognized one, so I halted.

A gold, circular emblem suspended from the ceiling and draped along the center of the rich maroon wall. It looked like a sun with rays jutting out from the center, but the beams were beveled like the spokes from a ship's wheel. And resting in the heart of the crest sparkled the largest ruby I'd ever seen.

"Brooke," Jaren said, reaching me and pulling me into a hug. It took me a moment to break my gaze from the emblem, but when I did, I was thrilled to see him.

I stood on the tips of my toes and pressed my lips to his. It was my rain after a drought, but I couldn't enjoy it with what hung before me. I pushed him back a step.

"What is it?" He asked, then lowered his brows in concern. "Are you okay?" He gently touched the side of my beaten face.

"Look," I said, mouth parched. I grabbed his arm and turned him to face the wall.

"Yeah. It's Zladislov's znak."

My knees trembled in fear. I gaped at him and my pulse pounded in my ears. "It's also the same znak the woman who tried to kill me at the airport wore around her neck."

The worry on his face mirrored mine, and my heart pounded so hard and fast that I thought I might hear it echoing in the hallway.

I grabbed his hand and ran alongside him toward the door that I had burst through moments ago.

Turn the page for a sneak peek of Dirty Blood by Heather Hildenbrand.

DIRTY BLOOD

1

"C'mon Tara, you didn't even give tonight a fair chance," George said. His blue eyes were a mixture of pleading and irritation.

I returned the pool stick to the rack on the wall and tried to think of a fair answer before I turned to face him again. I was careful to keep my voice down; the tiny pool hall was pretty crowded for a Tuesday night. The smoky haze that hung permanently in the dimly lit air gave the illusion of privacy around our corner table, but I noticed the couple next to us was already glancing over, trying to look like they weren't listening.

"George, you were an hour late picking me up because you were working on a press release with your agent." I stepped closer. "Your agent," I repeated, shaking my head. "Seriously. You haven't even graduated yet, much less secured a scholarship. Why do you even need an agent?"

He ran a hand through his hair, evidence of his impatience, though he was careful to keep his tone light, in an attempt to win me to his way of thinking. "I told you already, my dad set it up. And a lot of the pros got one early, especially the big timers. And I'm sorry I was late, but I'm here now and I'm focused on us." His expression became accusing and he added, "More than I can say for you."

I rubbed at my temples, trying in vain to massage away the stress headache that had become a trademark of our relationship. "I'm sorry, George, but I'm not the one who messed things up. And I don't fault you for a change in priorities. Football is important to you. That's fine, but it's pushing out everything else, including me. It would make it easier for you to just admit it."

"You're wrong, I can do both," he insisted, shaking his head vigorously. His loose blond hair shook with it.

"You've cancelled on me three times in the last week," I argued. "Not to mention standing me up two nights ago."

"Tay-" he began, using his nickname for me.

I put my hand up to silence him. I couldn't do this anymore. "Just stop, George. Stop with all the excuses. It's just not going to work. You should go. I'll find my own ride home."

George stared back at me and I waited for him to argue some more. The tone of regret in my voice had been obvious, but so had the finality of my words. Finally he sighed.

"I'm going to find a way to fix this," he said quietly.

I didn't answer. There was nothing to say. Reluctantly, he grabbed his jacket and left. I watched him until the door swung shut behind him and then turned back to our half finished game. I went to the wall and retrieved my stick, as if the breakup I'd just initiated didn't bother me one bit, and lined up my next shot.

I ignored the curious looks from the nosy couple beside me and focused on sinking the three ball. Only a small twinge of regret ate at me while I finished the game. I hadn't wanted things to end with George. We'd known each other since sixth grade, and in a lot of ways, he was my best friend. I cared about him a lot. But he'd changed in the past few months. At first, it was so slow I'd barely noticed. We'd go two days without talking – a record for us at the time – which slowly turned into a missed date or a last minute changing in plans. Then, he got an agent, and it was only downhill from there. And while I hated thinking I was throwing away everything we'd ever been to each other, I wasn't going to be a 'back-burner' girlfriend, either. A girl had to have some self respect.

With the game finished, and my pride somewhat still intact over letting a pool hall full of strangers witness my breakup, I pulled out my cell phone and dialed my friend Angela for a ride home.

"Hello?"

"Ang, you busy?" I asked, doubting she was.

There was a second of hesitation and then, "Um, Dave and I are having dinner."

"Dave? That guy from your pre-Calculus class?" I knew my surprise came through, maybe a little too loud and clear, and I felt bad for the way it had come out. "That's great," I hastily added. And it was great. Angela had been harboring a crush for this guy for like four months now. And it wasn't that she couldn't get a date; she was really pretty with her long dark hair and sexy-librarian-style glasses, but she was mortifyingly shy.

"Thanks. We just ordered so.... Is everything okay? Are you already home from your date?"Oh, yeah, I'm fine. Never mind." I decided against interrupting her. "I'll talk to you tomorrow and I want details."

Angela giggled and I pulled the phone away from my head to stare at it like maybe it had just morphed into another life form. Angela never *giggled.* "Okay, see you tomorrow," she said.

We disconnected and I dialed my friend Sam. Even if she was out, I wouldn't feel nearly as bad interrupting her; Sam was always 'out'. Unfortunately, all I got was voice mail. Darn. I disconnected without leaving a message. No point. She rarely checked it anyway.

The only option left was to call my mom but I quickly dismissed that. No doubt she'd have questions as to why I'd gotten myself stranded in the first place. Which would lead to what happened with George, which was something that, even though I loved her, I didn't really feel like discussing with my mother. It wasn't that she wouldn't listen. The problem was, she'd listen too eagerly. My mother was a classic worrier, and because of that, she hovered. She always wanted to know every single detail of my day, down to what I'd had for lunch and who did I stand next to in gym. And it seemed like the older I got, the worse her worrying became. No way was I calling her.

With all my transportation options exhausted, I sort of regretted letting George leave. Only sort of, though. If he'd driven me, it would have extended the argument or his pleading attempts to change my mind, which in the end would've pissed me off. And I was still hoping to maybe salvage our friendship.

I turned my rack of balls in to the bar attendant and walked to the door. I stood there, staring out the foggy glass of the front window, and considered my last resort. There was a bus stop a few blocks away. Not ideal in the middle of February in northern Virginia but it was all I had. I yanked my arms into my coat sleeves and headed for the back hall, past the restrooms, to the back door which would give me a minimal shortcut through the alley that ran between the building and the public parking lot on the other side. The cut-through would shave at least five minutes off my travel time, which was five minutes less I would have to stand in the cold -and I despised the cold.

I slipped out the metal door and pushed it closed behind me, making sure it clicked. A few yards to my right, a streetlamp cast a yellow beam onto the asphalt, but I turned left, towards the bus stop, and into the darkness that was my shortcut. I walked slowly until my eyes adjusted and then picked up the pace. The dark didn't bother me; I'd made this shortcut dozens of times. The parking lot coming up on the right was free parking and I used it more than the meters out front whenever I came to this part of downtown. I passed the lot, wishing I'd driven separately so that my hand-me-down Honda – and its wonderful heater – would have been waiting for me, instead of the drafty city bus. Matter of fact, I wished I hadn't come at all. George's tardiness would've been the perfect excuse to change my mind. Especially when we both knew our relationship had already hung in the balance, precariously leaning towards 'breakup' before we'd even made it out tonight.

It was quiet and my boots thudded loudly against the asphalt. I hurried to reach the bus shelter, hating the bite of the cold air, and glad that the surrounding buildings were high enough to keep the wind to a minimum. I drew my coat tighter around my neck against the chill that seeped its way into my skin, giving me goose bumps from head to toe.

I hated goose bumps because it meant the hair on your legs grew back twice as fast. And I was always getting them, because of some weird cold chill that would come over me. Even in the summer, when everyone was wearing shorts and bathing suits and having shaved legs was sort of a priority. When I was younger, I complained to my mom about it a few times and she would always say that Godfreys were thin blooded and easily chilled. Then she would stare at me, with an odd expression, and disappear; either into the backyard, to weed the flowerbeds, or the pantry, to reorganize the canned goods.

The tingling of the goose bumps subsided and my thoughts wandered back to George, and all the history between us. Like in sixth grade, when he'd tried growing his hair out, saying he'd wanted a surfer look, but really, I'd had no choice but to tell him he just looked... grungy. Back when grungy was NOT "in". And seventh grade, when he'd shaved it all off again, after we'd watched a video on career day, about the army. He'd talked about joining for months afterward; talking about how cool it would be to shoot guns for a living. Then, in eighth grade, we'd each had our first kiss, though not with each other.

George had fallen hard for the girl until her family had moved away. She was military and her dad had gotten re-stationed. He'd changed his mind about enlisting after that. Ninth grade, he'd gone out for football, and made Junior Varsity MVP. He changed a lot that year, gaining a self confidence that wasn't there before. By the end of sophomore year I'd started to notice him as more than just a friend. Last summer had been awkward between us. I'd spent the entire time stressing over the uncharted territory of having feelings for him, and whether he might have feelings for me.

I'd never even questioned being with George. It felt natural and right. He was my best friend for so long that the only thing dating had really changed was adding kissing into the mix. Not bad, as perks go.

Up ahead, a movement caught my eye, pulling me out of my thoughts. I stopped short and felt my pulse jump at the unexpected company. I didn't usually see anyone else in this part of the cut-through but just past the next dumpster, a girl with long blond hair and pointy-heeled boots stood in the center of the alley, shaking uncontrollably. I took a step towards her, wanting to help in some way, and then stopped again, at the look on her face. She was glaring at me with a look of hatred so raw that it sent a shiver down my back.

"Um, are you okay?" I called out, still trying to understand why she was basically convulsing. Was she having a seizure? But she was managing to stay on her feet. Her gloved hands were balled into fists at her sides, and she was breathing heavy now. I tried again. "Do you need some help?" Something about the way she looked at me was making my skin tingle and crawl. I shivered again.

"Help," she repeated, through clenched teeth. "Right." Her words dripped with sarcasm and unconcealed malice.

Then, before I could think of something to say to that, her shaking reached its crescendo and then she ... exploded. There was really no other word for it. With a harsh ripping sound her clothes disappeared, scattering into the air in tiny pieces. In the same second, her body seemed to waver and then morph, leaving in its place the largest wolf I'd ever seen. I felt my jaw drop. Was I crazy or had that girl just turned into a giant dog?

I had a split second to stare at her and then she charged. The brown fur became nothing more than a blur as she rushed forward, teeth bared and claws extended. In that moment, I was completely sure that I was going to die. I didn't even have time to be afraid; it would all be over too quickly.

Then, somehow, though my conscious brain had nothing to do with it, my body reacted. Just before impact, I twisted aside, dodging her. Using my body's momentum, I brought my hand around and swung. I hadn't even realized I'd made a fist, but my knuckles connected and I heard the crack of bone as my hand slammed into the wolf's cheek. The hit drove it - her? - back a few paces but then it straightened and seemed to right itself. Its yellow eyes locked onto mine and it came again. I shed my jacket, and let it fall next to me on the asphalt; some hidden part of me knew I needed better use of my limbs.

Three more times I managed to dodge the wolf as it lunged. On the fourth, its claws caught on my shirt and raked down my abdomen on either side, driving me back. I stumbled and fell. My back slammed onto the pavement with a hard thud. Again, I accepted my inevitable death. I watched as she continued to come at me, slower and more confident now that I was on the ground. All I could see were razor canines aimed straight for my throat. I cringed and turned away, unable to look into those bright yellow eyes, knowing what was coming. When I turned, a glint of slivered moonlight caught a piece of piping nearby; probably meant for the dumpster but somehow landing here.

Again, subconscious reasoning took over and I felt myself reaching for it, my hand closing around the cold steel. With a grunt, I swung out.

I hadn't expected to actually land the blow or for the crack to be quite so loud. I felt the vibrations from it all the way up my arm but I managed to hold onto the pipe until I felt the wolf's weight go slack and it crumpled in a heap, half on top of me. I pushed it aside, which wasn't easy, and scrambled to my feet. After that, I just stood there, staring down at the giant mass of fur and wondering how in the world no one else had noticed what just happened.

As I stared, the wolf's form began to shake and then shimmer around the edges, going hazy, and then finally – it was the girl again. Her long hair covered her face in stringy waves, matting to her head on the side where the pipe had made contact. Blood seeped slow and steady from the wound to the pavement. Her body was naked and curled together, almost fetal, except for her knee wedged at an unnatural angle. I could see that her eyes were open and staring vacantly but I didn't linger on that. I couldn't. My eyes were wide and disbelieving as I gaped at what lay in front of me. I struggled to accept what I was seeing. No way. It was impossible. People couldn't be ... wolves. That was a myth. A way for Hollywood to cash in.

But there was no mistaking it. The girl lying in a heap in front of me was definitely the same girl as before. And she smelled, distinctly, of animal.

I kept hoping she'd move, or at least groan, from the pain of the head trauma. Ignoring the feminine details of her bare body, I stared hard at her shoulders and chest, looking for any sign that might indicate breathing. I didn't see any. And I knew, deep down, that I wouldn't.

My hands began to shake. Maybe from the cold, but I was too numb to feel the temperature against my skin. I took a step back and stumbled.

Hands closed around me, keeping me upright. I jolted and tried to jerk away from the unexpected contact. A strangled scream escaped my lips as the hands whirled me around to face my attacker.

"Whoa. It's okay. I'm not going to hurt you," he said.

I didn't answer. I couldn't really remember how to speak at the moment and if I could, it would've been a scream anyway. My breath came in uneven gasps and he waited until I got myself under control.

There was concern in his eyes but that didn't go very far with me. I noticed vaguely that his eyes were the same exact color as his hair, a sort of bronzed brown. The color was fascinating; unlike anything I'd ever seen, and they seemed to hold some dark edge that hinted at danger, no matter how gentle they got. The rest of him wasn't bad either. His face matched his eyes, rugged and hard edges from his cheekbones to his jaw. When he'd spun me around, I'd grabbed out to steady myself and even now my hands still rested on his shoulders, where I'd first gripped. Underneath my fingers, and the leather of his jacket, was solid muscle.

The fact that I was actually checking him out – just moments after killing a girl - was my first clue I was in shock.

"Are you alright?" His gaze swept over me without waiting for an answer, critically inspecting the rest of my body, not unlike the once over I'd just given him.

It dawned on me that he was trying to help, and thankfully, that dialed back my panic enough for me to find my voice. Then again, now that my brain was convinced the danger had truly passed, some switch seemed to release, giving me permission to officially freak out. "I think so." I answered automatically, without really knowing if I was or not. I felt numb and strange inside my own skin.

"Did she bite you?"

His voice seemed to come from inside a tunnel. I blinked to try and clear the fog. "What?"

"Did she bite you?" His voice was firmer now and his hands pressed down on my shoulders, trying to keep my attention.

"No," I answered, finding it easier to concentrate if I stared into his unwavering, gold flecked eyes.

"Good." A look of genuine relief passed over his features before his eyebrows arched downward with new worry. "Are you alone out here? Do you have a way home?"

"I-" I struggled to remember and kept my eyes fixed on his while I waited for the answer to come. "I was taking the bus. My ride left earlier."

His brows curved deeper at that and he shot an almost imperceptible glance at the exposed body lying behind me. His hands finally dropped away from my shoulders. "Well, I'm not going to just leave you here," he mumbled, almost to himself. He seemed to debate something a moment longer and then pulled a phone out of his pocket, hitting a single button.

"Jack, its Wes. We've got a situation. Liliana's dead." There was a pause as he listened to whoever was on the other end. Then, "No, it wasn't like that. It was a girl but it's ... confusing. I can't get a read on her at all." Another pause and then, "I'm in the alley behind Fleet Street. She'll be in the dumpster until you get here... No, not the girl, Liliana."

I blanched at that and felt new panic rising as he finished his call. Whatever else he said didn't make it past the warning bell ringing in my ears. He must've seen the look on my face, though, because he quickly put his hands, palms up, in front of him, and spoke soothingly. "I meant her- the girl you fought with. I didn't mean you."

I nodded, inhaling deeply to wash away the adrenaline that was coursing through me. I really needed to get a handle on myself. This was ridiculous. I probably looked and sounded like a moron, and the fact that I was shivering didn't help, either. It reminded me of the way the girl had been shaking, right before she-

"What's your name?"

His voice snapped me out of it, cutting off the replay my brain had been about to give me. "Tara," I answered in a voice that sounded much weaker than I'd intended. "Tara Godfrey," I repeated, louder.

"Tara, I'm Wes and I'm going to help you, if you'll let me. Can I give you a ride home?"

"A ride? Seriously?" I gaped at him. "I just killed that girl. We need to call the police, a coroner, somebody."

"I made a call and someone is on his way to take care of it."

I shook my head. "Yeah, that didn't exactly sound official. And you called her by name. Liliana. You know her? What's going on?"

"Look, obviously you saw what's going on," he said, a little impatient. "That girl wasn't human. And I don't think either of us wants to answer the questions that would come with admitting that to the police. Not that they would believe you in the first place. So, I'm taking care of it - discreetly. And unless you want to end up in a padded room, you'll do the same."

Okay, he had a point - especially about the padded room part. I mean, I saw it with my own eyes and I was still having a hard time with it all. I could guess how it would sound, trying to explain it to police or doctors.

It didn't feel good, lying about something like this, though. I'd just killed a girl - or dog - or whatever. But, maybe I'd be willing to deal with it - if I had some answers about what the hell was actually happening.

"Fine, I'll do it your way. But you have to give me something in return," I said.

He eyed me, wary. "What?"

"Answers. An explanation. I mean, seriously, this kind of stuff isn't real. Or isn't supposed to be, but here it is. And you seem to know a lot about it, so what's the deal?"

He sighed in response but didn't argue my demand. Maybe he'd been expecting it. "I'll tell you in the car. For now, we've gotta' get out of this alley before someone sees us. Come on."

"No way. We talk here and then I'll take the bus, like I planned."

He glanced down at my shirt with a wry half smile. "I don't think that would be wise. You would draw a considerable amount of ...attention."

I glanced down, too, and noticed for the first time that my shirt was all but destroyed. It hung off me like a rag with long slash marks running up both sides of my abdomen, along my ribs.

Underneath the fabric, I could see shallow slash marks on my skin. The wounds were raised and red and looked like I'd faced off with a cat. Oh wait. Dog.

I reached down to zip my jacket and remembered I wasn't wearing it.

"Here," he said, holding it out to me.

"Thanks." I took it and put it on, fully preparing to just zip it up to cover the damage. No such luck. The zipper wasn't just broken; it was completely gone, as was a huge chunk of my sleeve, near my wrist. Apparently the she-wolf had gotten closer than I thought with her teeth.

"Crap." I sighed, long and loud, letting him know exactly how I felt about this idea. "Fine, you can take me home."

"Let's go."

He turned and started walking, slowing his pace to match mine and blocking my view of the girl as we passed by on our way back down the alley. We ended up in the public parking lot. The lot was lit with yellow-bulbed street lights at each corner and in the middle. They were like glaring spotlights compared to the pitch darkness of the alley. My senses kicked into overdrive. Something in me snapped. Maybe I was finally coming out of the shock I'd been in – or maybe I'd hit a new level of "freaking out". Either way, at the sight of the lights, I froze.

I tried putting one foot in front of the other but it just wouldn't happen. I was shaking badly now, enough to make my teeth chatter, though I felt weirdly numb and unaffected by the cold. I didn't even have stupid goose bumps anymore. My heart began pounding, echoing loudly in my ears. Behind that was a rushing sound that made me lightheaded.

"Tara?" I heard Wes calling my name. I hadn't even noticed him standing there.

"Tara, we need to go. My car's over here." His hand closed over my arm and sent me over the edge.

I jumped away, startling both of us, and stared back at him in panicked fear. This was all just too much.

"Tara." Wes' voice was low and soothing. "I know you're scared but I'm not going to hurt you. I'm trying to help you. Let me help you." He took a step closer.

Some closed off part of my brain was yelling at me, telling me to shake it off and stop acting like a complete lunatic. But I couldn't seem to calm down.

"I can see that you're in shock," Wes said, still edging closer while I fought the urge to bolt. "I can't afford to take you somewhere to be treated so I'm going to do something for you. I'm going to help you forget – just for now. It should wear off in the morning, and if not, I'll help you remember. But for right now, it's better if you just forget for awhile. Okay?"

I didn't answer. Partly because I was scared if I tried to talk, I'd scream like a banshee, and partly because not a single thing he'd just said made any kind of sense.

Apparently he took my silence as agreement because he nodded and said, "Good, now just relax." He was using that same patronizing tone, the one meant to be soothing. But he was looking at me like I was some wild animal, ready to bolt. And he kept his distance. "Now just keep your eyes on mine. That's right. Just focus on me..." He murmured reassurances and somewhere around the third or fourth one, I felt myself being drawn in. I looked down but my body hadn't moved. It was my mind, something inside me, that seemed to pull closer and closer until I felt like I could reach up and touch him. "Right here, Tara. Just look here, in my eyes. It's going to be okay." I looked up and our eyes locked. His held a piercing stare that seemed to stab all the way through me and out the other side.

Then, it all disappeared.

Find more information (and books!) on Heather at her blog
heatherhildenbrand.blogspot.com
For more titles available through Accendo Press, please visit

www.accendopress.com

Acknowledgements are next ;)

ACKNOWLEDGMENTS

There's a saying that it takes a village to raise a child. Well, this book has been my baby for the past eight months, and a village has helped me raise it.

Heather Hildenbrand: When I started out on this writing journey, the only thing I was sure of was that I would come out the other end with a book. I never thought I would find you in the process. I knew I needed someone along the way to help me create a better book and to be a better writer, and when I put out the call for this special person, you answered. You have been more to me than a critique partner. You have been my mentor and my sounding board, but most of all, my friend. This book wouldn't be what it is without you. Thank you for your faith in me, teaching me that it's okay for my dialogue to sound real, and giving me courage when it was hard for me to find it on my own. You're the Louise to my Thelma.

Jenn Sommersby: You caught my friendship by being one of the funniest people I have ever met, but you held it with your pure heart and brilliant mind. Our late night chats and worrying spirals mean more to me than I could ever express. I can't imagine my life now without you in it. Thank you for teaching me how to be a better writer, and a better person. You are truly gifted, and I have been blessed to see how the sculptor molds her words. Your touch is prominent among these pages. Oh, yeah, and we're going to go GLOBAL!

Annie Duckworth: You've been one of my best friends ever since the seventh grade. You were there for me at the beginning of this journey and someone that I could go to when I didn't have anyone else. Thank you for believing in me enough to hear me ramble on about my dream.

Hannah White: You're my prison buddy in this crazy place we call life. Although distance stands between us, you have never been far away. Thank you for always being there for me and talking me through the rough patches.

K.C. Neal: Revising this story was most definitely the hardest part of this journey. On days when I was almost too petrified to continue, you were there to urge me forward. You said the things that I needed to hear to beat down those walls that I had built before my dream. Nothing bonds two people more than surviving a tough experience. Thank you for having my back as we crawled through the trenches.

Megan Duncan: You were the second writer I met when I jumped into the writing and publishing pool. And you're still here. Thank you for your support and encouragement when I felt I was floundering.

Matthew Merrick: You have been the biggest surprise to me of all. You started out as my funniest tweeter and ended up giving my book enough polish that it shined as brightly as it does. Your feedback and the detail in which you gave it, means more to me than I can ever express. You are a genius and the ladies reading this book should thank you for helping me make Mirko that much hotter. Thank you. For everything.

Jessica Estep: You run a tight ship in the blogging world, and I am so blessed to have you. Your input into the blogging and marketing world has given me an edge that I don't think I can ever repay you for. You are one of the nicest, most clever people that I know. Thank you for helping set up the blog tour and answering every question I could ever think of!

Kelly Frew: Thank you for being the Croatian language specialist that I needed.

I know this is getting long (I did say a village), so I'll cut to my family. Mom, thank you for always believing in me. I have always felt that my dreams were attainable, because you knew I could reach them. Brandon, thank you for trusting me enough to let me run with my dream. And thank you for all the nights you went to bed lonely because I had other people talking in my head. I love you forever, and God truly shined down on me when he sent you to unclog my sink. Brian, Spring, Serena, and Trent; I am the person I am today because of your love and support. I couldn't ask for better brothers and sisters, or friends. I love you.

About the Author

Angeline Kace writes young adult paranormal romance. She's a Scorpio living in the Rocky Mountains with her husband and two dogs. She loathed dogs and their "stick everywhere" hair until she fell in love with a pit bull.

For information on new releases, giveaways, or anything else to do with Descended by Blood or Angeline Kace visit her website at: www.angelinekace.com

Lightning Source UK Ltd.
Milton Keynes UK
UKOW051134111011

180142UK00001B/21/P